the Vodka
dialogue

the Vodka
dialogue

Kirsty Brooks

HODDER

A Hodder Book

Published in Australia and New Zealand in 2003
by Hodder Headline Australia Pty Limited
(A member of the Hodder Headline Group)
Level 22, 201 Kent Street, Sydney NSW 2000
Website: www.hha.com.au

**National Library of Australia
Cataloguing-in-Publication data**

Brooks, Kirsty.
   The vodka dialogue.

   ISBN 0 7336 1717 4 (pbk.)

   1. Women private investigators - Fiction. I. Title.

A823.4

Text design and typesetting by Bookhouse, Sydney
Printed in Australia by Griffin Press, Adelaide

'If women dressed for men, the clothes stores wouldn't sell much—just an occasional sun visor.'

Groucho Marx

When I was twenty-five and looking for a career, I was told that it's the difficult things in life that are worth doing. Unfortunately, I found a lot of things tricky, which left me slightly dazzled by choice. But when I turned twenty-nine I decided to take control of my life. I figured I could think on my feet and fight like a girl. That's how I got into PI work: playground tactics and a lack of direction. A desperate nosiness didn't hurt either.

Unfortunately this glossy CV didn't help me much when I was hiding under the bed in a stranger's house some two weeks into the business. And if the police arrived they would soon realise I hadn't exactly used a key to get in, unless by key they meant a rolled-up copy of *Hustler* magazine rammed through a window. Those babies can really pack a punch.

My name's Cassidy Blair and I didn't need any porn the first night I started work.

'Quit channelling your mother, Josie, and zip me up.' I felt like I'd been vacuum-packed into a gimp suit.

'I can't, Cass. Like I said, it's too tight.'

'There is no such thing.'

'There is when there's a hunk of girl flesh between the teeth of the zip.'

I peered over my shoulder, then moved backwards towards the mirror. 'You're right,' I eyed the V of pink skin that ran between the soft folds of the leather dress. 'I guess I shrank it.'

'Yeah, by eating all those M&Ms.'

I ripped the dress off over my head and tugged at my G-string. 'What am I going to wear? How am I going to lure a guy who thinks Tony Danza's the king of the world?' I watched Josie try to sit down in her tiny clothes. Best friends should always have a visible flaw but there was enough of Josie showing tonight to make me think she was the exception to the rule, which, let's face it, wasn't going to turn my frown upside down. 'I used to be a rollerskating waitress, for God's sake. There's got to be something tacky here.'

'Cass, you've got *stacks* of tacky clothes, just nothing actually sexy.' Josie might be my best friend but she was light years away in terms of taste. While I read *The Face*, she flicked through *Harpers Bazaar*. She was doing this job as a favour to me, but it looked like she already regretted the decision. She was probably cursing the cocktails last night.

She held up a green mini-dress. 'How about this?'

'Too short. My thighs are like two slabs of Spam.'

Josie sighed. 'Thanks for painting that picture for me. What's this?' She held up a long pink tube. 'A pair of tights? A scarf?' She held it at arms-length, her tone changing. 'Possibly an old condom.'

I grabbed it. 'Ah, the vamp slut girl from *Buffy* dress.' I rolled it over my head and Josie grabbed the bottom of the fabric, pulling it down.

'I bought it for a Halloween party last year in Melbourne,' I told her, trying to smooth down the rolls of stretchy fabric. 'I went as Vampire Slut Girl and, once again, I didn't get laid. It was a beacon for the lovelorn plagued by body odour. It's slutty but I don't feel as though I'm giving it all away.'

'No, you're just highlighting it in hot pink marker pen.'

I checked my reflection in the mirror. It looked okay. 'Can you tell I ate chocolate mousse for lunch all week?'

She sighed in that garden-salad-for-lunch kind of way. 'It's a *Halloween* dress, Cass, not a magical dress.'

I looked like one of those pink balloons that people twist into shapes on street corners. There was a chocolate mousse-shaped lump where my flat stomach was supposed to be. I sucked it in. I looked okay.

As we gathered our stuff together, Josie went for one last look in the mirror. 'I might be checking my dignity at the door, but I'm not leaving behind my bag,' she said, grabbing her Fendi purse. 'Are you sure I can't wear a coat? I feel naked.'

'You *are* naked,' I said, 'except for the strips of fabric covering your nipples. But you're naked for two hundred and fifty bucks, and it doesn't get much better than that. You don't even have to touch these guys. And I'll buy you a cocktail to sweeten the deal.'

I gave myself one last glance in the mirror and then slammed the door to my little apartment. What used to be an old city office had been gutted, then blasted back and painted deep brown. It was cold in winter without the heater, but I loved it. Bright and airy, it was one hundred per cent better than my old place in Melbourne. The word hellhole took on a whole new meaning when you'd spent unemployed and friendless days in a dank Brunswick bedroom. Adelaide offered at least a careless wave at daylight.

I'd stayed in Melbourne for six dreary months before I ran whimpering back home to Adelaide a year ago. My friends blinked back their self-satisfaction and helped me resume my old life. I guess they knew they were stuck with me, so they bogged in and made the best of it. I borrowed their clothes in return, having thrown all of mine out in a fit of New Life-itis. The Halloween party story epitomised my entire time interstate. I'd tried hypnosis to cleanse the experience from my mind but all it did was give me nicotine cravings again.

I shivered slightly as Josie teetered behind me down the footpath towards the car. Five hundred bucks just to see if some guy would flirt with us. I wasn't entirely clear on exactly how far we had to go; I just knew it was for a good cause.

'So tell me again why we're doing this,' Josie asked as she tried to stuff her breasts back into the tiny multi-coloured halter-neck top while I started the car. 'These undies are flossing my bottom every time I move.' She'd stuck gaffer tape under her boobs to hold them up. I wore a push-up bra that made me feel as though I could rest my chin on my super cleavage. Neither of us were excessively busty, but right now we looked as though we should be making faux love to a pole in a smoky room.

'It's Amanda's fiancé. Amanda from the shop. Were you listening to anything I said last night?' I pulled into traffic.

'Mainly it was drowned out by that boyfriend of yours belting out hits from the nineties,' Josie muttered, slipping her feet out of her shoes and rubbing her toes. 'If I ever hear "Smells Like Teen Spirit" by Nirvana again I'll stuff my ears with other people's snot.'

'Josie!' I was shocked. Josie was never crude. Her idea of vulgarity was wearing last season's Gucci slides. Maybe the crass outfit was having an osmotic effect on her personality.

She glanced down at herself and groaned while I took a corner a little too fast. We were nearly there. 'You're a giant musk stick and I'm a colour-blind junkie. How much lower can we go on the "We don't watch the Fashion Channel" spectrum?'

'Five hundred bucks, Josie.' I reminded her. 'And he's not my boyfriend.' I pulled into the car park a couple of blocks away, paid for a ticket and slipped it onto the dash. We took a couple of minutes to tug our outfits out of various crevices and then headed towards the pub.

'I own a restaurant, for God's sake,' said Josie as we approached the building.

'You own a café, and I'm not exactly between jobs myself at the moment. We're doing this as a favour.'

'You work in a DVD shop, you big gorilla.'

'Sssh. You're making me all sweaty.'

'Oh yeah,' she said, glancing down at her protruding nipples. 'And our big concern here is not being gross!'

I ignored her. She snorted quietly to herself, then took an audible breath. 'What does he look like?'

'Dark, tall, like a cop, only not too bright. The dimmer switch gets readjusted every time he has a drink, so Amanda wants us to move in once he's had a couple, but not so many that all his brains cells are dead and he'd try to chat up the cigarette machine. He's due to meet his friends here at nine o'clock.'

Josie looked at her watch. 'It's nine now.'

'I know. The dress fucked up my timing. We'll be fine. We just need to get into position. If he's by the bar, we sit there. If he's in a booth, we have to put ourselves somewhere within his range of vision, giggle a lot and not encourage anyone else.'

'What if we run into someone we know?'

I stopped and looked at her. 'You know anyone who drinks at the Redneck Saloon?'

'It's been revamped,' she wailed. 'It's all Irish pub style

now. You never know who might be wandering in for a quick drink. I might run into my sister.'

'Well, everyone still calls it the Redneck, so it'll be as embarrassing for her as it will be for you.'

'Only she'll be dressed,' muttered Josie as we pushed through the doors. 'I think I need that drink.'

I pasted on a big plastic smile, trying to cover the nerves that were fluttering in my stomach as though I hadn't stuffed myself with pizza some forty-five minutes earlier. 'You stay here and keep a lookout. I'll scope the bar.'

I was off before Josie could say a word. A table of sixteen-year-old boys had just noticed her and were reeling from the visual fleshfest. She really did look like someone had mugged her and left her in underwear. And big earrings.

I was a very bad friend.

She moved unsteadily around the corner just as a big guy in a green jumper scrambled out of a booth and walked right into her. She stumbled and fell, but he pulled her to her feet. I ordered two cocktails and threw the money on the bar, straining to hear across the crowd.

'Hey, lovebox,' green jumper guy shouted at Josie. 'When do you want to get married?' The music from the Irish juke-box had mercifully ceased some minutes before and everyone within ten feet could hear him. 'I'm free tomorrow. We could have a bridal shower. Together. In the nude.'

I made my way through the crowd with two pina coladas, picturing the carnage about to unfurl as Josie sliced through his ego. Josie was Kathleen Turner; all sultry pout and steely eyes but I couldn't tell if men ever noticed her cynicism, so preoccupied were they with her belly button. I had recognised one of green jumper's friends in the booth from the photo Amanda had shown me. It was Tony, our quarry.

'Wow, what an offer. Only—'

'Binky!'

I squeezed through the crowd, arms high to protect the drinks, my smile plastered on like whitewash. 'Binky, honey. Here's your drink.' I handed Josie the enormous cocktail and raised an eyebrow. 'Now, who are these good-looking chaps?' Tony's gaze had honed in on my eye-level nipples and I moved slightly, watching his gaze follow my boobs. He was leaning so far over green jumper's shoulder I thought he'd dislocate his neck.

'Well,' Josie pointed to the far corner, 'I was just about to sit dow—'

'No, Binky,' I tried to giggle, but it came out as a death rattle. 'We can't leave these boys alone. You never know who might snap them up.'

As they sat back down in their booth, we discovered to our noisy, girlish joy that the big green jumper man was Bob and his friend in the baseball cap and enormous trousers was Simon. I'd already staked out the tall, muscular 'Guido the Killer Pimp' type and I was right: it was Tony. He appeared to have the brains of patio furniture, or maybe it was just the dull lights in the pub not doing him justice. I gave Josie a significant look, which she acknowledged with a roll of her eyes.

Bob went off to buy us all another drink while I turned my attentions to Tony. Our brief had been to flirt, not touch, and see what Tony's response would be. We weren't to push the envelope; there was no point putting Tony in the unlikely situation of having sober women giving him the eye. Clearly the man wasn't playing with a full deck, but Amanda wanted to be sure that that didn't mean playing strip poker with bimbos.

I tried to see what Amanda saw in Tony. She was attractive, especially since she'd had a very expensive nose job. Okay, maybe she was a little brainless, but she earned great money in an architectural firm when she wasn't working nights at DVDWorld to pay for her upcoming honeymoon. Tony looked like he couldn't spell façade. All I knew about him was that he drove a truck, liked country and western music and had a penchant for sex in department store lingerie change-rooms.

'Tony?' I smiled, leaning as close as I could without stuffing his nose into my chest. 'How do you spell façade?'

Tony turned to me, his dark eyes impenetrable below a heavy forehead and poorly cut hair. 'Is that a sort of cocktail?'

Conversation wasn't necessary, but I kept an ear out for Josie's lines as she poked me with the toe of her white plastic stiletto. There was always something to learn from a girl who'd dated two solicitors and a judge before she got busted by all three at the Law Ball. Only the judge actually broke it off, though. It took the others months.

'You know, you'd look great on one of those cars at an expo,' said Simon, eyeing Josie's distended chest. He looked around at Tony as though he'd had a brainwave. 'She'd look great on the hood of a Porsche. Whaddaya think, Binky? You expo material?' He turned, his nose pink from the beer and his eyes blazing. Clearly he was a hood ornament fan.

She grimaced. 'Some days, it's all I can think about.'

I nudged her with my strappy sandal. I was actually kind of fond of men, but these guys were like dogs; as long as you kept the tone right, it didn't matter what you actually said. But I didn't want to risk having to go into damage control. That might involve touching.

Bob returned with the drinks and slid into the booth beside Josie, effectively cutting off her escape. I turned my hundred watt smile on Tony and he dropped another couple of IQ points. This was a pretty pleasant way to make some bucks. Sort of like being in a zoo. With cocktails and dim lighting. In a maelstrom of tight pink gladwrap.

'So, Bob,' Josie said, smiling. 'Seeing as you're the drinks guy, here's a pickle for you. I'm all thirsty.' And she licked her lips so slowly that I'd drained my glass by the time she'd finished. The men were becoming dangerously dehydrated, and they watched enviously as her tongue disappeared inside her mouth.

You're on in ten, Ms Monroe. Josie put on her best starlet smile and I could feel the testosterone competing with the sweat in the air.

My mouth hung open in surprise as Josie smiled, running her finger around the rim of her frothy cocktail glass and licking off a dollop of cream. Tony grinned at me as I tried to turn my shock into an erotic mime with a cigarette. I could almost see the unspeakable sex acts run through his mind as I burned a little hair. I had to move this thing along a bit. I was expecting Zara to drop by later tonight for takeaway, my sandals were starting to hurt and my Swiss finishing school friend was turning into the town bike before my eyes.

'So, Tony,' I said, my big cheerleader smile plastered on my face. 'You ever done it with more than one girl at a time?'

When I opened my front door to a knock some forty minutes later, Zara involuntarily jumped back on the tiny landing and almost fell onto my grouchy neighbour's door. 'What the fuck are you wearing?' she yelped. 'Chewing gum? I can see your pubic hair.'

'You can?' I looked down absently. 'No wonder my jokes were such a hit.'

'Boy, oh, boy,' said Zara, pushing past me. 'I leave you two alone for ten minutes and bimbos invade your bodies.'

'We were on a job,' said Josie, coming into the room from the only contained room in the apartment: the bathroom. 'We were trying to see if one of Cass's colleagues was marrying the right guy.'

'And is she? Because if he found either one of you attractive he should be calling 1800-CHEAP-PUSSY.'

'Real sweet of you, Zara. And yes, he wanted the Cass package. And the Josie package, and just about every other package with "Girl" on the label. Scary stuff.'

'Why do you end up with these weirdo jobs, Cass?' said Zara, flopping down on the couch. 'You're a smart woman. You could be running your own company by now.' She looked around hungrily. 'Got any chips?'

'I don't want to run any damn company, and no, I have no chips. I thought you told me you were getting pudgy.'

'I am. I'm whining about it all the time,' she said, picking up a wooden box from the coffee table. 'What's this?'

'Present from Moody Boy,' cut in Josie, laughing. 'It's a wish box. Cass gets to keep her wishes inside it like any good little eight-year-old girl.'

'Funny ha. It was a sweet gesture,' I said. 'I know he's not my type, but he just seems to be everywhere I am. I like him. I don't want to fuck him.'

'He doesn't know that, though, and accepting the gift honours the giver.'

I groaned, opening a bottle of wine, then throwing a take-away menu on Zara's lap. I really didn't need another drink. What I needed was ten thousand bucks.

'Leave Declan out of this, guys. I know what I'm doing.'

'I don't know what the hell I'm doing,' I muttered some three hours later as I trimmed the split ends from my hair in the lights surrounding the large bathroom mirror. I had a teenage boy pining after me and I bought clothes from mail-order companies. 'It's really pathetic, Jock. I'm Mrs Robinson at twenty-nine.'

My little parakeet squarked at me and I let him out of the cage and cleaned the tray. He pooed on the couch and then flew into my hair. I loved it when he sat on my shoulder when I was home, and no matter what I did, he always managed to slop poo into my jeans pocket. Four out of the five nibbles on my ear were very affectionate; it was a little sad how desperate I was for contact sometimes. His constant chattering was a comfort noise and I didn't like to admit that I appreciated the company. Some people grow them in their belly; others buy them for $9.95 at the pet shop. I thought I'd definitely made the right choice.

I owed ten thousand dollars to the Visa card company and my $435 a week at the DVD shop wasn't going to chip it away as fast as the interest rate was going to bump it up. The negatives of living in my apartment (no garden, occasional vertigo, cranky next-door neighbour Mr Crabtree) didn't outweigh the positives, and I would chain myself to my Smeg fridge to avoid getting chucked out if I had to.

I suspected maybe I had spent too much money on matching underwear—but then I dismissed the thought. I just loved the way the expensive stuff felt on my skin. I probably spent one hundred dollars a month; that was only twenty-five dollars a week. Most people spent that much on CDs and magazines. I spent it on underwear. Colours, lace, G-strings. It was a carnival of unmentionables. I've considered cutting down to just a G-string a month and checking out the sales, but that sort of budgeting can really mess with your head.

I went to the window and gazed out over the city of Adelaide. The stars were masked by clouds but the hills loomed up behind the city. I looked back into the glow of my apartment. I liked my lifestyle. I liked my capsule home. There was no way I could go back to sharing a house with—well—*other* people. I was going to have to find a way to make some money, and fast.

Unfortunately, wisdom tends to come packaged up in the past tense. It's a feeling that as you grow older (and thus more wise) you're more capable of understanding human nature and the world around you. I'm only twenty-nine, so I'm clearly a couple of notches under score on my wisdom belt, and Amanda was making sure I didn't forget it.

'But he didn't try to kiss you?' she asked in DVDWorld the next day, her eyes dark and oddly glittery. Perhaps it was the light.

'No, he tried to eat me.'

'You just said it was Simon and Bob who followed you to your car.'

'Yeah, but I left out the bit about Tony's, um, handicap.'

'You let him drink too much! I warned you. I can't accept what you have to tell me if he was completely smashed.' She leaned back against the corridor wall and tried to stare me out.

'He had three beers while I was there,' I told her, folding my arms across my chest. 'And by handicap I don't mean drunkenness. I mean erection.'

'But he was drunk.' I could see she regretted ever giving me the job in the first place. She was obviously hoping to be proven wrong.

'Well, I hear when men are drunk, they can't complete the sexual act. Tony was trying to fulfil his quota right there in the booth, so the handicap wasn't exactly a blanket restriction.'

'But he didn't kiss you?'

I could feel my temper rising. 'He was having trouble locking lips because he was so focused on getting my hand down his trousers.'

'But you led him on.'

'That was the whole point!' I yelped. 'You told me to flirt with him!' Boy, I needed a drink.

'Yes, but not to make him think he was Hugh Hefner.'

'Hugh Hefner's an old geezer with more money than Viagra,' I retorted, hands firmly on hips. 'There's no way your fiancé would be allowed in the mansion. Now are you really disputing what I said? Do you want me to run you through it again?' I waved away her protest. I had tried to be nice about this, but Amanda's attitude was pissing me off.

'We sat down; the boys talked to our tits. We were trashy and flirty but we didn't touch them. I made a slightly off-colour remark and Tony grabbed my hand and shoved it down his trousers. Before I could pinch his testicles, Josie clambered over the table and brained him with her Fendi purse. We left, with Simon and Bob right behind. Tony has a big vein running along the top of his penis, no?'

Amanda's eyes were wide. The look on her face said yes.

'Because somehow he'd unzipped while we were drinking and when we left the place, he was slumped in his chair with his tackle out. He'd also suspiciously gone out without boxers on. Now that's not something you see every day, which is probably why the cops brought your fiancé home. I guess Simon and Bob bailed after we left them in the car park. Josie carries a lot of stuff in that purse. I wouldn't test her.'

'I'm not paying you to embarrass me.'

'Well, so far I haven't received a purse of gold doubloons and Tony seemed well-equipped to embarrass himself without our help.' I took a breath and leaned against the corridor wall between the X-rated section and the cartoons. 'There's no way I'd try to break up your wedding. I'm a goddamn wedding fan. The dancing and the frocking up and the romance.' I stepped back to let a couple of teenage boys make the trip to the sex shelf.

I turned back to Amanda, trying not to look at her fake nose. She'd asked for a Christina Applegate, but someone had made it just a little too perky. It was definitely more Michael Jackson now. 'I'm not saying Tony's a swine; I'm just saying he wasn't sending us away. I took her arm and pulled her towards me. 'Amanda, that's the truth.'

Her red eyes looked up at me. 'I was just so ashamed. They said he was exposing himself in public. My friends could have seen him.'

'Well, if it helps, he's got a very large penis.'

'*Too* large!' she wailed and then suddenly spun on her heels and took off after the boys. 'You guys see the sign,' she screeched. 'It says *Over 18*. I wanna see some ID.'

I wandered back to the desk to resume sending people home with movies, chocolates and chips. I had on a twenty-dollar G-string and it was itchy. I've never understood why lingerie manufacturers make their tags so scratchy; I end up cutting them all off and then don't know what size or brand anything is. I handed a woman with two teenage children a plastic bag crammed with dairy milk and video nasties, drooling a little at the purple chocolate wrapper.

I was the opposite of an aerobics instructor. My internal mantra was to bulk our customers up for winter and help them conserve energy. It was very environmentally friendly.

Two hours later I took a break, picking up a sandwich and grabbing a fresh air chaser along the highway that housed Adelaide's largest DVD specialist. Some of our customers really needed to take their lurking to the deodorant counter of their local chemist.

Suddenly I heard a bang and a squeal of brakes. A bright yellow Mazda convertible stopped some fifty metres ahead of me and then reversed back to idle next to me on the kerb. I kept walking.

'Cass! Hey, baby. How ya doing?'

I snorted under my breath. 'Fine, thanks, Malcolm.' I kept walking. 'Now, let me see.' I put my finger to my chin and gazed into the blue sky. 'No one's tried to steal my car, or bitch about me to my friends for at least a couple of weeks. You been out of town?'

'Now, baby, don't be like that. I was only trying to help.'

'You told everyone I was a lousy lay!'

'I did not.' He chuckled like a newsreader. 'I told them that your ex said you gave a weird blow job.'

I had a vision of pulling him out of the car by his spiky black hair and mashing his face into one of the trees lining the street. Instead I just took a deep breath and kept up a steady pace. No way was I going to let an ex-housemate make me lose my temper. It was altogether too *Big Brother* for me.

'Malcolm,' I said, flicking my hair over my shoulder and unclenching my fist, 'that meant I didn't give him one at all! Ever. You giant turnip. I never even shagged the guy. We kissed once. He was just trying to get back at me, which explains his motivation, but not yours.'

I stopped walking, stepped over the grassy verge and leaned over the passenger seat, one hand on the dash, the other on the seat. 'So tell me. What brings you into this neighbourhood? On your way home from stealing this skanky car?' It wasn't really skanky, but Malcolm lived and breathed by other people's opinion, even mine.

He ran his hand over the steering wheel. He wore well-tailored clothes that always looked as though he'd stolen *them* as well: too big, too well-ironed, too non-greasy to be his own. He lived on a celebrity diet of *Video Hits* and making up bullshit about all the sex he was having. He also loved to shop and today he'd clearly been busy maxing out his Visa card. The car was littered with bags.

'You think it's skanky?'

I looked behind him as a stream of cars raced towards us. There was no parking lane. He'd have to move out of the way before he got plowed down. 'Yeah, and that's only the fur-lined seats,' I said, as he scanned the car for signs of trash, ignoring the cars heading our way. Quietly I reached into the foot space on the passenger side and picked up a large brown Haigh's chocolates paper bag.

'This is for being a bitch, Malcolm,' I said, turning on my heel and walking quickly back the other way. Malcolm shouted and threw the car into reverse, but the cars were upon him and they beeped insistently to force him forward. He pulled out, shouting muffled obscenities at me as he went.

I opened the bag when I reached DVDWorld and tucked a coffee truffle into my cheek. This definitely made up for the morning I'd had. But I still had to make sure Amanda gave me the money by the end of closing. I wasn't going to make much of a sexual sleuth if I couldn't rough up my clients for payment.

By the time I'd sent some teenage girls home with *Risky Business* and *The Breakfast Club,* I'd given Amanda enough evil eye to get her skulking to her handbag. She handed me an envelope of cash just as I pulled the security grille over the front door. It was 12.30 a.m. and I was pooped.

'Thanks, Amanda. I'm sorry it didn't work out the way you'd hoped. I was really looking forward to the wedding.' I tucked the envelope into my shoulder bag after flicking through the green notes. 'I sure do love orange cake.'

'Oh, I guess I'll still go ahead with it. My mum's made the dress, and she'd kill me if I backed out now.'

I stared at her. 'But, he, um…'

'At least now I know to keep an eye out. I'll sleep better knowing what he's really like.'

I frowned as she walked away, all stiletto boots and slinky skirt, large hair and small dreams. I was going to yell something like, 'But his dick is too big!' but I figured it would be classier just to walk away with the cash.

I climbed into my little five-year-old Laser, trying to buck up my spirits with the thought of two hundred and fifty dollars and the rest of the Haigh's. I'd already eaten a smidge too many and was feeling unwell, but I was sure I'd recover by the time I'd slipped into trackies and pulled out a book.

Unfortunately, Amanda and her crazy ideas about romance were tugging at my thoughts, giving me the feeling I get whenever I go on holiday: that I've forgotten something important. Probably it was just the usual anxiety about love and romance, and guilt that I'm not yet married with three kids. I'd had a few relationships, a couple that had lasted longer than my toothbrush, but many that had caused me to say 'men suck' under my breath whenever a cute guy walked into my line of vision. Marriage with anyone I'd dated so far was listed under 'Nightmare Scenarios: Emergency Use Only'.

I was never good at restraining myself or learning from my mistakes when it came to romance, but I was extremely good at writing mental notes and sticking them to my conscience, most of which consisted of warnings. There was really nothing worse than giving up my brains and heart to the first guy with chocolate eyes. Especially if he thought I could lose a few kilos.

Three days later I was sorting through the Hs in the horror movie section and whistling 'Que Sera Sera' under my breath when I felt a tap on my shoulder.

She was tall and broad, as though she'd just dropped out of the rowing team to concentrate on World Wrestling Entertainment. She smiled, which made her look like she'd just swallowed some tinfoil.

'Can I help you?'

I'd become calm, service industry girl after the boss had come down on the entire staff—apparently sales were down. All two managerial eyes were on me, and, as a result, I was as tepid as half-hour-old bathwater, and it was really getting on my nerves.

'You're Cassidy Blair?'

I nodded.

'I have a friend,' she said.

I waited. Her impulse-purchase top was straining against the weight of her breasts. Something was going to pop and I didn't want to be in the firing line. I took a step back and she advanced towards *Halloween II*.

I gulped. 'Well, good on you. Friends? Me, I just watch the show. The real thing is so time-consuming...'

I trailed off. Now her nipples were poking like bullets through her top. One false move and she'd take out an eye. The woman was armed with an arsenal of fashion faux pas weapons.

'A friend said you might be able to help another friend of mine. Problems with her boyfriend. Very discreet. Name your price.'

I opened my mouth to say something along the lines of how investigation work wasn't exactly working out for me, and that I'd hung up my sleuthing G-string, when I remembered the Visa bill.

'Seventy dollars an hour, plus GST. And expenses.'

I tacked that last bit on after being blinded by her multiple flashing rings. Her hair was freshly cut, she smelt like Chanel No. 5 and she glistened with wealth. I knew greedy pigs always finished last, but I had started burning the Visa statements and it was getting way too Retail Therapy Intervention Show drama for my tastes. The adrenaline rush was peaking and I clutched a DVD to my bosom for support.

She nodded. 'Fine. Here's her card. Call her after eight tomorrow night on the number at the bottom. She'll explain the situation.'

She moved to leave, and then turned back towards me, catching me mid-grin. It fell off my face like pastry crumbs. 'And your confidentiality is very important.'

I nodded and she stalked heavily out the door. Not that I was one to talk about excess weight. I'd long ago been indoctrinated into the women's magazine mantra: 'You Must be Thin to Attract a Mate', thus I had not pursued love for nigh on twelve months and, frankly, it had not pursued me with any intoxicating vigour.

Unfortunately there was now a roll of fat wobbling precariously at the top of my leather miniskirt which really needed to disappear. I'd dispensed with the blue man-trousers of our uniform and wore the DVDWorld shirt over whatever was clean. It was not popular with the boss, but so far it hadn't been blamed for a direct effect on sales. It made me feel as though I hadn't exactly sold my soul. Maybe just rented it out by the hour. I spent the rest of the day intrigued by my WWE visitor.

That night I went to a gig with Jail-bait (aka Declan). Declan was a *Party of Five* reject wrapped up in a Ramones

T-shirt. I had grown very fond of his odd devotion to me, however, which left me in something of a moral (and sexual) bind. Aesthetically, it was difficult to find fault, and after a couple of pints, I found myself aching to touch his virgin flesh. I avoided this temptation by reminding myself he'd only just started pre-school when Rick Astley hit number one with 'Never Gonna Give You Up'.

The band was loud, the beer was frothy, and, slowly, I felt a smile creep back upon my face. The events of the past few days had unsettled me, and I had the distinct impression I was waiting for something to happen; good or bad, it wasn't quite clear. I wondered if my pro-wrestling visitor was it. I was certainly waiting with some excitement for tomorrow night to find out more about my possible client. And by excitement, I mean fear.

Declan, on the other hand, seemed to have been infused with the elixir of life from the moment we met outside the Big Star record shop on Rundle Street. Later he wore a grin as wide as the path he'd cut as he danced his way to the front near the stage. I remained cool, aloof and wary of the sweaty stench of thirty-odd drunk teenagers (and let's emphasise the word 'odd') and therefore felt like an elderly citizen lurking up the back at a school sports day.

This was why I wasn't taking Declan seriously romantically. I didn't think dating a nineteen-year-old would help my efforts at sophistication, but hanging out at venues like this wasn't making me feel that great about myself either. I wasn't so much a cradle-snatcher as a skateboard-snatcher. It was cute; it just wasn't my vision of the future.

I nursed my beer and resisted the urge to bum a cigarette

from the chain-smoking tootsie shimmying away beside me in a white vinyl jumpsuit. Kids sure don't shop, or dance, like they did when I was a teenager. If you flashed back I'd be Molly Ringwald in *The Breakfast Club*, bop dancing in a knit tube skirt and wide-necked top, feeling uncomfortable if I let the outfit droop down one shoulder rather than stretched between the two.

A late bloomer, I'd woken up three times with exploding orgasms before realising it was imperative I tested this out for myself with a witness. It took four weeks to get Simon, my next-door neighbour, to zing me with the same pizzazz, but it was worth it. Those skills are still with me, although unfortunately I wake up more often with the echo of a groan than I do with a man beside me.

Sometime in the last few years the word 'Man' has taken over from 'Boy', as in capital B, Boyfriend. And apparently they're now often called 'Partners'. But I have decided to disregard this fact, figuring the pole had been raised without my consent. Unfortunately it seemed that, unlike your early twenties, in your *late* twenties if you drag someone home for a couple of hours of intense sexual aerobics, you keep quiet about it. Apparently it is now cooler to buy matching watches and go on picnics as a group—of couples.

Also, my DVDWorld position didn't exactly endear me to the corporate climbers, so the picnic/dinner-party crew wasn't the best place to look around for a personal gym partner (and not in the 'I'll spot you while you do a hundred sit-ups' way). I found myself drinking too much champagne and flirting with the wrong person. All I really want is someone to whisper 'Darling' to me without adding 'Please settle down and take a deep breath'.

After unsuccessfully urging Declan to pursue the girls who were dancing with him, each hoping to be noticed, we both walked to the taxi rank, laughing drunkenly about how the lead singer looked like he was desperate for a wee during the first set. As always, Declan tried to kiss me, I did the cheek thing, and I sent him safely home in a taxi, my loins screaming for vengeance. He really was very cute and I was surprised to discover that I had a conscience. I had certainly had occasion to doubt it.

As I jumped on the late night bus, which took me the three stops to my house, I tried to ignore the voice that told me I was messing with Declan's head by seeing him. I knew next time he called, I'd have to say no, very firmly. Over the phone. So that I wouldn't lose my nerve. He was wasting his time with me. While I loved the idea of kissing him, I knew I couldn't do it. What I needed was a grown-up.

Instead, I stopped off at the service station and picked up a copy of *Hustler* magazine and an Aero bar. There's nothing like bad porn to make your life look good. The chocolate was just a chaser.

The next night I called the home number scrawled on the back of Helen Since's business card. She picked up on the first ring, and launched into her spiel before I had finished introducing myself. Fifteen minutes later, I had drained my wineglass after the bit where she explained how much money she was going to pay me. I could afford another bottle, if not two hundred.

'So it's not just an accident. You really think he's cheating?'

'Yes. First the hairs, but then the bed smelled different. I narrowed it down to Miracle, such a girly fucking scent.' She sounded mad. I was glad she was paying me a lot, because I didn't want her to test me on my 'Standing Up To a Bully' skills, which were minimal.

'Okay. But maybe his sister…' I trailed off. Her cold silence told me that my experience of relationships was pathetic. My experience of cheating was good, but I'd always been gullible enough to accept excuses and apologies. Especially when they came with gifts. It had happened enough for me to realise that it was just safer not to get into anything serious. If you don't care, you don't care that they're secretly fucking someone else. It's simple, really.

'Well, okay. What do you want me to do?' She'd already given me his home address and their love history, which basically consisted of meeting at an after-work drinks party for a friend and then buying lots of wine together and drinking it. They'd been dating now for a year and she was expecting to move in with him soon. Her apartment was coming up for renewal in four months, and she was panicking.

By the tone of her voice, the past few weeks had slammed down a side order of frustration along with her cold dish of romantic mind games. Or maybe I was just being judgemental. I had no one to play romantic mind games with, unless you counted Declan, which I didn't. His habit of wiping down my bar stool with a coaster probably didn't even register on the Romanc-o-meter.

I agreed to visit Helen at her work to get a deposit on the job and a photo of my mark, Daniel. I also provided her with my contact details and a reference (Josie). Then I called Josie, organised to have her expound on my superior sexual sleuthing skills, before hanging up when call waiting popped on her line. Helen was clearly cautious.

Then I heated up some cannelloni, curled up on the sofa to watch *Buffy* and promptly fell asleep, apparently *in* the food. I woke the next day with red streaks from the tomato sauce. Funky, but not very consistent with my responsible, small business owner look. I pulled my hair back into a tight ponytail, and went out for parrot food, mangoes and flowers. And who should I run into on the street but Malcolm?

Add some dramatic weight gain, a cold sore and some cross-country cycling and the morning would be complete.

'Looking sporty.' I eyed Malcolm's trainers and striped tracksuit with trepidation. *GQ* must have had a rogue fashion advisor this month.

'I've forgiven you for the other day,' he said, with what appeared to be a solemn glance at my hair. 'I'm inviting you to my birthday party next week.' He handed me a lime green invitation decorated with nubile girls.

'Wow. Thanks, Malcolm.' I could tell he was walking a fine line between throwing a sulk and frosty silence, but it was as though my mouth worked independently from my brain. 'Are these scantily clad girls actually going to be there or is all this porn a lure?'

He frowned, then swept his hair from his eyes and smiled so that a little bubble of spit caught in the corner of his lips. 'I'll ignore that caustic remark because you don't know about my new place. What sophisticated woman could resist spending an evening in my new jacuzzi?' He let his gaze travel up and down my body as if to imply I didn't quite make the grade.

I stepped back, knocking his gaze from my tits. 'Last time I counted, every single one of them.' I breathed deeply in an effort to get some uncologned air. 'On second thoughts, maybe more.'

'That's not very polite, Cassidy.'

I laughed. 'Boohoo, Malcolm. Maybe I should distract myself from the pain with a *crappy blow job.*'

Luckily I was walking off, invitation tucked into my handbag, so I didn't catch whatever he shouted as I swung into Coles. I was certainly one peg short of being a happy camper when he was around. Sure, I was still cranky about the dud rumour, but I was probably going a little far. Anyone would think I was bitter.

Previously our acquaintance had been spiked by small, sly betrayals, but telling everyone I was a turnip in bed was really something I could hang my abuse on. The opportunity to be rude to Malcolm was almost worth the indignity of Zara informing me that my vegetative bed manner really had been the latest news, and sadly Adelaide is the kind of place where you just can't avoid people you don't like.

Okay, I was no acrobat in the sack, but I had my moves. And sure, they hadn't changed much since I first started practising, and therefore they were the equivalent of the moonwalk, but they still worked. I mean, maybe not *lately*, but they'd certainly had their day in the sun.

After impulse-purchasing myself out of fifty bucks, I staggered home, cardboard box of shopping under my arm, trying to read the front page of the paper.

I grumbled up the stairs and sucked in a breath when I saw Mr Crabtree shuffling past on his way to the communal window, bucket in hand. Oops.

'Miss Blair,' he croaked, sounding for all the world like Marianne Faithfull. 'You missed your shift again.'

Twenty years stripped off me like dead skin and I swallowed the urge to shuffle from foot to foot. I put the box down in front of my door and patted my hair. A little bit of cannelloni sauce was still stuck to my scalp.

'I'm sorry, Mr Crabtree. I've been busy with work and I—'

'I know. You forgot. You have holes in your head. I will do

it this week, but next week, if you have not cleaned this sill until it shines, I will have to report you to the maintenance officer.'

I glanced at the sill. It looked pretty white to me. 'Sure, Mr Crabtree, but remember, it's not actually listed on my strata agreement.'

He glared at me, all Julius Sumner Miller eyebrows and yellowing teeth, then turned back to his wiping. I pulled out my keys and pushed the box inside. Jock squarked hello as I kicked the box until it hit the kitchen island. He flew up to the paper lantern lampshade hanging from the ceiling and watched me like a surveillance camera.

I put on comfort music (Air Supply) and spent an hour in the bathroom, washing and deep-conditioning my hair, exfoliating and even puffing powder all over me like a self-contained snowstorm. I emerged, white, sore and feeling like I had been de-flead, ready for incarceration. I put my wet hair into two long black plaits and tied little red bows on the ends to cheer me up. Then I tucked into a bowl of Froot Loops and considered what Helen had told me over the phone.

She'd discovered girl-related items at Daniel's house: it smelled like perfume, there was a long red hair in the bed, another had floated towards her in the bath ten days ago and certain items had been moved, as though for aesthetic improvement. That was the clincher. Helen was convinced Daniel was having an affair, but she'd already asked him rather pointedly one evening and he'd denied it. Now she felt there was little else she could do without jeopardising her relationship with him. She wanted this mess, and her suspicions, cleared up, whether it meant losing her relationship with Daniel or not, although I suspected the latter was preferable, especially as she was going to such expense. And something kept bugging me.

When she mentioned the hair, her voice had cracked, and she sounded much happier retelling the bit about his denial. She really loved this guy.

It was eleven-thirty in the morning. I was working at DVD-World after I met Helen so I decided to wear my business suit with my default job briefcase, which currently housed my four-hundred-dollar instant camera and a fake clipboard. I had cobbled this together before Amanda had outlined exactly what was expected of me on my first PI job. Initially I'd had a vision of staking out Tony's work, infiltrating his home and intimidating his friends.

This new job, however, looked more promising. It also looked more dangerous and exciting, and required better footwear. I'd take almost any job except another one involving see-through pink Lycra, but what were the chances?

I got some paper, a pen and laid out some plans. Firstly, if the problems were happening at Helen's boyfriend's house, then I had to stake it out. Luckily I had a nondescript car. Secondly, I had to have a cover in case someone spotted me hanging around the neighbourhood, but I'd figure that out once I got to the house and looked around.

In the meantime, I did four loads of washing, partially cleaned the flat (wiped surfaces and kicked junk under the sofa) and then called Zara who was at home faking food poisoning so she could spend a few hours in the X-files chat room, reliving old episodes. One thing about Zara was that she was smart. Not street smart, like I pretended to be, but book smart, the best kind. She worked for a dot.com that survived the crash because they ran a porn site sideline, doing all the programming for the only sites on the web that actually made any serious money.

She was perhaps a little pudgier than me, but it suited her. She was cute, like an apple. I was running over the edges, like an uncooked apple pie. All this boils down to the fact that I hoped her smarts would be able to help my infiltration.

I was in Emma Peel mode and I needed some hot-headed and steely determination to overcome my fear. I swiped on my favourite lipstick—red to contrast with the black hair, and put on my sassiest underwear (red again). If I was heading into unknown territory, I was going to do it looking good.

Two hours later I was wedged into Zara's home computer chair, downloading information about all manner of dodgy surveillance gear: cameras that looked like power sockets, microphones that you could wedge into almost anything, pens with tiny cameras. Her day off left me with plenty of time to pick her brains.

'So, you think this stuff is going to help you figure out what's going on?' she asked, a pencil in her hair, another behind her ear, her eyes glued to the screen and a *South Park* T-shirt tight over her breasts. She must be quite the vixen on ICQ.

'Yeah, I think there's something among all this cool stuff that'll do the trick.' I did a wizzy on the chair and squeezed my eyes shut, then stretched them wide. The screen was making me zone out. 'Only I used the term "cool stuff" as a euphemism for "daggy geek things",' I added.

She didn't break in her typing, but her face flushed slightly.

'Sure, daggy geek things,' she repeated. 'The same ones that bought me this computer you're using?'

I flushed and gave her a squeeze. 'Sorry.'

I suspected I sometimes took my friends for granted. And that I might be getting my period. I also figured there was a reason she'd bookmarked PatienceandLove.com.

'Sometimes you get very weird ideas, Cass.'

'I know,' I said, suitably humbled. It was true. The many and varied love affairs. The choreographed dance to 'Eye of the Tiger' at the school formal. There were many reasons to look back in fear.

And I guess going on *Wheel of Fortune* wasn't a high point and probably I shouldn't have drunk all the champagne in the green room beforehand. Sure, the stage fright was unexpected, but it came across okay on telly and who the hell knows what 'thither' means anyway?

I arrived at Helen's work later that afternoon. It was a tall brownstone with too many cornices, and I was regretting the second bowl of Light'n'Salty chips, but with Zara's print-outs in my bag, I felt professional enough to exude a certain authority. Little did I know I was entering the lair of the High Priestess of Control, and that didn't just refer to her undies.

I was buzzed through by a snippy secretary who glanced at my suit as though she could tell it was last season's. Then I realised the woman who had visited me at DVDWorld was Helen, not her friend. Man, she was suspicious. I kept quiet as she grabbed her bag, coat and walked back outside with me. No farewells to colleagues, no cheery comments to Miss

Pernickety. Clearly she was the boss, and she didn't like to fudge the boundaries between the tiny minions and their great and glorious leader.

Her shirt was still straining over her boobs, but clearly no one had had the guts to tell her it was a bad look. She was scary and not in a good way; sort of like a wide and kinda ugly Anjelica Huston. I found myself scurrying along beside her in a form of pathetic servitude. I was guessing she not only wore the pants in her relationship, she was boss of the entire slacks industry. I wondered how Daniel had the guts to cheat on her. Probably his self-preservation instincts had been crushed in a freak industrial accident. Or maybe he was just driven mad looking up her enormous nostrils.

We went to a café about three hundred metres from her building—a long, deep, interminably groovy venue. We suffered the indignity of perching on low wooden benches like school children, only to be shouted at by the staff under the guise of service. In fact, it was more like being *in* the service, but I kept my trap shut. I figured scary Helen would deal with it, but she just ordered me a strawberry smoothie and herself a long black. Perhaps she had a soft spot for the waiting staff. She passed me an envelope containing two thousand dollars and a photo of Daniel. He looked like Hugh Jackman's shorter, stockier brother—appealing in a drunk-at-the-office-barbecue sort of way.

'In other circumstances I would have drawn up a contract for you, despite the fact that you said over the phone you don't use them. To be honest, I'm uncomfortable not being able to do this, but I also feel it would be best in the long run if there's no legal documentation tying the two of us.'

I tried to read her expression. She'd obviously watched *The Rockford Files* while I'd been glued to *I Dream of Jeannie*. When she'd asked me about contracts earlier, I hadn't given it another thought, but I mentally checked this under 'To Do Once Solvent'.

'Why is that?'

'If something goes wrong, if Daniel finds you on his property, I don't want to be linked to it. It would have repercussions and reflect very poorly on me. Do you understand?'

'Sure, sure.' I said, aware I was now in the shit. Knowing I'd be arrested for breaking and entering with no alibi or excuse. I slipped the money into my briefcase when the drinks arrived, pulling out the print-outs at the same time. 'Now I have some ideas—'

'I don't want to hear about what you'll do, or how you'll do it. I just want some information by the end of two weeks. I want to know who this girl is, if it is in fact a *girl*, and what their relationship is. That's all. The money is a deposit. You can clock up your hours and send me an invoice at the end of the two weeks. If it takes longer or costs more, I don't mind. I suspect it will.' She stirred her coffee, drained it in one gulp and stood up. I pushed my chair back in surprise but she brushed me away.

'Stay here. Finish your drink. I just wanted to make my position clear. His home and work address are in the envelope too. Call me at the end of the week with whatever you have, then we'll work out what to do next.' And she left.

For a moment I felt rebuffed, as though I'd been stood up on a date, but then I remembered the two thousand bucks and whistled under my breath. I sipped my drink until the staff gave me so many frosty looks I got goosebumps and then walked to the bank. I would slowly chip off my Visa debt and be carefree again. But I had to start planning. How exactly was I going to do the whole break-and-enter thing?

When I was seventeen I'd dated a rebel whose nickname (Achilles Neil) had been born from more than an excessive use of hair gel and some poor life decisions. Neil Tasker had been in jail three times and breaking and entering was his speciality.

Sure, incarceration didn't bode well for his career as a villain, but he knew how to get in and out of a place without detection (a skill that came in handy while I was living at home) and his weakness was flattery of any kind. Unfortunately his skills tended to be slightly reduced when drunk or stoned, which he was quite a lot. I was guessing this hadn't changed. I wanted his advice on staking out Daniel's house and needed to set up a. meeting. The only problem was, he hated my guts.

The next morning, trying to cross the road before I got run down by the bikies that had been screaming around the corner for the past eight minutes, I attempted to convince myself that I hadn't made a mistake. And eight minutes was a long time when a gang of teenagers on the other side of the street were calling out offensive things to me with rap blasting from their stereo.

I'd slept badly the previous night, my dreams like a *Funniest Home Video Show* of my entire relationship with Neil. All six months condensed into a collage of dirty looks, inappropriate sex and the odd bitch slap.

The street was garnished with defective cars and I walked carefully around garbage as I counted my way down from 350 to 112. My sister-in-law Denise had cheerfully informed me that her old school friend's brother Charlie was Neil's parole supervisor, managing in one conversation to remind me of my poor choice of boyfriend and the regretful lack thereof at the present. She gave me the address while implying

the question, 'You're not going to fuck him again, are you?'
Only she preferred the term 'love play', which made me feel
like I needed a romper suit.

Parked in front of Neil's house was a silver Saab which
my admirers had clearly already tried to access, judging by
the post-alarm bleeps of the indicator lights. I didn't normally
notice cars, but this street was so down and out that any non-
graffitied surface looked garish. Perhaps Neil had made it big
in the looting game and kept the address for the image.

I knocked on the door and stepped back, surreptitiously
wiping something greasy from my knuckles. I forced myself
to turn and stare nonchalantly at the road when I heard a
noise inside. My heart was throbbing between my ears. The
Saab now wore a festive hat of garbage.

Suddenly a curtain flicked in my peripheral vision.

'Yo?'

I whirled around. Boy, oh boy, Mum was right all along.
I had bad taste in men. Neil stood there, twelve years older
but not a day cleaner, or straighter. Eyes pink from the effort
of smoking three bucket bongs before breakfast, he still wore
his clothes inside out as an effort to cut down on the household duties. He was also disarmingly cute, in a skinny Ben
Affleck kind of way, and he was all trouble. Things hadn't
changed much.

'Neil?' I was nervous and there was definite squeakage.

'Who's asking?'

'Cass. It's Cassidy Blair. From...' Where? The backseat of
your Kingswood? The roof of your parent's garage? The soft-
serve machine undercarriage during your sister's shift at
Hungry Jack's?

'Cass!' His face broke into a creased smile and he held the door open, motioning me inside. 'Come in. It's the day for visitors. I've got cake.'

I whistled relief through my teeth as I stepped inside. Thank God for massive amounts of THC wiping away his memory of me dumping him for Don la Rox, the drummer in a short-lived Duran Duran cover band. Last time I'd seen him we drank too much at the Schutzenfest and had one of those bogan-style public brawls. I'd kicked him in the shins with my purple Doc Martens and he'd thrown up on my black, furry shoulder bag. It was no Jane Austen moment but it was swift and it was final. At least, I assumed the latter was correct.

I hoped the end of the house might offer some respite from the stifling air as I followed him down the long corridor. I was also cautious about who the other visitor or visitors might be. I didn't want to get involved in some *Dog Day Afternoon* style scenario. I needed to ask some embarrassing questions and I didn't want to get second-hand stoned from what smelt like last week's harvest.

The light through the kitchen window suddenly struck me in the eye.

'Sorry, the place stinks. I'm just opening the window.'

The voice was deep and unfamiliar. Once he'd moved from the window's silhouette my heart leapt into my throat and I was thrust into an alternate reality, where everyone was weird. It was Neil's older brother, Sam. Only he'd been hybridised with David Duchovny to create this Supernerd with floppy hair and a cold expression. I imagined for a second I saw sparks fly but then realised it was probably just a tiny spray of spit as my mouth responded to the sex on legs standing before me. This was a monumental disaster.

Sam Tasker was the nerd who had always looked at me as though I was a weird bug stuck between the pages of his science book. He didn't look this way now. In fact, his face wore an expression of complete calm. A practised blankness.

I cautiously walked towards the chair he offered. I'd seen that expression before—from people in uniforms thrusting little bags with tubes attached through my car window and then asking me to step out of the car. Jeez, if I'd known it was going to be like an episode of *Studs* I might have dressed up a little. I mentally kicked myself, *Get what you need and leave.*

Neil was right behind me. 'Hey, Sam. Look! It's Cass. Remember, from the roof?'

Sam's expression shifted slightly. 'I remember,' he said, his voice offering up only the slightest hint of a smile. Probably he was trying to find a clean spot to sit. He eyed my leather pencil-skirt.

'You want some cinnamon cake?' asked Neil.

'No thanks. I just came around to ask you…' I trailed off, noting the look on Sam's face. 'I'm not,' I stuttered, turning to Sam. 'I mean—I haven't seen Neil for a long time. I've—' I felt ashamed of myself because my first instinct was to distance myself and prove how much more together I was than Neil, but, really, what could I say? I work at DVDWorld? I tempt other people's life partners for money? I have no boyfriend, husband, children or pets with teeth? I rarely see my only brother after the incident at Christmas two years ago when he and Denise argued right through lunch and presents?

It was altogether too depressing. It was really no wonder I was a semi-satisfied spinster.

It was going to be a long visit.

I couldn't ask Neil the ins and outs of B&E in front of his brother, who I suspected was a cop, or a security guard, but more likely a cop. His stature was too straight, his manner too disapproving without saying a word. He wore nondescript clothes, but the car didn't hold true. I guessed the Saab was not a company vehicle.

I'd known a few cops in my life and they all had something chilly about them. My friend from university, Gus Stamp, abandoned a perfectly useless arts degree to become a cop and his good humour is about the only thing that keeps him from going crooked, which, frankly, I thought would be a lot more fun. That and his annual appearance at the Sydney Gay and Lesbian Mardi Gras as a Charlie's Angel.

Cops knew human nature. They'd seen terrible things and it came out in their manner. They knew what you'd be capable of if you were desperate. Sam was looking at me as though he could see that side of me and I wasn't too happy about it. Unfortunately it was also sort of sexy. I whimpered. Maybe he'd just seen me on *Wheel of Fortune*.

So I sat down and ate cake. I told a couple of fibs about my work (administrative assistant), my home life (two dogs) and my reason for still living in Adelaide (glamorous overseas trips 'keep me sane'). I don't know why I lied. I only know I grew quite enamoured with the pups, Dougal and Oscar, laughing about their exploits and when Sam left I abandoned

them as a conversation topic with some regret. They were playful little scamps.

We waved him off as he hopped into the Saab, now fes-
tooned with an entire garland of household refuse. Someone
sure had eaten a lot of pot noodles. When we strolled back
to the kitchen, I got right to the point.

'Neil, remember how you stole Mrs Davaner's earrings?'

He turned to me in confusion. 'Ye-ah.'

'Well, I'll forget all about it. Okay? So, *poof*!' I sparked
my hand in the air. 'That's forgotten. Now, you want to tell
me a few things about keeping a low profile on a surburban
street? How do you break in somewhere and not get detected?'

I was trying to be tough but there was something about
him that almost made me falter. Was it the fact that I'd once
thought I'd loved him (well, him and Nik Kershaw), or was
it that he seemed so damn marginalised? It was as though a
journalist was about to crash through the door and do a
story—'Druggies in our town. And now they want welfare!'

I swallowed hard. 'Do you really need any more bad
news about you circulating? You think your folks would want
to know?'

'Hey!' He sat up straight. 'Are you threatening me?' And
instead of looking angry, he looked surprised. And hurt. Jesus.
This wasn't going as well as I'd hoped. I barrelled on, trying
to ignore his expression. I had to remind myself as much why
he had been annoying enough to dump, and why I couldn't
afford sympathy.

'Remember when you threatened to tell my parents I'd
smoked dope down on Parker Street?' Parker Street had a
nightclub that played the best alternative music in town.

Unfortunately it was also raided by the cops almost every night for drugs and illegal gambling. I'd been a regular once I found a girlfriend who agreed to act as a cover for me. It had changed the way I thought about music. And accessorising with safety pins.

'Yeah,' he said softly and I gulped. It really wasn't enough to bargain with. It was nothing, kid's stuff. We'd done mean, teenage things to each other all the time. That's what we did. We had no place in the world yet, so we were crazy with it. I was just about to apologise, to smile in embarrassment, when suddenly something of the old Neil surfaced and his eyes sparkled to life. 'And I can still tell them, you know.'

'Neil, I'm no longer a private-school girl. No one cares a fig about that shit any more.'

'Oh yeah?' he said loudly, but something still wasn't right. Was he angry or just tired? I watched him carefully. 'Well, how about we test that out?'

I kept my feelings in check. 'Sure. You do that, Neil. Unfortunately, they're both dead, and Mrs Davaner is alive and well and living in Glenelg so we'll just have to settle with you telling me what I want to know. I suspect the last thing you want is for something like that to pop up and bite you on the bum.'

I actually had no idea if it would still be an offence, or if his parents were so sick of him that this new offence would be a drop in the ocean to them.

He seemed to deflate like an air mattress, the effort draining the energy from his limbs. He flopped into the kitchen chair. 'Okay. You want a coffee?'

'Sure.'

I was relieved and everything about him had swooped

back in a flash. His immaturity, his lack of guile, his vulnerability, and the flashes of kindness that had kept us together.
I stood up to try to hide my discomfort and put the kettle
on the stove. He sat staring at his hands, looking twelve years
old. I turned away quickly and washed a couple of mugs that
had been sitting in the sink.

'How'd they die, Cass?'

'Old age, Neil,' I muttered. 'They were in their seventies,
remember?' I was fifteen years younger than my brother and
my parents had both died from heart failure. I reminded
myself every morning that it had nothing to do with dying
my hair blue at university, or dating a body-art technician.

'So, you think you might share some tips about surveillance?'

'Why'd you want to know?'

I poured the coffee and sat down.

'Because I've got a job and I need some tips.' I paused,
seeing his face. 'Not *your* sort of job. It's legit; a bit of Nancy
Drew, without the Hardy Boys.' I'd decided to be honest with
him. I also couldn't think of a lie fast enough. 'I need the
work, Neil.'

He spent the next two hours outlining his approach to
the 'job'. He seemed utterly unconcerned for the victims, or
the homes he robbed. Or, I guess, unaware of them. He
seemed to simply see them as obstacles to the treasure and
himself a kind of pirate.

'You've got to watch the neighbours the most. Make sure
you keep an eye on the entire street, not just one house. Check
out the houses around this guy's place; check garages and res-
idential parks for cars. Get there early. Plan it well. What are
the routines? Is there an alarm or just a sticker? Look for the

box, the outside wiring, the alarm speaker. Is there an organised Neighbourhood Watch? A security firm? Somewhere for you to sit unnoticed? Who are you going to be? You need an identity and you need to be friendly with everyone, but not too friendly. You don't want them to remember anything much about you once you're gone. Leave no identifying characteristics in anyone's mind. Be unobtrusive.'

The list went on. I wrote some things down, repeated others in my head until they stuck. I drank three cups of coffee and was soon jumping like a bean. The air was punctuated by my fake Rolex alarm beeping as it did every day at four o'clock. I had no instructions for it and, until I finished this job, no way of replacing it with an authentic version. By the time I left, Neil had smoked a couple of joints, drunk two beers and made us both toasted cheese sandwiches. We were still wary of each other but we'd made a strange sort of peace.

Afterwards, I sat in my car with a grim feeling in my gut. I had all the information I needed to keep an eye on Daniel but I wasn't excited. Most of what Neil had told me was common sense, although to be honest, the meeting had highlighted the fact that I'd never had much of that, especially when it came to boys. I'd thanked him and kissed him on the cheek, promising to drop by again, but hoping I wouldn't have to. I didn't belong in his world anymore and he didn't deserve my pity either.

Every time I watched him absently scratch the scabby puncture wounds on his inner elbow I was reminded of why I wanted to do this job properly: to get a good reputation, start a proper business and be proud of what I did, which was probably how Sam felt. If he really was a policeman, I wondered how it was for him, dealing with guys like his own brother every day. I just knew I didn't want to end up on the back roads of life. I didn't want to ever answer the four messages left on Neil's machine from his increasingly cranky dealer. Neil was clearly trying to be his best for me. I owed him the same.

Coincidences are a funny thing. Sometimes it's like two worlds collide, other times, it's like a big fucking set-up. A bloopers show with you as the reluctant star. I admit I was feeling pretty paranoid as I watched Sam's Saab travelling at a steady fifty-five kilometres an hour three cars back in my rear-view mirror on the way home from Neil's, but when I pulled up in front of my apartment, killed the engine and crawled out, I saw him pull into a park a block away. I swore quickly to myself. He was sticking around.

I grabbed my bag and walked back up the street towards him. Slowly, like a stroll. I didn't want him to peel out before I could find out what his story was.

He was on his mobile phone when I walked up parallel to the car, but as soon as I knocked on the passenger-side window he rang off. I was expecting him to get out, so when he leant over and unlocked the door, it took a moment before I climbed in. The leather smelt good, it was twenty-four degrees and he favoured Radio National. He clearly enjoyed having a James Bond car about as much as I loved having a capsule home. Maybe I'd been wrong about him, but I didn't think so.

'Something tells me you're going to say you were just in the neighbourhood.'

He nodded to his right. 'Don's has great ravioli.'

'They close at 3.00 p.m. for coffees. It's now—' I checked my watch to give myself a moment to catch my breath, '4.28 p.m.' I was having trouble concentrating and the shock was giving me a hot flush, which I was desperate to contain. The car seemed too small for us both and he smelt sort of nice. Like fruit shampoo mixed with sweat.

I was a bad blusher, all pink neck and reindeer nose. What was going on? Sam used to tell me to keep it down because he was playing Dungeons & Dragons. I remember the sad, grey-flecked slacks he wore to his school formal, for Christ's sake. Hopefully he couldn't remember the electric blue, air-conditioning duct, drop-waisted formal dress I wore for mine. The bow was as big as my head. The eighties should exist only as an acid flashback.

Thinking about those slacks, I flicked a glance to his legs. Bad move. Not only did he have deep grey, wool trousers on, but his legs looked good in them. Too good.

'So, are you going to tell me why you're here or shall we just catch some rays?'

'I wanted to know why you visited my brother.'

'Are you his watcher? Because he's no vampire slayer.'

'You know what I mean. Neil's in trouble. I'm trying to find out why he's in so deep.'

'I guessed as much.' My voice sounded thin. I was exhausted. 'I don't have anything to do with that. I swear I haven't seen him since I left him pashing the pavement at the Schutzenfest. I just needed to ask him a couple of questions, that's all.'

'What sort of questions?'

'Uh, hair grooming tips? Who cares?'

'I do. He's my brother.'

'Yeah, well, he's not mine. What he does is his own business. I was just visiting.'

I noticed the temperature gauge on the dash go up a degree. I turned to look at him, his face a sculptor's dream: all angled and alert. There was something around his eyes, though. Something I didn't remember. Maybe his lashes were darker or his stubble just long enough, but there was a distinct bad cop side emerging from his good cop façade. I wouldn't say it was unattractive, just unnerving. I had to remind myself he had an IQ higher than my bank balance and he was not going to be easily fooled. So I lied again.

'It's just something stupid,' I grinned. 'My relationships haven't been very satisfactory. You know? I just wanted to,' and here I lifted my hands and cricked my pointers into little quote marks, '*understand* them.' I was going to add something about my biological clock but I might as well have said I was selling my eggs for crack cocaine, judging by the look on his face.

'Yeah, I see.' He was trapped. He could either sympathise with this outrageous statement, which frankly was making me a little nauseous, and try to pretend he'd seen *Bridget Jones's Diary*, or reel back in fear of the hormonal woman. He was too honest for the former and I watched his body language shift and the chill settle into the car interior as he went for the latter.

Triumphant, I patted his knee, in an effort to be pally, and maybe to test the elasticity a little. Hmm, tight, with the satisfying friction of leg hair. Before he could respond I jumped out of the car, winked in a 'My hormones are driving my every gesture' type of way and slammed the door. I walked calmly up to my apartment building but my legs were itching to sprint, which was odd, considering I was crap at it. He really had a strange effect on me and I wasn't sure I liked it.

Once back in the apartment, I sneaked up to the window overlooking the road and saw his car was gone. The rest of the street revealed nothing.

'Good,' I muttered to myself, knowing I'd done the right thing for the job.

It had been necessary to get him off my back. The last thing I wanted was a cop on my tail, especially a crooked one, or at least one who could get a good rate on European cars. I busied myself getting ready for work and set my mental alarm clock for six a.m. the next morning. I was going to get down there and check out Daniel's neighbourhood, record his departure time (he worked at a mobile phone company), then his routine. I wanted to get inside for a decent look around.

This thought sent a rush of adrenaline coursing through my veins. I needed some excitement, and if I wasn't going to date creeps or take drugs (those Christian television ads had a lot to answer for), I figured poking my nose in where it didn't belong would be good enough for a while.

My arse was like granite. The street was wide and I looked suspicious sitting in my car on the side of the road when there were only three cars—a blue Volvo, a yellow Toyota and a white Beetle that had pulled in while I'd been sitting here. I'd missed seeing the driver get out but the car had uni student written all over it. Everyone appeared to have carports. I was sitting like a lurker with his hands down his pants, slouched behind the wheel. After an hour I was dying for a wee. After two I'd forgotten my bladder and my eyes were drooping. Six a.m. was a very early start and I was cranky by nature, so the mood in the car was grim.

A flash of green caught my eye as cars started moving out of the driveways. It was like *Edward Scissorhands*. Five minutes later a dark blue hatchback zoomed out of number 17, my target house. As I'd stupidly parked opposite number 14 in an effort to be invisible when he pulled into the street, all I could see was a dark head, but I rolled the car quickly along the road until I could see the garage door slamming into place.

'Super,' I muttered to myself. Now what? I was bored and my bladder was still pressing on my vital organs. I should go home and clean up. Jock had eaten some bad seed that morning and shat all over the rug. Parakeets were good pets but they had occasional bowel control problems.

I pushed the car door open and slid out. There was a public park with a tiny barbecue area almost opposite Daniel's house. There might be a skanky loo there for me to use. I was shuffling along, wishing I was still wrapped up in my doona, when a woman who had been very ill-advised at the hairdresser's came barrelling across the street with her pram and offspring in tow.

'Harry! Watch out for the lady. Penny! Don't go on the swings until I tell you! Put your hat on! Ooh, it's just a cat, don't chase it. *Penny!*'

I momentarily thanked God and all her minions for the fact that no one wanted to have sex with me and risk pregnancy, and headed towards the stone-flecked block behind the slippery dip to relieve myself. I managed to pee all over my undies trying to avoid the daddy-long-legs rendezvousing on the edge of the toilet seat, and by the time I'd crunched my way over several cockroaches, I decided it was time to go home.

I had a lunch date with Josie and I wasn't working that night. We were going out 'somewhere decent'.

'You need to meet people,' she'd told me while surreptitiously eyeing my electric blue capri pants. 'And you need new clothes.'

I was never going to meet my perfect mix 'n' match but

perhaps I did need to make some effort to seek a mate. A boyfriend would be nice. Maybe one the same size as me so I could borrow his clothes. That would solve both problems at once.

We'd finished lunch at Josie's café and she was telling me about Carl, the cocky Englishman she was dating. She wasn't convinced he was going to get a fourth date and neither was I. The man smelt like Old Spice and danced like he was directing someone to put up wallpaper: point, point, point. We also had a plan to meet some nice guys, although, according to Josie, not 'the usual shrapnel you pick up at the kebab bar or the taxi rank at four a.m.,' which I thought was a bit harsh, so it was wine and lounge bars all the way. Men with ironed shirts and controlled facial hair.

But frankly, I had nothing to lose except my dignity. And my experience told me that meeting men in bars was a confident and steady step towards heartbreak. 'I think tonight we should keep an open mind and just see how it goes.' I put my sugar in my coffee and sat back against the vinyl padding attached to the wall. The café was empty and the blinds drawn. 'And by "See how it goes" I mean, "Get drunk".'

'Yeah, that's what I need, more alcohol.' Josie eyed the six boxes of spirits we'd just dragged into the café from the delivery van. The café was small and quaint, quite unlike Josie's usual style. She'd owned and run it for two years and was always talking about doing it up, but eventually we just accepted it would never happen. She had great taste, but she was also a little lazy, like me. She was hoping to get a full alcohol licence so she could serve drinks without customers buying food as well. Alcohol made a good profit and Josie wanted her bar, the Easy Lounge, to pay for a trip overseas next year, hopefully without brainless Carl.

'Carl is pissed off that I'm not meeting up with him later.' She rested her long legs on the coffee table in front of us. Her hair, once long and red, had been cut short a few days earlier into a dominatrix-style bob.

What I really needed were some ugly married friends who shopped at Kmart rather than Victoria's Secret. Having a friend like Josie was like trying to date at the Sexual Wimbledon with the top seeds against me. I just had to face facts, I was on the end of the dating food chain. Josie was still looking grumpy.

'Ah, Carl,' I said. 'His sense of humour is surpassed only by his misogyny.'

She sat up. 'You think he's sexist?'

I tried to laugh but it came out like an evil cackle. Zara and I were determined to extricate Josie from Carl's clutches before she did something stupid, like get married and go live in a castle.

'He hates that you own this place, he pretends to his friends that you spend all day baking in that kitchen over there, *and* you never wear heels around him.'

'He's short!'

'He's a *moron!*'

'Cass,' Josie suddenly sounded all serious. 'You know, you're getting all sort of...' She paused, her frown exaggerated by the low lighting in the café. 'Cynical.'

'Is that good?' I asked cautiously.

'Maybe, but you always seem a little critical when we talk about men. And anything else that makes you uncomfortable.'

I'd been smiling nervously but I could feel my face fall. 'Oh.'

We sat there in silence, me pretending to think about what she had said but really trying to hide my embarrassment, while Josie smoothed her perfect bob and picked dirt out from under her French-polished nails.

'So, you want to meet at the Steam Bar?' I wiped biscuit crumbs from my long denim skirt as I stood up.

'Sure, see you there at nine.' Josie carried the cups to the counter. 'Oh, and Cass?'

I turned around.

'What are you wearing?'

I hitched my bag on my shoulder. 'Why?' I asked absently, trying to figure out whether I could justify picking up some chocolate on the way home.

'I think you should dress a little more conservatively tonight.'

'I do dress conservatively!'

'I know, Cass. But some men get intimidated by the leather skirts, the scorpion necklace and boots. Especially the boots. Have you still got that long blue dress with the split?'

'Yes, but now I call it the dusting rag. The split sort of split.'

'Okay, your long green silky one. Is that a household item yet?'

'No,' I muttered sullenly.

'Well, maybe wear that.'

I grumbled under my breath as I left. Intimidation was a good thing. It sorted the wheat from the chaff. Only problem was, the wheat (or was it the chaff?) consisted of Declan, the bass guitarist and the wino on the corner who offered to braid my hair every morning.

I'd put Helen's money on my Visa card and had a hundred bucks in my wallet. I also felt a twinge of excitement, despite the doubts over my appearance. Going out was *going out*, after all. I didn't know what was going to happen. It could be the night of my life.

It could be the night when I look back and think wistfully of my wobbly stroll down the street, never knowing that I was going to meet the man of my dreams only minutes later. Someone who loved my cooking style ('the oven is a handy cupboard for out-of-season outfits') and my personal grooming ('bright colours distract from unsightly bulges'). Not aware that my life would be changed forever. That I'd finally find someone who loved everything I did, or most things anyway.

God, someone stop me before I barf. Apparently I swing wildly between cynical and hopelessly romantic. I was definitely getting my period.

I'd rescued the long green dress from the bottom of my wardrobe, put my hair in curlers so it was a bit bouncy, softened my make-up and sprayed myself with Romance. I knew on anyone else this outfit was perfect, but on me, looking out behind the rapidly flopping hair, I felt feeble-minded and more than a little itchy. I had transformed myself into one of those girls for whom men bought drinks and lit cigarettes. I was my own nemesis.

I held onto the railing carefully as I descended the stairs

to the Steam Bar, the darkest, coolest and most expensive cocktail/wine bar in town. I was wearing my spike-heeled boots, which weren't good for anything much except stalking in a bossy way from the bar stool to the loo and back. I wasn't looking forward to trying to dance, but it was a compromise. Boots for me, dress for Josie.

Dancing was important in this whole dismal game. A couple of shimmies on the brightly lit dance floor and hopefully men who looked like Brad Pitt would be intrigued.

If you didn't get out there under the spotlight, you could spend all night on your stool drinking martinis in the dim atmosphere of the aquarium and no one would even know you were a girl.

'Do you realise this is costume number two this week?' I whispered to Josie as I sidled up behind her in the lounge area. At least there was a better stylist during this shoot than on the Tony Incident set. Unfortunately she was already sitting with two guys, which should have been no surprise, but I had sort of hoped to have a girl's night, despite promises of meeting loveable scoundrels in Hugo Boss. She was wearing a short blue halter-neck dress, strappy sandals and her Fendi handbag/deadly weapon. She didn't look like she felt she was playing dress-ups, probably because she wore those sorts of clothes all the time.

'Cass, this is Ron,' she said, pointing to the dark-haired guy in a blue Ralph Lauren shirt. 'And this is William.' She smiled at William with his grey suit and tousled Hugh Grant hair and I swallowed nervously. Josie's heat-seeking lust missile was loaded and ready to go. She was always attracted to the most block-headed wanker in the room, especially if it looked like he drove a BMW. She had a very weird fetish for having sex in Beamers. I never asked why and she never told me; I'd just heard the stories. I accepted an offer of a cocktail from Ron and sat down. I guessed Carl and his castle were travelling in the romance slow lane tonight.

I spent the next hour laughing at lame jokes and restraining myself from rolling my eyes when William's anecdotes became repetitive and eventually slurred. I usually went for the scruffy, sexy, 'I know what a carburettor is' type guys who drank as much as Ron and William but were at least good to look at.

When I got up to go to the loo, Ron and William stumbled up too, which made me smile until I remembered they were wankers. Sure, private school education had something going for it, but it hadn't taught these boys empathy. Ron had spent the last ten minutes telling us how he'd fired his cleaning lady this afternoon because she used his stereo when she was working. 'She put Joe Cocker back in the Jimmy Barnes case.'

'You sad fuck,' I muttered to myself as I wobbled towards the ladies. Walking carefully around the enormous pillars separating the lounge from the cocktail bar area, a tall guy with white-blond hair and a rugby shirt stepped in my way and smiled in that smug, 'I've got you now' sort of way.

'Hi,' he said.

I tried to move around him but he stepped to the left. 'You here alone?'

Christ! I was not in the mood for this. Suddenly he stepped forward, right up against me, as though he'd been shoved by the crowd, but I could see a good foot between his back and the people vying for drinks behind him.

'Back off,' I said over the noise. I knew there was a reason

I didn't dress like this very often. I pushed him away but then his hand swept up and grazed my left boob.

'Hey!' I pushed him solidly in the chest and stepped backwards in case he took a swing. He smelt as though he'd rinsed his mouth in Wild Turkey. I was tempted to brain him with the big glass ashtray on the bar but my temper had got me into too much trouble in the past.

'Stupid bitch.' His face was red and suddenly it seemed huge.

There was no other way to the loos and it was starting to get urgent, so I tried to push past; his breath washed over me like toxic vapour and he wobbled slightly. I located his foot quickly so when I stamped down sharply with my heel, I was already moving.

Sweat trickled down the small of my back as I pushed quickly through the crowd. I could see the bartender signal to the bouncer to get the human partition out of the club. My heart was pounding but I was glad of the drinks I'd had. Confrontations always made me start shaking after a while, no matter how righteous I feel at the time.

As I rounded the aquarium I felt an arm on my shoulder again. The man was an idiot. I pulled away and then my heel slipped on the shiny concrete floor. I flung out a hand, clutched at the arm that had grabbed me and straightened myself. I caught a whiff of aftershave and my tummy did a flip before I even glanced up.

'Great shoes.'

I looked up into Sam's eyes and dropped his arm. I didn't need to go to the loo anymore. 'I'm glad to see you can run if you need to.' I could almost hear the 'young lady' tacked on the end, but his smile was warm. He was a casserole of contradictions and I didn't trust him.

'You often grab at strange girls in nightclubs?' I steadied myself against the bar. Here I was in a nemesis dress with Hugh Grant and his inbred brother, while Sam stood there in his grey rollneck jumper and wool trousers. When had I called up a demon from the underworld to mess up my life? Admittedly it was already in some disarray, starting with sleaze and culminating in scratchy bimbo clothes.

'You can't grab girls in public places,' I said, trying on my best ice-queen expression. 'I'm beginning to think you're some kind of creepy cop slash security guy and, either way, don't you have to take an oath? As in "I promise not to be creepy in public"?' I swept my arm up to hitch my bag and walked off, blood pumping through my veins so quickly that my neck felt red and hot. My heart in my throat, legs threatening to give way, I pushed open the toilet door and nearly knocked out a girl in a leopard-skin dress as she frantically wiped party drugs from her nose and scrambled out behind me. I locked myself in a cubicle and sat down on the lid.

Sam did something to me that I didn't like. He'd known me when I had a temper even worse than I do now, with teenage hormones jump-starting everything I did. He was there when I got stoned at the Festival Theatre during the break for *Oklahoma*. I'd been drunk at his birthday party. I'd thrown up in his *Star Wars* rubbish bin, for God's sake.

I flushed the loo, reapplied my lipstick and went back out, straining my eyes to find him and apologise. He'd surprised me, and he'd been patronising, but I'd reacted rather badly. I was also worried that my response had been inspired by the throb in my groin when he looked at me and not the grabbing in a nightclub. I was furious with myself, and I knew I'd spend the rest of the night cringing if I didn't correct it right now.

The only problem was, the bar was as dark as a cave. To find him, I had to approach every group on every couch and bar stool. I'd rejected two offers of a seat, three drinks and a foot massage before I found him. He was facing away from me, curled on a couch with another guy and three girls, all of them drunk, two of them appearing to be sitting *on* him. Things really had changed since the chess club.

I flushed to the tips of my stupid hair and backed away. What a twit I was. He didn't care at all. I made my way back to the couches where Ron was in the middle of telling a corker about how he'd climbed out of the window in boarding school and put undies up the school flagpoles. Josie was too drunk to realise how dull the conversation really was and her skirt had ridden up to reveal the lacy top of her stockings. William was staring at her leg in an erotic haze. It was going to be a long night.

I'd decided my hangover was grim enough to warrant serious treatment and I was sitting on the bench in the park opposite Daniel's house, munching on potato chips and pretending to read *Rolling Stone*. I was looking at an article about Kurt Cobain when someone flopped onto the bench beside me. I jumped and may or may not have let out a girlie squeal.

She was about three years old, with brown hair in long straggly pigtails and a white plastic smock over a party dress. She had somehow managed to smear vanilla ice-cream all over her face like a tiny Marcel Marceau.

'You're from Daddy's work, aren't you?'

I stiffened, my mind reeling as I tried to remember exactly why I was here. Brad Pitt had a very anaesthetic effect.

'You're here because Daddy's worried about Roger. Well, you tell him he's okay. That he just had to get his bottom shaved, but now he's okay.'

I had to move cautiously, so I hesitated a smile.

'Who's Roger?'

She giggled, licking the last bit of ice-cream from the mushy cone she held in her left hand and then proceeding to chomp on it like a carrot.

'You're funny. There he is. His bottom is still sore though,' she added as she pointed to a scruffy terrier trying to pee on the baby swing, only it kept moving and he kept dropping his leg in disappointment before it swung back into range again. I grinned.

'He's your dog?'

'Mine.' She nodded and called him over but the dog ignored her.

I looked around.

'Where's your mother, honey?'

'Mum's making cakes.'

'She knows you're out here with Roger?'

'She yelled at me for spilling.' Her face fell and she wiped ice-cream from her chin with the sleeve of her ruffled dress.

I stood up. I had a feeling mum would be yelling at *me* if I didn't bring her home. I took the girl's sticky hand, wedging the magazine in my backpack. 'Does Roger have a lead?'

She giggled again and looked up at me as she happily hopped off the bench. 'Silly! It's not far!' And she pointed to the house across the park. Right next to Daniel's place. I couldn't back down now, though. I held her hand as we walked, me bent almost double. My car was parked down by the letterbox on the corner, near the rusted white VW Beetle. I called Roger, who came trotting up behind us and we all crossed the street together. So far, there was no movement behind the windows at number 17.

I knocked on the front door. Roger was busy licking the

little girl's face as I heard movement behind the door, then it was wrenched away and replaced by a wild-haired woman holding a wooden spoon caked with what looked like radio-active glue. I recognised her from the park the day before and now the girl looked familiar under her ice-cream face. It was Penny who hadn't been allowed on the swings. I hoped they didn't recognise me.

The woman grabbed the girl by the shoulders.

'Penny!'

'I'm sorry,' I said, by way of introduction. 'I was just over in the park,' I pointed behind me, 'and she sat down with her dog. I thought you might be worried.'

'You got kids?' She looked at me as though I was trying to sell timeshare. I could smell something burning.

'Er, no,' I said uncertainly. 'I don't.' I smiled, trying to look regretful. 'I see them around a lot though.'

I peered past her shoulders. 'I think something's burning.' I was doing the concerned citizen thing here pretty well and was feeling good about myself right up until the point where she pulled Penny inside, grabbed the dog and then shook her wooden spoon at me, throwing little gobs of yellow stuff on my face. A dollop hit my lips. It was definitely icing.

'She's only a child. She can't play in the park alone!' And then she slammed the door.

I stood there for a moment, staring at the streaks in the paint on the door, before turning around and walking in a daze back to my bench. I had no choice but to stick around, although I was dying to go home and have a bath. I'd been there for five hours and my hands were grimy with park bench dirt. I wiped the icing off with a tissue from the bottom of my backpack, but it was still sticky, so I rinsed my face with Evian water like a supermodel. Now my nose was pink.

I got out my magazine again. It was only two hours before Daniel was supposed to return from work, and I wanted to look as innocent as possible for Penny's mum in case she decided to call the cops. I was also trying desperately to lose myself in Brad Pitt before I let myself remember kissing Ron outside the Hilton nightclub at four o'clock that morning.

I shuddered as I recalled him offering to walk me back to my apartment, but he did give me a fifty to catch a taxi home, which I broke this morning at the deli up the road. I told myself I'd never drink cocktails again. Certainly not any named after genitals anyway.

'Hey Cass,' said Zara, walking carefully into my bedroom balancing a tray of coffees. 'Pamela Anderson called. She wants her tits back.'

'She can have them,' I was trying to tuck a shirt into one of Zara's work skirts and vacillating between the grey pinstripe and the dark brown wool. I settled on the pinstripe. 'Did you bring one of *your* work shirts? This one doesn't fit over the ridiculous tits.' I looked in the mirror. 'It *really* doesn't fit.' There were little oval-shaped gaps between the buttons which flashed my new C-cup bra stuffed with gel-caps like runny little stress balls. I'd never had a bra that had three rows of clasps. It was like an Olympic sport to get the damn thing off. It was a wonder those porn queens ever got laid. Well, I wanted to be Ms Not Me and I figured the tits helped.

I hadn't realised Zara was standing silently behind me, the coffee tray in her hands, until I moved out of the mirror. Her expression was blank but her eyes were shiny. The tray was rattling slightly as she put it on the bed and I could see her hands shaking as she settled it on my hot-pink duvet.

I started to apologise, my heart sinking as I realised I really had hurt her. I had no shame. 'I didn't mean you had ridiculous tits. You have *great* tits. I wish I had your tits. I'm—'

'Can you just stop saying *tits*?' she said furiously.

'I'm sorry,' I said, feeling horribly despondent. 'I just don't have any shirts except for DVDWorld ones, or lame slogan T-shirts. Your clothes are just much more professional than mine.'

I knew I was babbling. Was this what it was like to be a sexist old man? Things just popped out and it was only when someone called you on it that you realised you'd said something really stupid and hurtful, and you deserved to die lonely with cats.

I went around and hugged her, but she kept her arms by her sides so it was like hugging a parking meter. I felt terrible. 'Zara, I know I've been a bitch lately.' There was only one thing to do. 'I'm just stressed out. If I tell you something, will you promise not to tell anyone else?'

She hadn't moved, but I could tell she was interested. Her left eyelid flickered.

'Okay.' I took a deep breath. I was never one to reveal my weaknesses, assuming that if you just don't draw attention to your faults, no one would notice them. In fact, that's sort of why I dress loud—to distract people from my expanding middle. And my personality.

'Two things. One, I'm totally in debt and it's getting worse. I'm like Demi Moore in *St Elmo's Fire,* only not so cute. And my friends are normal, and better looking.' At this she nearly stopped frowning. 'I'm paying it back very, very slowly and the interest is eating up my beer money and I feel like trailer trash because I've never been in debt and it's crap.' I sucked in a breath. 'Second thing, I hate my job at the DVD place and I really want this thing, *this* job, to work.'

There was a terrible silence in which all I could hear was the echo of my squeaky voice. I was building up to a *Party of Five* moment and it wasn't helping my mood.

'You're in debt?'

I nodded, unbuttoning the shirt and readjusting the gel-caps in the bra. I could feel my cheeks heating up from the emotional overexposure.

'God, you stress out easily.' I could tell she'd cheered up because she was acting all grouchy again. It's always good to hear how people around you are sliding into a terrible decline. I loved going to the Brickworks Markets to watch the matrimonial tension develop over the cheap incense burners and carved wind chimes. It was very *They Shoot Horses, Don't They?*

'How much do you owe?'

'Ten grand. Maybe eight with this job, but if I screw it up, I'll be back to square one.'

She stopped short. 'Oh, okay, that's a fair bit, but nothing you can't handle. And I agree, you should do this properly and then you can run your own PI business. Like in *Moon-lighting*. Was it *Moonlighting*?'

I nodded.

'Okay, Cass. You're not the only one in debt you know? Pretty much everyone I work with lives on twice their income. It's society.'

'Sure.' I tried to smile but it wasn't working well. I had to snap out of it before I got miserable and blubbery and then needed chocolate. Confession was one thing; streaky mascara was quite another. And I couldn't afford to put on another kilo.

She opened her sports bag and fished around, pulling out a soft grey shirt with a mandarin collar. 'Now put this on, have a coffee and then I have to meet Justin.'

Justin was her geek buddy. They both went to Nerd School together and were bonded together forever. Josie and I figured eventually they'd screw each other's brains out. I should mention here that Zara hadn't actually had any sex in her whole entire life—not even out of curiosity, which was weird but we figured it would change soon enough. By the time we realised it might not, we'd become used to it. In the meantime Zara and Justin would just go to science fiction movie marathons and listen to Kate Bush a lot.

'Okay,' I said. 'Thanks.' I checked the mirror. Not bad. I was stern, dull, camouflage woman. It was perfect. Costume number three. 'And there is a third thing.'

I poured the milk and sat down on the edge of the bed, watching her carefully. Zara used to be chess captain at school when Neil had already dropped out of school to be in his skanky punk band, Flaccid Erection. She used to get genuinely cranky every time Sam was around because he was such a daggy swot. Sam would get very intense about chess, complaining about rules and lighting and was generally the geek of Nerd School. Nowadays he'd be courted by girls hoping to date the next Bill Gates, but back then even the science club steered clear. Zara decided that he gave chess a bad name. (She was also Book Club Treasurer and leader of the South Australian Branch of the Official Devo Fan Club. To her, chess was frivolous and social and his anal behaviour ruined it for her.)

'I saw Swotty Sam the other day,' I said, stirring my coffee idly. 'He looks like a secret agent and drives a Fuck Me car.' Little apples of colour suddenly tinged her cheeks and she stared hard at me. In every society there is the same familiar but desperate social food chain, and for Zara, Sam was dung beetle. He was a year ahead of us but that hadn't added any pizzazz to his reputation. I think she hated him because he was a tragic version of herself—too close for comfort and all that. But since then she had admitted to guilt trips about putting mashed-up Chicken Crackles in his pencil case just before the year ten chemistry exam.

'I'm afraid I think he's rather cute. Which is weird,' I added hurriedly. 'Am I just not getting out enough, Zara?' I was secretly hoping she'd disagree, of course, but she looked too shocked to say anything. This was bad, I realised, so I kept babbling.

'But he thinks I'm acting like a desperate twenty-something, and he knows I'm nearly thirty! And I had sex with his brother. Only three times, admittedly, but still...' I ran my hands through my hair in panic. 'And how am I going to be sexy when he was the one who mopped up all the blood when I tried to pierce my nose? So there's no chance. He's gorgeous, in a strange, patronising way, but I cocked it up.'

The silence that suffused the air when I finally finished, breathless with fear, was punctured by a gasp that sucked the remaining oxygen between us. It was like being in Apollo 13.

'*What!*' She dropped her coffee mug, which bounced on the bed and then splashed its contents all over my skirt. '*You have the hots for Swotty Sam! You're fucking kidding me!*'

And Zara never swore, not even back when Sam beat her in the Westpac maths competition, nor when I said 'A bird in the bush is worth two in the hand' on *Wheel of Fortune* and missed out on the Jason Recliner. I watched the coffee spread across the skirt and the warmth soak into my stockings. I guess I would have to wear the brown wool instead, which probably went better with my shoes anyway. Well, there was a crisis averted.

I strode up to Daniel's door with a heavy heart and an oversized and embarrassing handbag. It said in big white lettering that I was a keen reader of a trashy women's magazine. I wasn't too happy about this. I'd figured earlier that my choices of a backpack or hot-pink raffia beach bag weren't going to improve my disguise, so I'd adhered to Zara's advice and taken the promotional bag she'd never used. It was frightening how feeble I'd become once she'd yelled at me for misinterpreting Sam's 'pathetic boy crap' as hot babe action.

This gig was going to be the making of me, but I could

also very easily fuck up and find myself in a prison with women named Jaynelle forcing me to do their laundry. I knocked twice, clutching my default clipboard to my chest and trying to peek through the curtains without moving my head.

No answer, which was no surprise. I'd seen Daniel leaving home every day at the same time. I resisted the urge to glance around, and instead walked purposefully along the veranda and down the steps to the side of the house. A child protection fence ran across the walkway between the green corrugated iron wall of the garage and the house. A concreted pathway led beyond it to a small garden. I lifted the latch quietly and walked through. That was when I heard the dog bark.

Frozen, my briefcase in hand and mind swinging wildly between options, I remembered my carefully prepared cheese sandwich. I opened my briefcase, balancing it precariously on my knee and expecting any moment to be knocked down by the dog. Pulling off the plastic, I flung the sandwich with one fluid motion as a yellow shape came bounding around the corner.

It barked again, but then growled low in its throat. It snuffled the sandwich, moving it around with its nose and levering it into its big hairy mouth in one gesture. A golden retriever. Not known for their ferocity, but I'd been flattened by them in the past. Their enthusiasm is equalled only by their saliva.

'Hello?' A woman's voice to my left brought me upright and I clutched the clipboard tightly to my chest again. A head popped over the fence. It was Penny's mother. Third time unlucky. I figured offensive was the best defensive, so I took a deep breath. My heart was throbbing.

'Hi, I'm Sandra from Adelaide White Ants Specialists—the environmentally sound pest control service,' I said, all perky like my tits. 'I'm here in the neighbourhood this week making evaluations of properties for the council.' My cover story didn't hold up to much scrutiny. She was frowning.

She didn't recognise me in these clothes. It was a good disguise. Or perhaps she was just stupid.

'Why haven't you been around to my place yet?'

'I'm working—' My mind raced to remember, '—odd numbers first. It's random. Then, if the council want a full investigation, they'll complete the survey.' I threw in my wild-card, just in case. 'They're thinking of declaring the suburb a National Trust area, so they need thorough evaluations. You'll receive a letter soon.'

I figured that the potent words *National Trust* should give me some prestige, but Penny's mum fell into a sour mood before my eyes. 'But Rod and I are putting up extensions. They won't let us do that if it's heritage, will they?'

'Perhaps not, so you'd better get your skates on. It won't be confirmed for another six months.'

Her fretful face disappeared from the fence and I tried to hold in the sigh of relief. It lasted only a second when I realised she was probably calling her husband right away. He'd be onto the council within a half hour and I'd be a cooked goose. Just as I was about to puke from fear her face popped back up.

'Rod's such a lazy bastard, he'll never get the plans in before then.' Her face broke into a smile. 'So there'll be no rumpus room? I can have my herb garden?'

I nodded gamely. Did this mean she wasn't calling the council? She disappeared again. I'd done it.

'And you say the letter will arrive soon? I'll just take it and hide it. He'll never know until it's too late.' I heard a screen door slam. The woman obviously didn't have the farewell concept down pat.

I found the dog chewing on a sneaker around the back. The other one was scattered across the yard in a maelstrom of rubber and stitching. No wonder he'd taken so long to get around to guard dog duties.

I wasn't pleased. Helen hadn't mentioned anything about a dog, or nosy neighbours. What other surprises were in store? A glance around under the gutters and the windows revealed no sign of an alarm system: no stickers and no pur- poseless boxes. That didn't mean there weren't any.

Then I spied the key on the inside of the back door. A double glass door.

If only Helen was a more agreeable woman, he might have given her a key to the place by now and all this rubbish would be unnecessary. She might even be able to snoop around under her own steam. Instead, here I was feeling all anxious and wishing I'd worn a spencer under Zara's shirt. It was get- ting cold.

The dog ignored me as I walked past the glass, noting the garden was overgrown and the trees blocked most of the light. It was a small yard, with a patch of grass as big as a large living-room carpet. Flowerbeds built up from large wooden sleepers kept the weeds at bay. Five shaggy trees lined the garden fence, keeping the area cool and dark. Unless

Penny's mother did some quick pruning on her side, she probably wouldn't be able to see me.

I climbed over the sleeper on the far right, pushed through some bushes and fumbled along the rough whitewashed wall. A human-sized bathroom window sat hidden by the trees. I shook woodchips off my skirt, put my folder down at the bottom of the tree by the bathroom window and wedged my sensibly shod foot into the V of its branches, which spread low to the ground. The bark cut into my hand, but I yanked myself up and leaned forward, pushing against the glass louvres.

This was a lucky break. I was a master at removing louvres. After once living with hopeless stoned boys who always put the bolt on the front door without checking that I'd come home for the night, I'd grown used to yanking out the louvres on the back sunroom late at night and thundering drunkenly onto the linoleum below. Stoned paranoia worked well in terms of domestic security, but it was a minor payoff for all the loud, late night munchies.

Taking out a little tissue box, its slot exploding with nasty lubricated rubber gloves in a carnival of colours, I pulled on a pair, realising too late one was bright green, the other hot pink. I looked like I was in Wham.

I wiggled one louvre loose on its rusty bracket and slid it out. Working away on the rest, I found two were rusted firmly in place. I had been sliding them towards me and flaking off the bits of rusty metal, but these two had apparently been repaired recently and wouldn't budge. I waggled them around for some time without result, then stretched down to where my bag rested in the tree branches. I pulled out one of my magazines and rolled it up tightly. Gripping it with both hands, I raised it above my head and brought it down on the edge of the first stuck louvre.

Dropping the magazine, I lunged just in time to grab the louvre as it began its descent into the bathroom, praying I hadn't squealed in panic, then laid the thick glass in the crook of the branch next to my bag and repeated this process with the second one, this time making sure I kept one hand on the louvre. This cautious approach took longer but the glass soon came loose and before long I had them all resting in various branches of the trees, which I hoped I could reach from inside to replace them.

I had two choices. Attempt to hoist myself in legs-first and face a happier landing, or squeeze through head-first, reminiscent of the drunken sunroom adventures circa 1995-96. I peered through to my landing deck. The toilet beneath the window didn't even have one those smelly pink shag covers to break my fall.

Not being particular limber, or smart, I chose the head-first option, mainly because I couldn't get up high enough to go legs-first. After a minute of wriggling, and wishing I had a soft towel to cushion my hips from the edges of the window, I shuttle-boated into the tiny bathroom. It was an ugly fall, but I gathered my dignity and managed to soak up most of the blood with toilet paper, which I then had to flush to remove the evidence.

The cut on my wrist from the desperate grab at the toilet roll holder was sore but not deadly. I couldn't say the same for my mood, however. I reached back to get the louvres, replacing them carefully in the rusted slots and wiping up the freckles of rust that had sprinkled the window ledge and the back of the toilet. I trusted the fact that I could let myself out again via the glass door at the back. I checked the area for evidence, it looked decent enough. I limped into the hall and looked around.

To my right was the lounge and kitchen area, with a couch against a wooden bench separating the two. Most of the light came in from the French doors, but two low, insulated windows, a foot from the ground on the far side behind the television set, featured internal blinds that were open. There was one shin-high window on either side of the outside gate.

The room was messy, but I picked my way carefully over the rubbish and took the key from the lock in the door. I figured if I covered my tracks well enough, I'd be able to come and go as I pleased. I could copy this key and then replace it. I could wedge the original under the mat by the doors after I'd copied it, so if he noticed it was missing and then couldn't find it, he'd just think it had dropped out and he'd missed it in his search.

Assumptions can be a dangerous thing, though. Not as dangerous as rock-climbing, but occasionally as sickening. As I stood there, smiling at my cleverness, I heard a clang and something flashed in the corner of my eye. I didn't have time to be scared, I just turned my head and saw legs move past window number two behind the telly. Someone had come through the side gate. In two giant strides I made it across the room and crouched behind the lounge room chair that matched the sofa, facing the French doors.

My heart pounding as though I was running long distance, I heard a woman talking. Using a high-pitched dog-conversation voice, she sounded like she knew Daniel's dog. Was this the other girlfriend? I slid down onto my knees, praying my arse wasn't sticking out too far, and listened. God, what if she had a key? Bile rose up in my throat. I swallowed and tried to blink away the tears that had come to my eyes. I wasn't naturally brave.

I heard more chattering and then suddenly, again, the over-exercised calves of the intruder went past the window, then some little yellow legs followed by a warp-speed wagging tail. A click of the gate and they were gone. I was just glad I hadn't peed my pants.

Pins and needles were creeping into my legs and I wiggled them around on the floor, sitting out like a doll and resting my back to the wall. I knew I had to move but I didn't have the guts just yet to do anything but curse quietly under my breath. I kept wiggling and looked around, trying to gauge Daniel's personality. Bright Ikea- and Freedom-style furniture abounded and there was a rash of photos on the sideboard between me and the TV set. His mother looked like Lenin and the rest of his family appeared to have some form of halitosis as they were all either scowling or photographed alone. A nasty business.

Crisis over, I stood up and decided to get out of the limelight of the lounge room. The door adjoining the central corridor of the front of the house and this modern extension was stained glass, new, kitsch and out of sync with the modern edge of the lounge room. I was never fond of that old-style

romantic flower motif. It reminded me of dusty pink orna-
mental soap and lace curtains (i.e. my sister-in-law, Denise).

I pushed my way through the door and relaxed in the
semi-darkness of the closed corridor. All four doors off the
hall were closed. My eyes slowly focused in the semi-
darkness and I clenched my fists to stop them shaking. I was
never good with deathly silence; it always made me want to
break spontaneously into the hits of a Broadway musical.
To control myself, I whistled quietly as I opened the door
to the first room on the left. I was halfway through 'My
Little Buttercup' by the time my eyes had adjusted enough
to the light. The blinds were up about a third on the windows so I could see everything fine and dandy.

This was either a junk room or someone hadn't taken their
anger management classes at all seriously. Clothes were strewn
about, boxes of wine were opened and half-empty, and the
large, dark wood wardrobe that stood across from me to the
left of the window was spewing clothes. Girl's clothes—either
Lenin had passed away, Helen had started moving in already
or he had an ex-partner who hadn't quite moved out yet.
I picked up a pink scarf. Pretty. There were five boxes of
clothes and the same again of wine. It all looked slightly dusty,
so I was guessing it wasn't anything urgent or unknown to
Helen.

Standing in a corner, with boxes stacked against it, was
an antique bookcase—with a two-door cupboard below, and
the glassed-in bookcase starting at waist-height. The glassed-
in section was locked. I opened the cupboard below, pushing
the boxes to one side. Nothing but an abandoned dinner service, and an ugly one at that. Big roses blossomed next to

big, red satiny ribbons. It was enough to put you off your food. No key for the glass doors, though.

I peered through the glass. There were lots of musty paperbacks and a couple of those fake leather books with 'Photo Album' embossed on the spine. One was still covered in plastic. The key could be anywhere. I moved the boxes back and scanned the rest of the room. Nothing.

I closed the door and moved on down the corridor, swiftly segueing to 'Xanadu' as I tried to fill the still air around me. The other rooms were less messy, one bedroom at the front on the right with a large wooden bed, a weights room opposite which was also sort of dusty, and a dining room next to the bedroom that featured some regrettable wine stains on the carpet and circles on the table. Someone needed some coasters.

Realising I would have to stick around long enough to avoid running into the dog-walker, I went back to the front bedroom and went through all the stuff. Porn in drawer three of his bedside cabinet under some socks, boxers in a pile on the bed and shoes in an Ikea shoe tower next to the chest of drawers. Suits hanging in the wardrobe revealed nothing; pockets in jeans and tracksuits netted another big zero. There were two leather jackets that looked largely unworn; one brown, suit style, the other a longer black suede. Both pockets were empty. I was looking for phone numbers, but I had an inkling I was covering old ground.

If Helen was going to pay me a couple of grand, she wanted me to do more than she was capable of. It's well known that if you poke around, you're bound to find shit you don't want to find. I was the shit collector. Not unlike the dog-walker, I guess. Right on cue, I heard the gate clang shut, a high-pitched voice and some barking—then silence.

I peered through the front curtains, and watched as the woman's perky bum power-walked down the drive towards the street and disappeared past Penny's house. That was fast. I checked my watch. Only twenty minutes had gone by. I wondered if Daniel knew his dog-walker was such a slacker and if he was paying her for the cheapskate service. One escape route open again. I just had to avoid catching Penny's mum's eye after such a prolonged inspection.

I stood in the room and looked around. Now where would I hide stuff from a new girlfriend? I ran my hands under every jumper in the drawers, carefully between T-shirts and then pulled out every drawer to see if anything was taped along the sides or back. I couldn't anticipate how devious or neurotic this fellow really was. I hit paydirt when I fumbled under the powdery drawer liners, probably a present from Lenin.

I lifted the jumpers out of the drawer carefully and removed a bunch of paper. There were print-outs of emails and a couple of letters pressed flat from the weight of some dreadful, woven leather belts. My heart was thumping and I could feel the sweat sheen itself over my skin like a protective shield. I'd dated losers before. I knew what it was like when they fucked up. I also knew some guys just couldn't say no, no matter who they were with or what they felt.

Adolescence has a lot more power than we give it credit for, and every rejection and bad hair day gives rise to a desperate need to be popular later in life. It's hard to say no when you're used to hearing it from other people. An emotional back-up plan is always tempting for anyone who doesn't like to be alone. I was guessing Daniel was one of those people. I put the jumpers back and sat down on the floor against the foot of the bed to start reading.

—Original Message—
From: Vardia Salance
           [SMTP:VardiaSalance@southern.com.au]
Sent: Wednesday, 6 February 2002 11:46 am
To: DanielGlass@southern.com.au
Subject: Wednesday

Dear Daniel

Wednesday's fine for the meeting. I thought you wanted it Tuesday. What about the catering? You think Wendell's organising it? I thought Dick was talking crap about the whole Melbourne incident. No one cares anyway, so I hope you're not concerned. How about talking to Felicity and finding out if there'll be a Christmas party this year? I was hoping to get some karaoke.

VS
Vardia Salance
Promotions and Publicity
Southern Mobile Phones
'We're in your range'

I read two more but it was dull stuff. Unless Daniel got a woody over the thought of dueting to 'Two Less Lonely People in the World' with Vardia, I was wondering what the fuss was about. The emails were all work related and all from Vardia.

I felt my eyes moistening in boredom as she discussed the dramatic beverage disaster at the last board meeting. I - pictured spiked drinks and Rohypnol numbing the defences of the management, until I discovered she meant someone had spilled coffee on the CEO's report. If only she'd had a look at Daniel's dining room. Maybe Daniel had been the bumbling one and Vardia was just trying to be subtle. Either way, it was more boring than the sports section and my arse was sore. Why the hell was he printing and saving these?

I took a quick glance at the letters but my instincts told me I'd been there long enough. Now I had a key to the house I'd be like Cool Hand Luke. I carefully replaced the papers and brushed down my clothes so it wasn't obvious I had been crawling through windows. All was well until I heard a key in the lock and footsteps in the hall just a few feet away from me.

I froze. My skin turned to ice under the sweat as foot-steps thudded down the hallway. My mind was racing. Had I left anything in the living room? I looked wildly around but I knew my bag was still behind the armchair in there. I swallowed my breakfast again, which clearly wasn't going to settle any time soon, and dropped silently to the floor in a crouch, then down on my hands and knees.

Ignoring dust balls and an abandoned condom wrapper, I crawled silently to the bed, which had some space under it, but wasn't wildly high. Cursing the chocolate mousse lunch week for the second time, I slithered under the bed, holding my breath. Clearly the cleaner hadn't bothered to do any excess work under here. Tiny hills of dust were knocked to the ground and puffed up around me like fog as I crawled forward. I breathed as shallowly as I could, but by the time my feet were under the bed and my bottom was pressed flat against the planks holding the mattress in place, I realised I should have gone in feet-first so I could watch the door. As it was, all I could see was the dusty skirting board. I paused, listening.

I heard a clang coming from the living room and took the chance to quickly swivel around, letting my head and feet poke out the opposite sides of the bed as I moved, hitting various objects as I went and slipping on some forgotten porn mags. That brief exposure to the rest of the bedroom again emphasised the closeness of the planks to my head. I pushed away an old pair of shoes from the corner of the bed closest to the door. They too were covered in dust.

I laid my head on my arms and closed my eyes, trying to calm myself. I just had to hope whoever was there wouldn't notice the bag or my presence and pray that I didn't sneeze. I guessed fainting from fear might be the best thing in the end anyway. Then I heard footsteps making their way up the hall towards me. A trickle of sweat made a break for it on my forehead, ran slowly down my temple and slipped into my eye.

The heavy tread had prepared me for a man, but it was a very cranky woman with tennis shoes and faded, scuffed old jeans who stomped into the room. She went around to the side table next to the bed, the one with all the porn, pulled out a drawer and I could hear her riffling through the papers. She wasn't half as startled as I'd been by the *Food Fight Fannies* magazine sitting on top, so my guess was she'd been there before. They didn't look like Helen's feet—too small and I couldn't imagine her in sneakers. Maybe the slack cleaner?

She sat down on the bed with a huff and blew through her teeth a few times as though she was doing something stressful or exhausting. I couldn't tell which but I guessed the former. I looked at my watch and with a sinking feeling in my gut realised it was nearly four o'clock.

I'd been there longer than planned—the whole sickening honesty gig at Zara's had really kinked my cool. Time for my alarm to go off. Tennis Shoes had been here before and seemed pretty comfortable with the place, so she'd probably know if something was off—which meant I had to do something about my watch and fast.

With my tongue poking ever so slightly between my teeth, I gently unstrapped the watch from my wrist. Looking around for something to muffle the noise I found a dust-covered sock in the shoes I'd just moved. Holding my breath in case I cartoon-sneezed I eased the watch inside the sock, twisting the end and then turning the sock back inside itself. With Tennis Shoes to my left, I inched carefully with my forearms to the bottom right-hand side of the bed, as close to the door as I could, then I scrunched my arm slightly to give myself some back swing.

I was left-handed and my backhand was strong, so I felt more confident gripping it tightly with my knuckles facing the ceiling. With the sock tightly in my left hand, I swung along the floorboards towards the back of the room for velocity and then with a prayer let it go, watching it fly almost silently through the bedroom door and across the hall.

I sucked in a breath as it slid through the open door of the gym room across the hall and softly ricocheted against the surface, took a lazy turn towards the window and landed near the padded leg of what looked like a bench press.

Withdrawing my arm I was still dangerously close to the corner of the bed, but I didn't dare move. I was frozen, listening for any sound of suspicion; my heart was in my throat as silence hung in the air. I heard her sigh, close the drawer and then I stifled a squeak as my watch beeped merrily from the other room. She let out a girlie squeal before apparently slapping her hand over her mouth.

She padded carefully around the bed. My arm was only

centimetres from her feet as she left the room in search of the noise. I took that chance to slide backwards so that my feet rested against the skirting board as she entered the other room.

Not that I'd known, but it seemed that a sock with a watch in it wasn't an uncommon sight in a gym room because she made a nervous attempt at a laugh when she bent down to unfold it. She had her back to me so all I saw were skinny legs clad in pale blue jeans before she stomped back out again.

Then I heard the front door slam and released a huge sigh of relief. But I'd been unconsciously holding my breath and the gasp that followed sucked in enough dust to make me sneeze twice. I waited, fearful, in case she hadn't moved from the veranda in time, but after a few minutes I decided it was safe to leave.

I still had to crawl out, make my dusty, crumpled suit look corporate again and then sneak out the back door, unseen by Penny's mum. Daniel always returned home at around 5.25.

I shuffled about on my stomach, my bones groaning as I slid into a crouch, then stretched up, like an acrobat finishing a spectacular stunt, to get the crick out of my neck. I crossed to the bedside table and pulled open the drawer. Nothing looked amiss so I carefully lifted up *Food Fight Fannies,* catching sight of a vibrator and some pretty icky looking hairs stuck to it. I couldn't remember if that, or the hairs, had been there before, but either way—Euuw!

I grabbed the watch and then made my way quietly down the corridor, gingerly opening the back door to the living room and looking around before I stepped in. There was no one about, not even the dog. I spied my bag crushed behind the chair, looking wonderfully abandoned and unsuspicious. The dog was curled up in a cane basket beside the doors outside. He was sleeping, so the chances of another enthusiastic welcome were slimmer.

As I slipped the key into the lock and lifted the bottom latch, I realised that there was a good chance that the latch would be dropped again, before I had a chance to come back, especially if Daniel noticed the missing key. Not looking forward to the opportunity of reliving my toilet torpedo adventure, I popped some chewing gum in my mouth, munching a few times before the delicious strawberry gave way to the sensation of chewing on my own bile, then wedged the chewy behind the head of the latch. I stood back. If he noticed the latch hadn't dropped, he'd see it in a second, but if not, there was a chance I'd be able to return with my dignity intact.

I stepped outside, relocked the door silently and crept to the gate. Five minutes later I was in my car. The street was empty except for the Beetle. Probably they couldn't afford to run it except for quick, illegal dashes to the BP for the munchies. I remembered owning a car during my five festive years at Adelaide University and not being able to pay for registration. Riding a bike is only fun in good weather. Being called Butch Cassidy also didn't help my mood when I'd come home dripping, my carefully written lecture notes soaked through in my cheap backpack.

Back safely in my car, I sighed dramatically and gulped water from a bottle I kept in the glove compartment. I was exhausted. I stopped at the first pub I came to, walked inside, ordered a beer and finished it in minutes. I went over what I'd seen. Despite their mindnumbing content, I had to read the other letters to find out why Daniel had kept them and also look in the bedside table more thoroughly to see what Tennis Shoes had been up to.

I ordered another beer, this time a light, and watched some guys play pool for a while. As they showed off I slowly felt normal again. One seemed conscious of me, and I was worried that he'd come over, but he went off to the bathroom, leaving his friends without a fourth. It seemed fart competitions came a close second to pool so I picked up my drink and moved into the booth that afforded me a view of the car park. I checked my wrist and it was fine. It stung but it was really only a surface cut and the blood had dried.

I pulled out a cigarette, smoked it slowly, waved goodbye to the bartender as I went to the bathroom and then nearly tripped over the pool guy on the phone in the narrow corridor. He looked sort of familiar but I couldn't think of why. After my recent adventures I was relieved he hadn't made a move; it seemed that I was better at handling dogs than men.

Thankfully I wasn't working until the next day, and anticipated curling up on my couch with some Vegemite toast and red cordial. Comfort food worked well on my nerves. I got back in the car with relief.

Halfway home I glanced in the rear-view mirror and noticed a car roaring up behind me. I went to indicate to change lanes, thinking it was a hoon who couldn't believe anyone would drive at the speed limit, when all of a sudden I felt a crash and shot forward into the windscreen but my seatbelt held me back. I tried to grab the wheel as I flew towards the parklands across two lanes of traffic, horns blaring in my ears.

It was too late. Scrub and darkness loomed in my window and I banged into the steering wheel. I bounced over something, the seatbelt straining against my shoulder. The breath flew out of me and I slammed to a stop. The world became quiet except for my gasping and the chugging of the car. The branches of a tree were shaking against the glass with little scritching sounds and I snapped off my seatbelt, flopping back against the seat and trying to stay calm.

I mentally checked myself for injuries. My legs still moved; so did my arms. I rolled my neck. Okay, but I felt like I'd had a vigorous sports massage, all sore, strange and sort of stoned. I shut the car down. The silence was unnerving and I remembered the car behind me. I reached into my bag on the passenger seat and grabbed my screwdriver.

I'd started carrying it around after some guys approached me on the street one night, looking for cash. I eventually lost them by bursting into a Lebanese sweet shop and threatening the pursuing gang with a metal serviette holder. It was blunt, but effective. I'd scored a couple of ladies' fingers from the sympathetic manager, but I couldn't count on that sort of quick thinking every night, so I kept the screwdriver there just in case. I flung open the car door, hand tool extended like a dagger.

I struggled out, still shaking, hit a branch, stumbled, slipped on a pile of wet mush and flew headlong into some woodchips. A dark shape threw itself at me and a dull roar filled my ears. I rolled and screamed, thrashing about until I realised I was stabbing at the air and my legs were wrapped around rubber and chains. I lay there a moment, trying to catch my breath and listened. The roar was the traffic behind me. The attacker was a child's swing.

I carefully untangled my leg and sat up, alert to the movements around me. I was in a playground, a square climbing gym between me and the road. No one came up behind me, no car, no running madman. There was no one attending to the runaway car, just the sounds of the city.

I crawled towards my car and used the door to pull myself upwards, muscles resisting the movement. I checked the vehicle. Nothing was smashed except the bushes I'd unintentionally used as brakes, like a runaway rollerskater hitting a pile of cushions. My rear bumper was dented but not broken.

I fell into the driver's seat, keen to leave the scene of the accident before the hoons came around the block to assess the damage. I reversed, scraping the bonnet against the trees and bushes, and negotiated my way back through the playground backwards, my left arm wrapped around the shoulders of the car seat next to me. Crunching my way slowly over the surrounding woodchips, I bounced down over the curb and slid into the empty parking lane, swung around and pulled back into traffic once the lights up ahead created a gap.

I turned on the radio and drove carefully, putt-putting along as though I had an aquarium of fish next to me on the seat. When I pulled up into the parking spot on the street outside my house some ten minutes later, I wished for the fiftieth time that my apartment had undercover parking. The street was dark and, for the second time today, I was frightened.

I spent the day after the crash in bed nursing aching muscles and a groaning headache. I called in sick at work and then occupied myself muttering obscenities as Jock screeched for a while, pooed in my hair, kissed me and then picked at a pimple on my chin until it bled. I called Helen, making an appointment to tell her what I'd found so far and then comforted myself with chocolate. We played Russian Roulette with the remote (Jock has very trashy taste in daytime television), then I woke the next day with the idea that it might have been Amanda's Tony who'd sent me sprawling through toddler land. I couldn't think of anyone else who would be that mad at me.

Not only did it make sense, but Tony drove a truck, and it was certainly the high headlights of a truck that I had seen bearing down on me that night in the dark. And, on reflection, it was certainly possible the fourth guy at pool the previous night hadn't been so much interested in me as recognised me. I should have paid more attention, but maybe the guy on the phone was one of the guys from the Redneck. My world was closing in and it was making me twitchy.

I didn't have any enemies. Well, none that would bother to initiate that sort of drag strip action. The majority of the people who didn't like me were drippy boys who smoked too much dope, and they were only mildly annoyed because I got sick of them never doing the dishes. If Neil's behaviour was anything to go by, they'd have forgotten me as soon as I moved out. Most of them had lost their car keys, along with their minds, after bucket bong #32. Besides, I had a feeling I'd been driven off the road for a reason.

I was working with Amanda again that evening and prepared myself for a confrontation. When she walked into the coffee room some three hours after we'd both started our shift, I hooked the door latch, effectively locking out the rest of the world. I'd locked the front door. I was too angry to contemplate how my boss would react to finding us closed at this time. Amanda was too busy heating up her noodles to hear the click, but when she turned around to see me with my arms crossed and my face set with fury, she jumped back, knocking her head on the condiments cupboard.

'Cass, what's up?' she squeaked, her hands shaking as she put the noodles down on the table in front of her. 'You want some noodles?'

'Why would you be offering me your trailer trash noodles today when you never have in the past?' I asked, walking towards her and pulling out a chair. I sort of liked the idea of towering over her but my feet were killing me in my new patent-leather boots and I had to rest my sorry impulse-purchase arse. 'You got something else you want to share with me?'

'I don't know what you mea—'

In good *LA Law* style, I cut in, taking a punt. 'I know it was your fiancé who rammed me the other night. I can't believe you'd be such a stupid twit as to 'fess up to what we did.'

I slammed my hand down on the table, making the salt and pepper bounce in the air. 'You fucking turncoat.' This was really looking good. Clearly I'd spent too much time at Zara's watching late-night TV.

'I—I couldn't help it. They were mad, they wanted to find out who set the cops on Ton—'

Relief flooded through me as I realised I'd been right. Relief and triumph.

'That was the goddamn pub, Amanda. That had nothing to do with us!'

'I–I know, but they were mad, and I had to tell them something!'

I braced myself against the table and stared at her. 'Why? Why on earth would they think you knew anything about it anyway? It's ridiculous.'

'They said they recognised you from somewhere. They thought you were a friend of Samantha and they were going to go around there and–'

'And what? Beat her up? So you turned them in my direction to stop your sister getting hurt.' I slammed my hand down on the table again, hoping to move the serviette roll, but no luck. 'Boy, you're stupid. What did you think they were going to do? Give me a warning? They could have killed me. You're just lucky they don't know the girl who helped me that night or you'd be rolling down the aisle in a wheelchair.'

Okay, so I was getting a little too Al Pacino, but my temper had been let loose and I felt good. She was quaking in her hot-pink mules and I needed some payback for the lump on my head.

I took a deep breath but was caught short by the expression on her face. When I had mentioned Josie her pupils had dilated to points and I felt my skin blanch. 'You didn't!'

'I had to. They wanted to know everything.'

'He's your fiancé, not the bloody FBI. You don't have to...' I shook my head. 'Never mind. You don't know where she lives...' I remembered with a flash the discussions we'd had about catering for her wedding. Fuck. The café.

I jumped up. 'Do they know where Josie works?'

I could tell by her expression they not only knew, they'd probably already drained their cappuccinos.

I flew from the room, knocking over some teenagers balancing a week's worth of videos. I had a moment of Bruce Willis cool when I managed to leap over the revolving gate, but then tripped on the step by the door, and nearly sprawled on the footpath outside.

I slammed the car door and roared from the carpark, trying to figure out how long it would take me to drive to Josie's café. Too long, I figured, as I remembered the look on Amanda's face. I hadn't spoken to Josie since the crash.

While I'd known Zara from school, Josie was a relatively new friend from university days. We'd met after my boyfriend at the time had started talking about her. After one night when he'd mentioned the skirt she'd worn to a psych lecture three too many times, in a fit of teenage pique I confronted her in the uni bar. She was so nice I was mortified. She didn't even know who my boyfriend was, but we became firm friends and two days later I dropped him. Josie was lovely but she never hung out in the gorgeous gang. She hung with us: a nerd and a scatterbrain. We loved it.

I cursed not owning a mobile phone to call Gus, my only remaining friend in law enforcement. He was funny, earnest and a slick dresser, circa 1989. He also carried superior weaponry, which wasn't hard considering I was armed with only a pop-up umbrella and a screwdriver. He was just what I needed.

I raced through an orange light and then swung into the side street that housed Josie's café. Street signs told me to adhere to the new forty-kilometres-per-hour regulation but I had tears in my eyes at the thought of someone bailing Josie up, all alone, in the back room, and I just went faster. I pissed off more than one luxury car driver (the area boasted a row of those clothing stores like the ones they always flash in midday movies to indicate you're now on Rodeo Drive) as I screamed past and pulled up near the café. No cop car outside, so I ran in. Okay, I'm not much of a runner. I played the minimum possible team sports back at school, so my joints weren't prepared for the sprint.

By the time I hobbled in, clutching my ankle, I noticed three things that stopped me in my tracks:

1. Josie had painted the place dried-blood maroon.

2. She'd installed rows of long, low lamps that gave the place a 'pash me now' ambience.

3. She was sitting on a black leather cube nursing a huge brick of a glass with a slice of lemon in the bottom.

'Josie! Thank God,' I panted. 'Has anyone…? I mean, did you…?' I took some deep breaths, and then threw the bolt on the door behind me and limped over to another cube.

'Cass, what's wrong?' Josie's eyes were as wide as little casino chips.

'Amanda's bloody fiancé and his thugs ran me down, and I thought they might come in here too. I was worried.' I grabbed the bar phone, rang Gus and breathlessly explained what had happened. He promised to send a car over, so I grabbed a bowl of peanuts and flopped on the couch opposite her.

I took in more details as I glanced around; chrome brick ashtrays, succulents buried in grey stones and potted in white rock planters, sexy music oozing from the stereo. 'It looks great, Josie. Very *Wallpaper.*'

'Thanks. I won't be eating for a month, but I love it. The workmen have been here for the past two days, painting and doing the electrics.' She trailed off, her eyes bright. 'Hang on, there *were* some guys here. I didn't pay much attention. I was out the back with John, who rigged up the alarm system. The boys out front said they chucked them out.' She glanced at me. 'Might have been them.' She looked around. 'Thank God for redecorating.'

I nodded, eyeing Josie's glass. She caught my look and walked up to the bar, poured two more vodka tonics and brought them back.

'I didn't know you were fully licensed.'

'Got it last week. Coffees and baguettes can only get you so far. I'm staying open later, too. There're a couple of restaurant/clubs around here, off Darson Road, only five minutes' walk, and we're cross-promoting. Special deals, stuff like that. They don't want anyone just there for coffee or cocktails before eleven because they do dinner and then set up for dancing. They maximise their space, and now so do I.' She looked very pleased with herself, and I couldn't help smiling.

'Sounds good,' I muttered, sipping my drink. Dashing to the scene of possible danger had depleted my resources. When a police car screeched to a halt in the middle of the road, and two officers leapt out, I went outside and they drilled me with questions as we walked into the café.

Josie was busying herself folding huge red napkins in half as I explained the gig with Amanda and suggested they follow it up with Tony and his henchmen.

'You should have reported this sooner,' said the short, gruff one. Cops seemed to have an opinion on everything. I know Gus was always correcting my grammar.

'Sure,' I muttered. I *had* made a mistake. I was just too nauseous from residual fear to eat the necessary humble pie.

'Well, we'll send someone on a drive-by for a week and keep a lookout. Anything odd, you call us.'

I poured myself another vodka tonic once they left, leaving me officially too tipsy to drive back to work, so I cleared up the mess left over by the renovators in the back room and helped myself to a couple of biscuits. I didn't bother calling Amanda. Let her stew.

By the time I fell asleep in my own bed, it was three in the morning and I wasn't looking forward to working on this report for Helen over the next few days. I was, however, looking forward to revisiting my dream about cruising the Atlantic with Kevin Spacey. A recurring dream can really replace a love-life if you get it right. But I've noticed it's always handy to wake up before he takes off with the deckhand.

I spent the next morning tallying my hours and writing a version of a report to give to Helen when I saw her the following day. It had been a week since I'd started working for her and I felt obliged to continue our frosty interactions by performing all of my duties as a professional PI. Which, of course, I was not.

Counting the days at the stake-out and the investigations online, I tallied eighteen hours, give or take. I didn't include travel time, as I was charging expenses, but I did include receipts for petrol and bought a travel expenses diary. I moved backwards through time, vowing to keep a continuous record for the duration of the job. I even changed pens and writing style a few times in true subterfuge.

I'd done this sort of thing in classes at art school all the time. Painting by instinct on canvas and then working backwards, doing 'preliminary' sketches, cutting out pictures from journals and newspapers to support my artistic direction. It was a load of crap: I just liked splooshing paint around. I got the same kick out of fudging my inspiration as I did lying about my nightly facial cleansing routine. It was pointless but seemed to make other people happy (i.e. the latter had allowed my mother to sleep well at night).

In the report, I left out the cut wrist (which was healing well) and the accident with Amanda's fiancé. I glossed over the access to the house, detailing, however, the intruder and the dog-walker, Daniel's departure and arrival routine, and my plans for the next few days. When I called Helen she was in a meeting but she accepted the hours, said nothing about the dog-walker then hung up after arranging a meeting at a café for breakfast the next morning.

I went over to Zara's place that night with my report notes and typed them up on her computer while she made a pumpkin risotto. She was cranky and had opened a bottle of crap champagne she found in the back of the fridge. As I worked she started to whoop it up in the living room—playing Madonna very loudly and leaping about in her short green nightie like a reject from *Riverdance*—and I realised it must have been more than just her work that was bugging her.

'You having problems?' I asked as she sat down on the couch. 'How's Justin? Is he okay?' Zara was breathing heavily from the exertion as I blinked hard to keep my eyes open.

One glass of that champagne had made me slightly ill and very tired.

'He's fine. He's just fucking fine. Everyone's *fucking* fine.'

'You've played "Material Girl" four times now.' I handed her a glass of water with Aspro Clear, she drained it and then slammed the empty glass down on the wooden coffee table with no coaster. Something was definitely up. Zara was no smelly computer nerd; she took her hygiene very seriously and she always used coasters. She could slip coasters under glasses for Australia. Daniel could learn a thing or two.

Unfortunately she didn't feel the same about her modesty. 'Zars, you're unplundered garden is showing,' I said, pulling her nightie down over her thighs.

'Who cares?' she huffed. 'No one wants to pluck my flowers.' Then she burped. 'I never weed it. The soil's all dead and...' She seemed to struggle for a moment and then slurred 'like clay. Hard and crunchy.' The metaphors were certainly effective and I could pick up a definite theme.

'Who, um, were you hoping might take up the vacant position of groundsman?'

'No one,' she said, but her bottom lip was sticking out.

'Who?'

'Maybe someone at work.'

She hated everyone at work, including her boss and her sister-in-law, who also worked there. 'Working with porn is a taint that could never be erased,' she would say.

'What about working with porn being a tain—'

'S'bullshit,' she slammed a fist into the cushion beside her, noticing for the first time the dirty smudges on the cushion. She peered closer and then giggled. I reminded myself not to call to see how the hangover was coming along in the morning.

'What's bullshit exactly?' Romance and Zara seemed like opposing beasts. I'd toyed with the idea that she was a lesbian for a while until she watched *The Karate Kid* seven times. Being friends since before *Solid Gold* went off the air gave us frightening insights into each other's personalities but I'd wondered if maybe Zara was going to be celibate for the rest of her life.

'The whole bastard business,' she muttered, standing up unsteadily and stumbling into the kitchen. Returning with a glass of water and a packet of cheese biscuits, she flopped back down next to me, ripping open the packet like a savage. Soon her face was covered in little pollen-coloured specks.

'Zara, what is going on? If it's not Justin, it must be work. This is Cassidy you're talking to. C-a-s-s-i-d-y B-l-a-i-r,' I repeated, as though she was weak of hearing. 'I cleaned up your spew from the Night of the Many Fluffy Ducks. I watched *Foot-loose* with you three times in a row. I went to New York-style Electric Boogaloo dance classes at the WEA with you.' I was getting impatient and she hadn't offered the biscuits to me.

'It's just that—' she said with a tremor. 'I'm feeling *blue*.' She wiped her eyes.

Oh, thank God she said something, I thought wearily. 'Right!' I said, about to offer up some platitudes, but she cut me off.

'No! It's not all right. It's George. At work. I think I love George at work,' and then she burst into tears.

I stared at her, bewildered. No wonder she didn't drink very often. It wasn't so much that I was uncomfortable with emotion, it's just the snowball effect of the evening had really punched me in the guts. Zara rarely drank, let alone to the point of dancing. She was always neat and careful, never got upset, never talked about boys, or girls for that matter, in a romantic way. I was completely unnerved.

By the time she'd sucked up some snot and wiped it on her sleeve and my T-shirt, we had settled into the couch, with me patting her knee nervously. She told me she'd been email-ing back and forth with George. Flirty stuff, smiles over the coffee machine, blushing in the lift—nothing tactile. In fact, she'd only spoken to him directly in a meeting with ten other people present. And today, disaster had struck. She'd approached him in the cafeteria.

'Well?' Her pause was much too long. 'You like him, right? There's nothing wrong with that. This whole email love thing has gone too far. How can you test your chemistry with little smilies and electronic winks?'

'He smelt like cheesy feet. He had breath like a man who'd just eaten human flesh.'

I wrinkled up. 'Was it just a bad day? Maybe he'd had onions. Maybe he's in agony right this very minute because he knew he had fart breath and had forgotten to brush his teeth.'

'I sat there for hours this afternoon trying to figure it out. I couldn't approach him again. I mean, what if he thought I was interested, when I was just testing his breath again?'

'Zara, you *are* interested, aren't you? So what's the big deal? If he has fart breath, just tell him. And I have two words for you—*Swotty Sam*. You think you've got it bad. I've got the hots for a guy who used to run around the house in long under-wear with a bin on his head so he'd look like a Stormtrooper.'

'But would you tell Swotty Sam if he had B.O.?'

Luckily, Sam smelt like David Jones's perfume counter and expensive wool, but I could see her point. 'Okay, then. Buy him some Lifesavers: extra mint for that extra glint.'

'I spoke to Benny the mail guy in the lift.' She gulped some water and then went on. 'Benny's the office gossip. He knows everyone's business. He started chatting about everyone as usual and then just brought up George.' She blushed. 'I hate gossip but it would have been rude to ignore him. He said George's breath had wiped out two plants and no one would do Emoto with him anymore.'

'Emoto?'

'Emoto-response classes. It's a test for your emotional and rational responses to incidents at work. All that mumbo-jumbo crap, you know. George has to guess his responses himself.'

'Poor George.'

'I know.'

'Does it make you feel bad for him? Do you want to help him sort this out? It's affecting his work.'

'I think so...' She seemed to be sobering up. I pressed on.

'Do you like him enough to help him out? If he likes you, he'll realise how tough it was for you to say anything to him.'

'But we never talk. It might be too early.'

'It might be too late. He's probably wondering why no one talks to him anymore. He's probably scared, alone, worried.' I was a little caught up in the drama of it all now. Poor George. When Zara turned around to brush biscuit crumbs off the table I cupped my hands around my mouth and smelt. Nothing. But was it like thinking your own jokes are funny? I wrote Tic Tacs on my mental shopping list.

'He's not a child.'

'He is a little bit. Everyone is to some extent. It's horrible to think people don't like you. Does he have any other friends?'

'At work?'

'Yeah.'

She seemed to be thinking. 'I don't think so. He used to hang out with Derek but he got a job in Brisbane.'

'Was Derek a smelly too?'

'Derek wasn't a pine forest.'

'Maybe you should deal with this on a grander scale. Who organised the emoto-response classes?'

'Deirdre, the mumbo-jumbo girl in Occ Health and Safety.'

'Well, what about a class to look at interpersonal behaviour? Have everyone write down all the things about someone that might annoy others. Anonymous tips for people who don't realise they snuffle when they talk on the phone, or laugh too loudly.'

I remembered an incident when someone gave me a box of tissues for Christmas at the Rockin' Roller Disco because I was always sniffing. I'd pretended to laugh but it was awful. 'Don't wait until someone embarrasses him in public, tell him quietly and softly. Be a friend. Someone close to him should have done this before. Maybe they did but he didn't take it seriously. If you don't, you'll be embarrassed until it's resolved. You can't not let him know why you've gone frosty on him.'

She looked unconvinced. 'It might work.'

'Or you could send him an anonymous email.'

She brightened up. 'That's a good idea. Why didn't I think

of that? I could send him an e-card, and then I could say...'
She frowned. 'But what if he knows it's from me?'

'Well, if you phrase it right, he won't mind.'

'I guess.'

'Look, Zara, you said you loved him. Maybe you're drunk, but you should tell him the truth. Imagine if he's sitting there thinking, Wow, I sure like Zara, but if only she knew she had a little piece of snot sitting in her nostrils like an earthworm, I would have asked her out.'

'Yeah, you're right.'

'Okay, then.' I got up, brushing biscuit crumbs off my trousers and getting my gear together. I had to feed Jock and go to sleep.

'Zars,' I said, hitching up my shoulder bag. 'You do have an earthworm snot sitting in your nose.'

I let myself out, wishing there was a button I could press to erase bad incidents from the past. I know memories teach you stuff for the future, a self-defence mechanism, but it was tormenting to recall the lame stories I've told at parties, the time I forgot friends' names during introductions, the bit of poo that fell on my shoes somehow and made its way with me right through school assembly. It's a nightmare of mental self-flagellation. Better to focus on someone else's torment. I'd go back to Daniel's house in the morning after dropping the report off to Helen.

'Darling, I miss you. I can't wait to come home and make love with you again. Sometimes it's my heart that yearns for you, other times, my head. My fingers itch to touch you, my lips to kiss you...'

This was the third letter and my face was screwed into such an expression of disgust it hurt. Suzie, the volunteer librarian, was a wistful woman. I'd thought at first I'd hit pay-dirt, that I had something to hand to Helen to avoid the flaring face I'd been confronted with that morning, but I'd been wrong.

She'd read the report over cheesy bagels. I'd sipped a skim-milk strawberry smoothie, aware that I had to start doing something about my spare tyre. My stomach growled furiously every time a steaming plate of pancakes or eggs went past in a waiter's hand, but I ignored it. In my dreams the night before while I was sitting on Sam's lap in a liplock, my thighs had grown into enormous slabs of kabana sausage and he'd been squished. I had woken up covered with sweat.

Helen had nodded and tucked the report into her brief-case. I'd plucked up my courage and whispered that I needed to know what sort of contraception she used. She'd glared at me as though I'd slapped her.

'Why?'

'Because I found a condom wrapper under Daniel's bed next to his Dr Scholls.'

From her expression I guessed she was an IUD girl.

'We stopped using condoms after we both got tested,' but her face told me it was all my fault. Now I know what they mean by shooting the messenger. If I was going to take this job seriously, though, I'd be dodging bullets all over the place. Better get a Kevlar vest for my ego.

'It could have been an old wrapper,' I said hopefully.

'Sure,' she huffed. Those nostrils had their own atmosphere.

We decided that I would outline anything suspicious, embarrassing or likely to get me fired, along with the date and details, in another report at the end of the week. Then she could choose what she pursued with Daniel or not.

She wrapped an uneaten bagel in a napkin and stood up. 'Call me on Saturday and give me another report. I'm hoping for something more concrete by the end of the week.' Then she was gone. I figured the early departure was some kind of psych-out, a way of always having the final word.

I was also starting to wonder if she actually *wanted* me to find some dirt on Daniel. Maybe she just needed an excuse to break up with him. Maybe she couldn't admit she was scared of commitment. Maybe she secretly wanted him to be cheating on her because then it would be cut and dried; her suspicions would be justified and thus any ensuing guilt over employing me would disappear. Maybe I just had too much time on my hands.

But as I got my things together and prepared to leave, I realised Helen hadn't left. Well, she'd left the café but she was standing on the footpath staring at the ground. And then I sucked in a breath, because as she suddenly turned to walk off I saw she'd been crying, and her big nose was all red. I felt terrible, like somehow it was my fault, but I shook myself out of it. I'd had enough experience with guys to know they were capable of this, and a whole lot worse.

And I thought I'd found my evidence until I reached soppy letter number two and saw the date: nine years earlier. I checked the others. They were all old, as were the cards I'd found tucked into the bundle of letters, in a different handwriting and dated thirteen years ago. Suzie had a bad habit of drawing little love hearts instead of dots above her I's. Simone, the card writer, was prone to plush toy metaphors: You're my fluffy bear/little cuddle buddle.' It was sickening stuff.

I'd been there for an hour and it was nearly eleven o'clock. I checked the bookcase in the junk room again. Still locked. I should have asked Helen about it. Making a note to ask her next time I saw her, I scanned the rest of the room. I inspected the bedside drawer again. The vibrator was in the same spot but it had been cleaned. I poked about in the drawer.

It had been neatened. I made a note of the contents, time and date and I went through the same search as the other day, coat pockets, behind drawers, under drawers, between the mattress and base of the bed. The dust had settled again.

In a shoebox under a stack of old smelly sneakers I found an odd little collection.

The box contained a tiny dried pink rose; its faded green leaves clutching the outer petals like claws. Three marbles rolled around the box, hitting the edge of a bracketed silver frame. I pulled it out. A nude girl with long red hair, tiny features and an enormous monobrow glared out, reclining on a red velvet rug. In the opposite frame photo, a large alsatian drooled all over a rug.

I slipped the backing out but there was no writing on the back so I noted them and moved on. A small travelogue contained mundane details of a holiday, with the odd reference to a girl named Alex, or 'A'. I knew she was a girl because he said her breasts were like water balloons filled to bursting. Romantic stuff.

Well, this was more like it. I flicked through a couple of pieces of paper tucked between the pages; gleaning little but the fact that he'd seen *Cats* twice within the same week in February some seven years earlier and that he liked to park at the Discount Angus Street Parking Corp. Why these were saved I couldn't guess, but I wrote them down anyway. There was always the chance that Helen hadn't mentioned these things to me. She might compare my list with her own discoveries.

I crawled under the bed again, ran my hands under the dresser and wardrobe. I was still in council/white ants mode, wearing a long black pencil-skirt and green wool skivvy from the back of my wardrobe and I had to shrug the skirt up onto my thighs so it wouldn't rip. I brushed dust from my skirt and sleeves; I couldn't wait to wash my hands.

This morning I'd slipped quietly in the side gate and, seeing no one, dropped two sandwiches for the dog. He'd barely raised his head as I sauntered through and opened the back door with the key. The chewing gum was in place.

The blanket box in Daniel's bedroom was just crammed with sheets and pillowcases, so I stood on tippie-toes and unzipped the suitcase on the top shelf of the wardrobe. Once I got a look at the lumpy dark blue jumper and the stone-washed jeans I realised these were sad old eighties clothes he probably thought might come back into fashion.

'In your dreams, pal.'

I placed all the crummy clothes back on top and zipped it all up. I hefted the suitcase back into the wardrobe and moved the blanket box into place against the wall under the window.

I looked around the room some more. So he kept old crap, but among that old crap might be clues. Most people keep personal stuff in their bedroom, as though their presence protects it from prying eyes. I moved to the wardrobe again, where I'd already gone through the coats. There was a zippered suit bag which contained a suit of brown rayon with white fleck, kept perhaps in the hope that it might still woo women twenty years after it was tailored by Reef Co. in Bali.

There was another answer, though. As I looked over my list, with the letters and the bits of junk and souvenirs, I could see a pattern. What if Daniel kept all these things because they really meant something to him emotionally? What if the big bogan jumper from the suitcase was the one he wore on a date with Suzie, or the mustard shirt with embroidered panels was worn with Alex? I carefully lifted out the suit and found something that confirmed my fears.

Hanging behind it was a red satin teddy with little glittery diamonds splashed across the cleavage in the early nineties scattergun approach with a Bedazzler. Either Daniel was secretly dressing like a twelve-year-old girl preparing for her first rock eisteddfod or this was another souvenir.

With my notepad stuffed down my undies I moved into the stale sweat smell of the weights room. A couple of machines and a small stereo were as dusty as the windowsill, so I was careful not to touch anything.

On the mantelpiece sat a stack of CDs—including Triple J Hottest 100 #3, the soundtrack to *Fight Club*, the greatest hits of Barry Manilow and a couple of Chris Isaak's. Not bad, although he clearly hadn't listened to them for a while. I discovered a disgusting towel was the source of the stench and then realised I hadn't seen a laundry. I backed out of the room and went to look.

The dog was sniffing around the flowerbeds and I gave him a friendly wave as I walked around to the right, into the bathroom where I'd made such a spectacular entrance, and found the laundry. It was an unremarkable room: white tiles, slightly scungy sink, streaky mirror, tubes of toothpaste dangled from a cup suspended by what looked like a mixture of soap scum and dust. The laundry bin was full and when I opened the cupboard behind the door, I found a washing machine and dryer with a clothes hanger down the side between the machines and the wall.

A sudden shriek behind me sent me flying against the machines. I clamped my hand over my mouth as I realised it was the phone. My heart was thudding against my chest as I shakily closed the door to the machines and left the room just as the answering machine picked up. It was Helen.

'Hi darling, it's me. I know you told me your mother was coming over today to do your laundry, but I was wondering if you'd like to ask her for dinner sometime this week? Just a thought. If she's coming at two o'clock, she may well still be there by the time you get home. See you tonight.'

My heart didn't lag from its panicked state as I checked my watch. It was a quarter to twelve. But if I was expecting Lenin to arrive with her washing powder, I didn't want to take any chances. I mentally reviewed the house, checked the notes in my pants and let myself out again, but not before shoving the original key under the mat by the back door. I'd return tomorrow.

I slipped from the house, crossed the street and walked the three blocks to my car. I was getting nervous about the time I'd spent there, and was wondering if anyone had noticed me being there. I sat behind the wheel, filling in the gaps, trying to remember everything I could from the house. I didn't know what would come in handy later, but if Helen was going there tonight, whatever was different tomorrow would be due to her, and I wanted to make sure I hadn't missed anything.

I put on my big dark Jackie O sunglasses and started the car. A blast of Spandau Ballet hit me as I turned around, driving slowly past Daniel's house. Lenin hadn't arrived yet, but I blew out a sigh at the close shave. Thank God Helen had

had the brains to warn me. He must have told her after our talk this morning and she'd done the only thing possible.

I pulled up to the intersection between Daniel's street and the main road and idly watched a small group of school children crossing the road with their parents. It wasn't until they turned right and walked up the street and one of them, a thin woman, headed separately along Daniel's road alone that I realised she was wearing tennis shoes and faded, scuffed blue jeans.

I turned left and sped along the tree-lined road until I could turn again into another side street. These suburban streets all ran parallel until they hit the Torrens river that wound itself through Adelaide, from the crumbling kitsch outer suburbs and beyond. I'd never actually seen the beyond and guessed that the river itself was wider and bluer there than the murky sludge here, but I could be wrong. It had happened before on an almost ritual basis.

I broke the speed limit in the hope that I could catch her making her way into Daniel's place. I didn't want to think about it being a coincidence—I needed this. A one-way street came up on the left and I took it too sharply, nearly nicking a car on the corner. I slowed as I entered Daniel's street and drove past his house just as Tennis Shoes was passing Penny's in the opposite direction. She'd ignored the house. I pulled over to the left and checked my rear-vision mirror. With no one parked behind me, I had a clear vision of the road. I could see Tennis Shoes disappearing up towards the river, or, more importantly, away from Daniel's house.

Bugger. It would have been so perfect. If I'd seen her go in I might have been able to follow her home and piece something solid together. As it was I had few investigative skills and little in the way of street smarts, so I did a quick U-turn on the empty road, running through a list of colourful expletives as I nearly collided with another car. I was considering following Tennis Shoes just to see her safely from the area, when I noticed a blue sedan in Daniel's driveway.

While I was driving around the block, Lenin had arrived early. I drove slowly along the street, keeping a lookout, and eventually Tennis Shoes turned up outside a tiny deli further down the road.

Spindly chrome chairs and tables spilled out of a corner doorway filled with bright streamers. As I passed, looking for somewhere to leave the car, a man in a white apron emerged through the door carrying a cup. I pulled in around the corner. While the streets were empty, I didn't want to make myself any more identifiable than I had to.

I grabbed a denim jacket from the back seat, locked up and strolled back. I was grateful for the sunglasses, which allowed me to zoom in on Tennis Shoes's features as she hunched over the table. She was thin and exuded self-consciousness. She stirred the cup with long, unadorned fingers. It was a typical deli offering sandwiches, chocolate bars, hot chips and thickshakes. I ordered an orange juice and a muesli slice.

Of the four tables crammed up against the brickwork outside, she occupied the one furthest from the door, facing me, but with her back towards Daniel's street. I sat at the table next to her facing the deli and pulled out my magazine.

My practised anonymity died as I realised I was holding the copy of *Hustler* that I'd picked up at the service station and used to ram the louvre open. I popped the top on the juice, aware of her sitting hunched over on my right but I hadn't actually turned my head. I glanced casually around, sucking up every close encounter detail as I scanned.

She was very thin and looked the neurotic type—burning fat by thinking about how much space she took up and how nobody liked her.

I memorised her features as I picked at the slice. She had long, thin blonde hair, the type that makes a finger-slim pony-tail. Her skin was pale; her eyes were green, fringed with long lashes blotched with mascara. She wasn't exactly dressed for a secret rendezvous, but then what did I know? My last serious date ended with me vomiting in a plastic recycling box after drinking crème de menthe.

She stood up with a scrape and walked past me, away from Daniel's house. It happened so quickly that I choked and a little juice came back up my nose. I crept to the corner of the building and looked around. She was disappearing into the distance, her long legs blending with the footpath and shadows.

When I turned back to my slice, a little Murray magpie was sitting on the table pecking at the remaining piece so I shooed it away, threw the bits on the ground, picked up my bag and returned to the car. I'd do one last drive-by, then go home.

The dark sedan was still in the drive but this time the two front windows were open and I could see movement in the bedroom. I guessed laundry to Lenin meant a full spring-clean. I wondered what she would do with *Food Fight Fannies*.

That night at DVDWorld I discovered that Amanda had handed in her notice the day before. I guess the wedding preparations just took it out of her. A new boy called Barry had started and he was happy to let me alphabetise the shelves while he served. I liked alphabetising. I had to write it on my arm, but it was as relaxing as meditation—so when Zara turned up right after I had organised all the Cs, I was in a Zen-like state that even her distress couldn't suck me out of.

'Cass!'

'Uh-huh.' I looked up in a daze as she touched me on the shoulder. Her eyes were bright and her lids blotchy with red. She'd been crying.

'What's wrong?'

If this was about George again I would have to speak to him myself. He'd opened some emotional floodgates and I had no idea which comforting phrases were the key to closing them again.

'You know how you can do the quotes.' She held up her hands, pointer and abuse fingers aloft, crinching them quickly twice.

I nodded. I'd been known to do it now and then. Pretentious and sad, quotemarks always seemed to come naturally when I said the word 'interesting'.

'Well, do you think you can do the bracket?' She cupped her hands, fingers upwards, and thrust them forward as though she had a stack of books between them and she was sliding them onto the shelf with a sharp gesture. 'You think you can?'

I frowned. 'No.'

'You don't think that it's maybe kind of cool?'

'Only if cool is the word people use when they mean dopey.'

She hung her head, leaning back against the romantic comedies. 'I did that in a conversation with George today. I sent him an anonymous email.'

'Anyway,' she went on, her voice settling down a little, 'so I was nervous how he might take it and dropped by his desk. He was still smelly then, maybe more so because he'd been to the gym or something and he was sweaty. I started talking about the Hugh Grant movie on TV last night because I was a little nervous and I said Hugh was spunky, and then bracketed "despite the Divine Brown incident". I think it might have been a sad thing to do.'

'So do I,' I said, trying not to laugh. I was hardly an objective mediator in the cool vs uncool stakes, but I had a fair idea this crept into the latter. 'How did you get onto Hugh Grant?'

She frowned. 'I don't know,' she said slowly. 'Oh, yes, he said something about the fact that I had hair like Liz Hurley.'

'Well, that's a good sign.'

'You think?' She brightened.

'Definitely. Liz is such a handbag, but guys love her. She looks like she spends her days trying on frocks and her nights taking them off. She might even be smart.'

'Oh.' She was thinking hard, the plastic on the DVDs behind her crackling under the weight of her thinking. 'Okay.' She looked up. 'So the brackets weren't so bad?'

'Not so bad.'

'Great.' She paused, rubbing her face wearily. 'God, I feel like I spend my whole life recovering from clangers dropped on the ground like enormous piles of shit that I can never really clean up.'

'Me too.'

Now that I knew she wasn't about to cry again I moved on to the Ds, piling the cases on the floor. 'Everyone feels the same way, but how many stupid things can you actually remember me doing?'

'Quite a few.'

I smiled thinly. 'Okay, a better example. How many things can you remember *other* people saying that they might regret?'

A moment passed. 'Not many.' The plastic stopped crackling and she stood up, adjusting a pile of DVDs that were about to topple over. 'Hardly any, actually. I remember Carmen Johnson saying I was fat in high school, and Tommy Trevestos calling me Zoe that night we went clubbing, but they didn't seem the type of people to regret anything. Other than that, nothing really.'

'See! You spend time beating yourself up about things

and hardly anyone ever remembers them. Unless they were really personal, or really cruel. Which the fat one was, by the way.'

She nodded.

'And everyone forgets names,' I added.

'I know. It was just I thought I loved him.'

'Tommy?'

'Yes.'

'You'd only met him that night!'

'I'd taken some eighties drugs.'

'Oh.' Somehow I couldn't imagine Zara taking drugs. 'Coke?'

'Coke snorted through a fifty.'

'That's some decade you nailed there.'

'I know! And he was wearing pastels.'

'Christ. Are you sure it wasn't *actually* the eighties?'

'I think I would have remembered snorting recreational drugs while I was at school.'

'Yeah, me too.'

I checked to see if Barry was okay at the counter. He was chatting to two teenage girls dressed like Britney Spears and struggling to keep his eyes off the little girl bazooms.

'So, what do you think you'll do now?'

'About George?'

'Yes, about George,' I said impatiently. 'You still like him don't you?'

'Uh-huh.'

'Well, just wait your turn, it'll come together soon enough.'

'And I think I'm also a little in love with Lee Ryan.'

'Who the hell is *he?*'

Zara had never confessed her love for anyone before but in the last couple of days we'd had George, Tommy Trevestos and now this Lee Ryan. I was still reeling as I filed away *Deliverance.*

'He's from Blue, the band. He's not a real boy... Well, you know, he's a boy band boy. I just dream about him a lot.'

'Okay, I do that,' I said, although it was a teeny lie. I rarely dreamt about boys. I dreamt about being in a Smarties commercial fairly often though. The one where you get to drown in Smarties. I figured if I'm counting down to an ugly death (and the way I was going it wouldn't be long now) I might as well go with the drowning in confectionery scenario rather than a tropical disease.

'And I get up every Saturday morning to watch *Video Hits.*'

'That's okay,' I said, but doubt had crept in. Zara and Malcolm—poles apart but both addicted to the same music video show—the perfect cross-section of Australia.

'And I bought *Girlfriend* magazine because it had an article on him.'

'Target market—eight to fifteen?'

'Right.'

'You need some adult conversation here. Are you ready for it or shall we leave it until you're drunk again?'

'Drunk, definitely.'

'Is this becoming a regular habit, the magazine thing?'

'Yeah, well, after reading *Girlfriend* and hearing all the pre-teen complaining I felt much better about my life.'

I moved through to *Deep Impact.* My knees were getting carpet burn so I sat down on the carpet when I finished the row. The waistband on my skirt was very tight. There'd be no thickshake for me tonight, probably just the fries. 'Why the boy band?'

'They sing about love and really seem to mean it. They yearn despite their impossible good looks.'

'They pine.'

'Exactly.'

'That's marketing bastards for you,' I said, adjusting my skirt.

'I know I've fallen into their global domination strategy, but I love it when they get all sad. My heart turns to jelly.'

'And they're cute.'

'Yep.'

'And they dance together.'

'Mmmm.'

'Like in the rock eisteddfod.'

'I guess,' she said doubtfully.

'Zara! I'm surprised. These are *boys*. They'll try anything. You meet some pretty boy in the pub who tries a bit of a fake tear on you and you'll be pashing him next to the cigarette machine before you know it. Then he'll lure you home with promises of a back rub and it'll all be over. You want that for your first time?'

'No.' She gazed out the window. 'You know, some guy once offered me a front rub.'

'You mean, to rub your boobs?'

'Uh-huh.'

'But you said no, right?'

'It was the eighties night. Maybe my boobs had very sore muscles from all the bad dancing.'

'Well.' I was lost for words. 'All right then.' But I think we were both imagining the scene and, frankly, it was making me uncomfortable.

'It wasn't very sexy,' she said after a while.

Satisfied, I stood up, jiggling my legs to get the cramp out. The teens at the counter had gone, which was lucky for Zara. She might have wrestled them to the ground to steal their backpacks.

'What are you doing after work?' she asked.

'Sleeping. Got to get up early in the morning.'

'This whole *Columbo* thing working out for you?'

'So far,' I said. But my guts took a kamikaze into my throat at the thought of how close I'd been to getting caught. Several times. 'It'll all work out.' But I was just reassuring myself.

'That reminds me.' She fumbled in her handbag for a bit and then pulled out a plastic-bag-wrapped thing. I brightened. Zara always bought nice snacks.

'It's not chocolate, you know,' she said, seeing my face. She took a step towards me, 'It's mace.'

'Mace? But that's—'

'Illegal, I know.'

'But—' I sure was squeaky all of a sudden.

'I bought it off the internet. Arrived this morning.'

'But—'

'Justin's friend Graham from Illinois ordered it for me. He wrapped it up in an "Illinois is terrific!" T-shirt. You want the T-shirt too?'

'No.' I held the package limply.

'Don't you want to open it?'

'Maybe later. Thanks, Zars.'

'No problem.' She checked my face. 'You a widdle biddy bit scared?'

'No.' I was just feeling nauseous. Must have been the muesli slice.

'You need protection. Until you can punch someone properly, you should be able to disarm an attacker. I want you to learn a martial art, but until then, you're armed and ready to ruin someone's eye make-up.'

'Thanks.' I found myself glancing around the shop. There was no one around, but I could just see us on closed-circuit television, fuzzy in black and white. Me slightly whiter than Zara. What the hell had I got myself into? And now my square friend Zara was importing illicit items on my behalf.

'Don't sweat it, Cass. You think you're the only one who likes to break the law? Just keep it in your bag.'

'Okay.'

'Don't forget being lawless and brave and cynical. Oh, *and* the Visa debt.'

'Sure, yeah. Great.'

Barry turned to stare. He must have felt the draught as the wind left my sails and Zara left. She seemed to be smiling very broadly for a geek.

'Are you okay?' he asked politely.

'Yes,' I half-shouted and dropped to my knees to finish the alphabet in silence. You know what fad never caught on? Generosity to those less romantically fortunate.

The weather had turned bleak. I decided to dispense with the council worker suit for some nimble clothes. Black skivvy, pink mini-skirt, black tights, knee-high boots and three-quarter-length black leather coat. I was trying to think tough. Tough and sassy. Me and my mace. Like Bonnie and Clyde.

I dropped the coat in Daniel's hallway and went through to the bedroom again. Daniel's house was becoming a little familiar to me—odd but familiar. I'd arrived just before ten, missing Daniel's, and presumably Helen's, departure, sitting in the car reading until the street had cleared out a little.

As I reached the bedroom door, I felt something odd. A tickle in the back of my head. It ran the length of my scalp and made my hairs stand on end. Hackles. If I'd been a professional PI I would have listened to them but instead I just rubbed my head.

So I just walked in, humming Frank Sinatra's 'Fly me to the Moon'. Calm as could be—thinking maybe I needed to wash my hair because it felt creepy. The sight of Daniel sitting up in bed stunned me into silence, the tune dropping off so that I was left, one hand on the knob, the other frozen at my face.

I choked slightly on the smell of Vicks VapoRub in the room. I stepped backwards.

A huge wracking cough shook him from his sleep and I flinched, but his face fell slack again. He was heavily asleep, or over-medicated. A tiny chunk of phlegm flew from his mouth as he lay there convulsing, his body flinching.

I was struggling for breath a little myself. The coughing fit was slowing and my heart was beating fast, maybe faster than the day Tennis Shoes arrived.

He'd passed out. Either that or he had really poor control over his saliva. I took a quick inventory of the bedside table. Pseudoephedrine and pure codeine, night-time cold tablets, Panadeine, Sinutab and Sudafed. He'd self-medicated and was now doing the suburban version of Jerry Garcia.

Instinct told me to get out of there as fast as I could, but something had caught my eye. I crept closer—blood thumping in my ears as I kept an eye out for movement. On the bedspread, open beside him, was one of the photo albums from the locked bookcase. I lifted it gingerly and crept from the room, adjusting the dimmer switch on the light to increase the sleeping vibe of the room. I went into the gym room and slid down the wall, resting the book on my knees.

There were girls in every shot. Wistful redheads, stern brunettes, blousy blondes, anxious anorexics, exotic twenty-somethings. It seemed to be a retrospective of his life. Some photos had Daniel in them but mainly they were just the girls. I came across a picture with a folded edge and slipped it out. The date on the back of the photo was June 1998.

I started making notes. 'Skinny redhead, October 4th, 1997. Nervous blonde, 21st June 1993. Happy stoner in alternative clothes, March 1996.' It went on and on, right through from the mid-eighties to the present. Helen featured in a few shots, but not as many as spiral perm Mandy in 1988 and Diana who made it right through the early nineties until she cut her hair—and what a disaster it was. Long mermaid hair chopped into a severe Monica Lewinsky helmet.

As I flipped through the dates, I realised what was bugging me. The girls had nothing in common physically. One-night stands (they got their picture taken while asleep, which wasn't kind to some) took up as much space as the girls he'd dated for six months or more. Each photo featured a girl, and each did its best to focus on her, and not the background or the people around her. No wonder Helen was suspicious. There was something not right about this guy.

Maybe Daniel just kept these pictures as memory spikes. Could he be acquiring girlfriends for sport, and these were his trophies? Did he date girls to prove something to himself? Was he gazing at these pictures to make himself feel good? I checked his heavy snores, put the album back on his bed and crept quietly from the house—notes tucked into my bag. It was raining heavily outside and, as I ran to the car, I relished the thought of crawling under the rug on my couch and going through my notes. Then I'd call Helen and ask a few questions. It was only when I was driving home that I thought to check the bookcase for any other locked-up goodies. Damn it all to hell.

After doing three loads of delicates I was happily ensconced in my pink tracksuit pants and an old favourite shrunken They Might Be Giants T-shirt. I'd returned home to find the television warm. After witnessing Jock's skilful use of the remote control during my recuperation the other day, I had the distinct impression he'd become addicted to Jerry Springer and was now grouchy that I was home. I was struggling to light some scented candles to soften both our moods as I went through the next plan of attack.

I found the mace Zara had given me and weighed it in my hand. It felt wrong. And I was so clumsy that someone else could easily wrestle it out of my hands and it would be me with fire in my eyeballs, weeping myself clean. I put it on the desk and sat down.

I had a list of questions to ask Helen, starting with, who the hell were these women? She needed to open up a little with me if I was going to be able to make sense of this little mess. Were these girls the reason she wanted Daniel spied on? Was it the emails, the 'evidence' she believed she'd found, or was he just behaving weirdly?

The doorbell rang as I was turning the heater on and, as I opened the door, I ran through the Daniel options in my mind.

Sam Tasker stood in the hall in a dark suit and maroon shirt, looking like a male model/actor playing a Mafia boss. I gulped back my surprise, along with the sexual thrill that ran directly into my groin.

'Nice suit.'

'Thanks. Cassidy, I need to talk to you. Can I come in?'

He'd stepped through before I realised what I was doing. I shouldn't have let him in. He was law enforcement and my second job wasn't strictly legal. In fact, I had a whole bunch of misdemeanours clamouring for the swift and steady attention of the law: B&E, surveillance (i.e. stalking), lurking (an old-fashioned but still nasty crime), a myriad of fashion crimes and possession of an illegal weapon. And there were two racks of my smalls (or not so) hanging up on the wrong side of the wardrobe beside my bed.

I'd spent my teens writhing in illegalities and nothing had come to the attention of the police. Now, when I was starting to get my life back on track, I was facing some rather ugly and/ors (as in $30000 fine and/or three years imprisonment). I pasted a bright smile on my face as I followed Sam into the lounge room. *Sweet and innocent.*

He turned and smiled at me from the coffee table. He hadn't noticed the underwear.

'Nice mace.'

'Thanks, I–' Oh, bugger.

We watched each other for a beat then I re-wallpapered my face. *Bright and fun-loving.*

'Prop. It's a prop for the play we're, uh, doing.'

'Who's we?'

'Me and the local theatre group.'

'Not street theatre?'

'Not street theatre.'

'Not impromptu street theatre. Or made-up local theatre group?'

'No-oo.' I was usually a good liar, one of the best, but his eyes were doing funny things to my equilibrium.

'A *real* local theatre group?'

'Very real.' I knew nothing about theatre. 'We're doing, uh, *Fame*.'

'Right. *Fame*. With mace. Then I guess you're playing streetwise Coco.'

I walked over to the window. 'We haven't cast it yet.'

'We'll ignore the prop, then.'

'Probably for the best.'

'Until after the thespian revolution.'

'Yeah, uh-huh.' I concentrated on casually staring out the

window and not throwing my tiny replica of the Venus of Willendorf at him. 'You got it.'

Jock flew into the room, squawked, then curled up under a wing.

I was a little grumpy and frankly pretty disappointed that Jock hadn't taken a chunk out of Sam's face. Maybe I could train him to just rip that grin right off like a bandaid. 'That's Jock.'

'Hi Jock.' Sam moved to get closer.

'I wouldn't touch him,' I warned, mentally willing Jock to feel the call of the wild. Or at least nature. In Sam's pocket preferably. 'He's wild. Bite your hand right off.'

We both looked at Jock and I was furious to see he looked very cute and utterly harmless. What had happened to his Jerry Springer addiction? Wasn't violence now second nature? 'He's, um, got a mean streak.'

'Okay, well. So...' He paused, then turned away from Jock and looked straight at me. Goosebumps crawled up my legs like tiny insects. Eeek.

'You've been up to something, Cassidy Blair.'

'Wow! The full name.'

'What's your interest in 17 Riverside Avenue?'

The cheese and pineapple toasted sandwich I'd just scoffed took an ill-executed swan dive and landed badly in my gut.

Okay. Keep it cool. Always answer a question with a question; wasn't that what politicians did? But I was up against a master of the bullshit universe. He watched me carefully. His eyes were so dark I think the crash-landed sandwich had unravelled my gravitational pull. I wobbled slightly and then neatly tripped on my left foot. Swinging unsteadily into the couch, I tried to smile. It was like a drunkard attempting a dignified exit after vomiting on someone's shoes.

As I flopped onto the cushions I realised my mistake. I was now a few feet lower than Sam. And the problem was not just psychological. The man's button fly was now at eye-level.

He shuffled his feet for a moment and then eased into the chair next to me, putting his legs up on the coffee table. I flinched as his shiny black loafers slid on my stack of *Vogue* magazines, ostensibly hiding all the *The Face* editions I kept from the days when I thought a tartan mini-skirt and ripped stockings were the very pinnacle of obnoxious cool. I liked to flip through them and remind myself of the good old days when earning a living didn't seem as important as lacing my Doc Martens correctly. Elle Macpherson's smiling face disappeared under genuine leather uppers.

'I know you've been there, Cassidy.'

I switched my attention from his shoes to his face. 'You've been following me?'

'Uh-huh.'

That cheese sandwich was now definitely on its way up. 'So now what?'

'Hmm?' Was he really this cool now or was it all just an act? I tried to remember him cutting out all the Weet-bix vouchers for a *Neverending Story* poster but it just didn't fit.

'Well, are you going to arrest me or just crush my year's subscription to neurosis and bulimia under your shoes?'

He glanced at his feet and then hastily sat up, his feet tucking neatly next to an abandoned beer bottle and a Mars Bar wrapper. Christ, I was Homer Simpson.

'You read this—' he leaned forward to get a better look
'*Vogue*?'

'Yes.' I saw his look. 'Yes! What's wrong with that?'

'I just didn't picture you as a *Vogue* kind of girl. Maybe
more *HQ*, or even *The Face*.'

Damn it. How did he do that?

'I am a *Vogue* kind of girl. Very.'

I'd only subscribed because they were offering three boxes
of chocolates to the first two hundred subscribers, but the
point was, I could be a *Vogue* kind of girl if I wanted to.
I glanced down at my outfit. Well, if I wanted it really, really
badly.

'Okay.' He picked up a magazine and started flipping
through it. 'So what were you doing on Riverside Avenue?'

'Nothing. I was visiting a friend.'

'Daniel Glass?'

'Maybe.'

'You went to the Glass house to—' he paused. He seemed
to be acknowledging the joke, but only for a microsecond,
'—visit a friend. He lives alone.'

'Sure he does. I walk his dog.'

'He already has a dog-walker. Perky girl named Judy.'

Shit. 'Well, you know so much, you find out.' I stood up.
'I have work to do.'

'DVDWorld work?'

'Yeah, I just love going through that movie catalogue, planning my *big* weekend.'

I walked to my desk and slid my papers into a drawer—
everything about Daniel's house, the girls, the contents of his
drawers, the evidence of my B&E. I turned around, closing

the drawer with my arse. I smiled and for a moment the ice broke and he really looked at me, but then the wall came up again.

'I'm going to have to report it.'

I was tempted to go to the bathroom, but if I threw up it wasn't going to do much for my big show of innocence. Never again was I going to open the door without checking the peephole. A girl could lose a lot of weight doing that.

'Why?'

'It's my job.'

'Oh good, so what *is* your job, by the way?'

'Detective, special ops.'

I didn't think he was actually going to tell me, so I was flustered for a second. 'Okay, but why are you following me? There's got to be something bigger in this city than me fake dog-walking.'

'Sure, but I have to report it anyway.'

I put my hands up in a gesture of submission and crossed to the kitchen. 'You want some tea? Coffee? Water?'

'Coffee would be great.' He was rapping his fingers on the armrest. Okay, so maybe he was nervous too, but what about?

'Sure. I'll make you some coffee. I've even got biscuits.' I came back with the biscuits—Iced VoVos—and dropped the packet on his lap. He caught them but not before my eyes grazed his lap. It was a nice lap. Pity it was attached to an arsehole. I forced another smile.

'So tell me why you were following me.'

'You visited Neil. I thought something was a little suss.'

'You thought wrong. I visited Neil. That's got nothing to do with what I'm doing now.' Although that was a lie, it just wasn't the lie Sam thought it was. I didn't do drugs and I didn't know anyone who did. As I walked back to the kitchen I noticed Jock staring at me with one eye. Okay, maybe I did a bit of coke now and then, maybe the occasional recreational joint. But alcohol was a drug too and no one took it seriously enough. I'd rather be out with a bunch of friends on E than after they'd raided the minibar. Which gave me an idea.

'Okay, so what *are* you up to?' he asked, still pretending to read the magazine over the biscuits, but flipping the pages too quickly.

I set up the cups, put the kettle on and turned around, resting my palms behind me on the counter. 'First, tell me why you have to report me.'

'I have to report you because I got busted tailing you today.'

I frowned into the fruit bowl on the kitchen island (my mandarins were going slowly green). Okay, so that wasn't what I expected from Sam. I really needed to take control of this conversation or I was going to leave the apartment with handcuff accessories.

'What?'

'I followed you to Riverside Avenue today and someone called the station and reported a lurker. I got busted by the next-door neighbour, some neurotic woman with kids.'

A laugh bubbled out from my throat. Slightly hysterical, but still a laugh.

'You got busted by Penny's mother? *You!* A cop. Got busted for tailing *me*? What does special ops stand for? Special Opportunities for Comedy?'

'Yeah, that's funny.' His voice was low. Prickles popped up along my hairline. I remembered snotty Daniel this morning and the laughter in my throat subsided. 'Okay, so you have to have something to explain why you were there, right?'

'Right.'

'You don't necessarily—' I spoke slowly, hoping it would sound sexy. I thought about using my sexy walk, which, on reflection, had let me down a couple of times so I thought I'd better not risk it. 'You don't necessarily *want* to report me. You just need an excuse for why you were there.'

'No, I want to report you. You're up to something.'

But he didn't know what. Maybe he'd only tailed me today. 'You only think that because you're suspicious.'

'No, I think that because I saw you breaking into the house a couple of times last week. What are you doing? Drugs, stolen goods, what? You never leave with anything.'

Shit. 'No of course not. For God's sake. I'm not a thief.' I should have known it all seemed too good to be true. Paying off my Visa. Trying out a cool job. It wasn't in my blood. Gold jewellery and sensible working hours, now *these* belonged in my gene pool. No one in my family had even been divorced. We're just not that familiar with the court system.

Although, I distantly remembered my brother coming sheepishly home after getting drunk at nineteen and peeing on the football oval during an old boys match. I thought about a charge of Breaking and Entering.

Yeah, *that's* totally the same. The cops had let my brother off with a warning.

But Sam hadn't reported me yet so perhaps he was biding his time for some reason.

'Okay, I wasn't stealing anything, but I wasn't exactly being a Neighbourhood Watch officer, either.' I sighed in time with the kettle, poured two cups, brought everything to the table and sat down. He'd put the magazine on the arm of the chair, opened the VoVos and eaten three. He was working on a fourth. He had coconut all over his jumper and trousers and I flushed at the instinct to brush it off. I bet it was like brushing dust off a rock. The man had abs.

'I'm doing a surveillance job for someone, checking on her boyfriend. She thinks he's cheating,'

'Is he?'

'I don't think so. Something's going on, though.'

'The skinny chick?'

I sat up. 'You saw her?'

'Yeah, couple of times. Grouchy.'

'Uh-huh.' This was getting embarrassing. How had I missed Sam watching me watching the house? Well, I guess my watching involved more touching and moving and bleeding all over things, but it was still annoying. 'So, where–?'

'White Beetle.'

'Oh.' Damn. So much for the uni students with no rego.

We sat munching in silence. We finished off the packet halfway through the coffee, so I got up and fetched Tim Tams.

'You like your biscuits.' He said it with a hint of a smile, which was good, but I needed more than that to get out of this mess. I needed a 'Get out of jail free' card.

'So do you, it seems.'

It was getting dark outside so I flipped on a light. I knew I had a nice smile. I'd had lots of boyfriends back when I was wild and smiled a lot. Now I'm not so wild and I don't smile so much: no boyfriends.

I beamed at him. 'More coffee?'

'Thanks.' Then he frowned. 'Have you got a headache?'

'No. Why?' I said, moving to the kitchen.

'You're grimacing.'

'Okay.' My brain was buzzing on the caffeine and as I tried to relax my face I scrambled for ideas. I called from the kitchen, 'I'm having a glass of wine. You want one?' I kept my voice light. *Light and breezy.*

'No thanks.'

Damn.

'What's this?' He pointed to a notebook I kept to record my hours. My heart leapt for a second, then I remembered I'd stapled all the pages related to Helen and Daniel together and kept them with the file on the desk. 'What?'

He read from the page, '"Give me sweet nectar in a kiss, That I may be replete with bliss"–Strephon.' He looked up. 'Who's Strephon?' But he didn't wait for the answer. '"Give me but claret in a glass and as for kissing, kiss my arse"–Silenus.' Who are these guys?'

'I don't know,' I replied honestly. 'I wrote it down years ago on a scrap of paper. I found that scrap the other day, I just copied it out so I wouldn't lose it. I love it. I think I'm Silenus.'

He said nothing. I turned back to the kitchen without a word. What was wrong with being Silenus? I concentrated on relaxing and ignored the voice in my head that said, 'You prefer red wine over bliss?'

I opened a bottle of red that Josie had brought over months ago, hitched my boobs up when he turned his head to the window and while he rearranged my magazine pile, I squirted a bit of rose-scented hand cream on. Then I brought back the coffee plunger and the glass of wine, smelling all sweet and legal.

'So…' I made an effort to sound lazy, disinterested. Jail didn't faze me. No, sir.

'Yeah, so—' But he trailed off and we relaxed into silence, punctuated by the odd appreciative noise from me. I was trying to make the wine sound as delicious as possible without going too far into porn and, just when I thought I might have to put on some jazz, he spoke.

'Actually, wine does sound good.'

I resisted the temptation to punch a fist in the air and brought the bottle back with the glass. He smiled when he took a sip and then checked the label. Thank God for classy friends.

A comfortable silence prevailed. Either that or I was getting drunk. I ran my fingers through my hair. It was clean, but that was about all I could say for it. I could look nice on good days and like a demon from the mouth of hell on others. Tonight, I was just skirting the heat.

He put down the glass and turned to me. 'I guess I could explain where I've been by saying that I was following a lead that didn't work out.'

I contained myself. This wine was good.

'But if I do that, I want you to let me know if anything turns up.'

'Turns up where?'

'In the house. You said that you think something's off. If it's anything we should know about, you'd tell me, right?'

'Right.' It was too good to be true. Something was up. 'What do you want?'

'Nothing. But I'm going to keep an eye on you. I trust

you, but I'm still watching Neil. Something's wrong there too. You let me know if you hear anything and I'll stay out of your way on this.' I started to smile at this excellent solution, but he kept talking. 'Although… If I hear about you breaking the law again or doing anything stupid, I'll reel you in like a tuna.'

'Like a tuna?'

'Uh-huh.'

I'd have to remember to keep good wine in the apartment in future. It was a powerful tool of negotiation.

He got up, put the magazine back on the pile and brushed coconut off his trousers. I busied myself putting the coffee things away. There was nothing like housework to make a girl look benign and, therefore, hopefully law-abiding. So now he thought I was a hormone-driven, fashion-conscious, housewife type. Not perfect, but it would do in a pinch. Sure, he was cute, but he was also someone who could flip a switch and I'd be resisting cavity searches. I had to be very, very careful. The only problem was, I didn't respond well to being benign or careful. The housewife stuff wasn't so hot, either. At the door, he smiled.

'You don't read those magazines. You're no more a *Vogue* girl than I am.'

I had just put everything in the dishwasher so I closed the door with a thump. I walked around to the tiny lobby where he stood.

'What I do know is that you're an excellent liar. It's paid off, but I don't know if you can make the distinction between right and wrong.'

'There is no black and whi—'

'I know, only shades of grey. You used to say that in high school.'

'I did?' I tried to lean casually against the wall but felt propped up like a piece of wood. There was definite appeal in being attracted to someone who didn't know you'd once had a crush on Corey Hart and belonged to the Mel & Kim fan club.

'You don't read those magazines. You haven't even opened those little perfume sachets between the pages. Everyone opens those. Especially someone like you. Behind the tough girl thing, you're all scented candles and girly smells.'

Remember the cavity search. I took a deep breath. 'Sure, okay. No fashion icon here. You happy now?'

'Not as happy as when you poofed your boobs up like that.' He caught my startled look. 'The window reflects like a mirror. It was cute.'

And then he walked down the hall towards the stairs. I was about to slam the door when he added, 'And you have terrific underwear.'

My mouth may or may not have fallen slightly open. I shook my head and closed the door carefully. I was really going out in a blaze of humiliation.

I admit there was a microsecond when I thought, 'He thinks I'm cute!' but then I threw the biscuits at the wall with a low scream of exasperation. Chocolate sprayed everywhere, Jock woke up squawking and there was a pounding from next door.

I flopped on the couch and poured myself a large glass of wine. It was then that I noticed Sam had left behind three polaroids of me leaving Daniel's house. There was a post-it note on one saying, 'This is all there is.' I collected the pictures and threw them in the desk drawer. Time to talk to Helen.

I turned to get another glass of wine but then I slowly retraced my steps and opened the drawer. My bum looked big in that skirt. I slammed the drawer and poured myself a glass.

'So he never talked about them to you?'

'No. I didn't know he had so many ex-girlfriends. Are you sure?'

I showed Helen the typed-up notes. I'd borrowed Zara's computer while she was at work that morning. If the job worked out okay, I'd get a computer and then maybe I'd look up a few websites to see what else I could import, as in something I could use to detect nearby cops.

'Sure, I'm sure. There's a whole album there. He must keep the key on his key ring.'

She looked thoughtful. 'You know, he does keep a weird old key on his car key ring. I noticed it ages ago. I never thought to ask.'

'Okay, one mystery solved. These are ex-s. I don't think he's carrying on with any of them now, though.' I'd told her about Tennis Shoes but she didn't seem worried. Maybe the shoes classed the woman under 'domestic help'.

'But he *is* carrying a candle for them,' she said grumpily.

'He's keeping their photos, like he kept those emails. It's weird.'

'Everyone's weird. Haven't you got stuff from your old relationships?'

'Maybe...' she said cautiously. 'But it's all packed away. I don't look at it.'

And you don't wank over it, I thought. 'Maybe he doesn't look at it either,' I lied. 'Maybe this was a first.' The album gave me the creeps. 'Maybe he couldn't get Vardia's photo, so he held onto the emails. There might be other stuff. But I don't think he's cheating on you, unless you think holding onto mementos is cheating.'

'But it's as if he thinks this,' she gestured to the list, 'is as important as me. Or maybe that I'll turn into one of them. Just a picture. A souvenir.' For a moment a flash of vulnerability crossed her face and she looked young again, but then she straightened, frowned, and I remembered why she intimidated me. She had insecurities that she was never going to show anyone. I wondered how her relationship withstood such self-control.

'Why collect them all together, like butterflies?' She went on, 'Like that book about the creepy guy. I don't want to marry a creepy guy.'

'You mean *The Collector*?'

'Yeah.'

'I don't think he's got them all locked in his basement.'

She deflated. 'No, you're right.'

'You seem disappointed.'

She laughed.

'I know. Silly, isn't it? I guess now that I'm paying you, I want to find something for my money. I want results.'

'But that's not a good thing. Is it?' I watched her closely.

'I guess not. But this is interesting. He was getting boring; now he's complicated. I like complicated.'

'But complicated in a yucky way?'

'Describe these girls.'

I recalled as much as I could, but the thing about them was there were no consistent characteristics—younger, older, big hair, short hair, pretty, plain, big, thin, tall, short. Maybe he just wasn't very discerning. I looked at Helen's big nose and bulky features. I decided to keep that thought to myself for a moment. I was beginning to like her in a weird way. And I didn't want her to date someone freaky.

'Hey! Cassidy Blair.'

I whipped around to see Malcolm crashing between tables towards us, looking like the bastard child of Jennifer Lopez and Rambo. A red bandanna was tied over his slicked back hair and big sunglasses rested on his head. A tight grey long-sleeved top showing his wiry body (and another bandanna around his upper arm), white combat pants and black shiny shoes completed the look.

He grabbed a chair, turned it around and straddled it.

'Hi, Malcolm. Please don't sit down. Especially not like that. I'm working.'

'Me too!' He leaned forward, hand outstretched. 'Malcolm Ferrier.'

Helen shook back, somewhat bemused. 'Helen Since.'

'Delighted.'

My temper flared but I tried to contain it. Be professional. Everyone has dopey friends. I shouldn't let Malcolm faze me.

'You said you're working?'

Malcolm normally worked at his father's bakery. With his four sisters and two brothers, they made a decent living but their real source of cash was the allowance their grandfather left for them through their parents. I'd picked up from drunken conversations with the siblings that their parents hadn't exactly benefited from this windfall. Some interesting family dynamics in that house.

'Sure. I'm taking on the orders for Pop. No more flour for me.'

I turned to Helen, who was still staring at Malcolm. I guess there weren't many bandannas in high finance. 'Malcolm's family runs the Best Breads Bakeries.'

'And we service over two hundred cafés, restaurants and pubs around town.' He smiled at me. 'I just offered your friend Josie a good deal on dinner rolls.'

I smiled. Josie loathed Malcolm but he was overly generous with the breads and we still hadn't found a five-seed loaf to beat his. And every now and then I liked to flirt with his brother James. James is a honey. I would have seriously considered him were he not so closely linked to such a polluted gene pool.

'That's great, but Malcolm, I *am* working.'

He really had lost some serious IQ points trying to keep up with DJ Maxus and the local drug scene a few years back. He partied so hard he used sugar instead of flour at the bakery once and it ground the entire local catering business to a halt for a day while they tried to reorder ingredients and placate irate clients. He was a tepid drug user after that but it had certainly had a lasting effect.

'Okay, Cassidy. No need to be rude.'

'Yes, there is, Malcolm,' I muttered under my breath.

He got up with a flourish, nodding at us both. 'Well, be seeing you soon.'

'Maybe.'

'I heard that. Your friend Josie didn't seem so keen to get rid of me.' He turned to flounce off. For a straight man he had a lot of flourishes.

I laughed. Josie would have dazzled him with her wooing smile until she got free bread. Then she would have urged him out the door as quickly as her Chanel mules would move.

'I'm sure she's smitten.'

He turned around.

'Really?'

'Goodbye, Malcolm.' I turned to Helen. 'I'm sorry about that. Ex-friend. He doesn't know about the prefix. Bit of a problem.' She was staring at his receding back.

'You know him well?'

'Knew. Past tense. He's a little slow on the whole vibe thing.' I sipped my coffee. 'I can't believe I just said "vibe".'

'*I* can't believe he's your friend. I've seen him around. He's gorgeous!'

I choked slightly and recovered with a low cough.

'Really?'

'Yeah.' Helen was gazing at the door he'd just closed and my attention was caught by the scarf around her neck. I remembered the five boxes of women's clothes in Daniel's house.

'Do you know anything about the boxes in the spare room at Daniel's place?'

'Yeah, they've been there ever since I've known him. He told me they were his sister's things, but come to think of it, she never moved. I thought he was storing them for her. Maybe his mother's? No, they're not her style.' She caught my look. 'I went through them one day when he went to the shops. Well, through one box, anyway. I was curious.'

'Curious is good. But now we know he keeps mementos, those clothes probably aren't family storage. You think they might be more souvenirs?'

'Er, yes. Probably.'

'I can't really prove anything; there's nothing you can confront him with. It's not illegal. It's probably not even in those mumbo jumbo books about why men are bastards. It's up to you to figure out what you want. Do you want to marry a man who holds onto trophies of his past relationships? And, if so, do you want to confront him about it? There might be a perfectly good explanation. Maybe he never got laid as a teenager. Maybe he's insecure. Maybe he still loves them all. I don't know. But I'm going to find out about Tennis Shoes.'

She went to interrupt me but I put my hand up. 'I won't charge you for this, but if it has anything to do with Daniel and his relationship with you, I'll let you know as soon as possible. I know it's not part of the job, I just can't let it go. Something's wrong here and I want to find out what it is.'

'Okay, but I will pay you. I'm curious too.'

'Great.' I pushed my chair back and she put her hand on my arm.

'Cass, can you give your friend my phone number?'

I smiled thinly. I hated match-making. When she found out he was a lousy lay or she was an obsessive dental flosser it would all turn out to be my fault. 'Okay. I'll take that as word that you're not sticking with the whole "moving in" thing.' If she liked Malcolm she could have him. He had to be an improvement on Daniel.

I got into work to find Barry in a bit of a temper with a female customer. A young, pretty and highly amused female customer.

'Think of Bill Murray in *Mad Dog and Glory*. Bruce Willis did it in *The Jackal*, too. You don't want to see your good guys turn bad. You can see that every time you read the papers. You shouldn't spend–' He checked the box, '$5.95 on this when you could get *Pitch Black*.' He thumped the DVD in front of him. 'You love Pierce now, but after you watch this, you're going to want to complain to the B-grade actors' association.'

'But I don't care,' she said. As I came through the turnstile I could see why Barry was working himself up into a Rambo sweat. She was radiant, literally beaming. I know that look. She was either getting laid on a regular basis or she was pregnant. Or maybe I just read too many women's magazines. Maybe she just loved her high-flying career and had a very satisfying home life.

'Hey, look,' she said good-naturedly. 'I hear it's a good movie. I want to rent it. Here's my card. Scan it. Give me the DVD.'

'Give her the DVD, Barry.'

I flipped open the counter and took him by the shoulder.

'You go put out those weekly hire tape covers, okay? I'll take care of this.' Barry moved away like a zombie and I turned to the girl.

'Sorry. He gets a little heated about movie stuff. We have no life here.'

'It's good to see someone passionate about their work.' She smiled. She was definitely getting laid.

From the children's aisle he yelled, 'And Harrison Ford in *What Lies Beneath*. You don't wanna see that!'

I processed the rental and when she was gone and the store was empty I called him over. 'What's up?'

He looked sheepish. 'Sorry. It just bugs me. That's a bad movie. She hasn't even seen *Alien* and she's renting *The Tailor of Panama*.'

'It's her choice.'

'I doubt it. I think there's a guy at her to hire it. I saw her go straight to the horror movies, but then she obviously relented and brought this over. She'll regret it, I bet. Clichés just aren't what they used to be.'

I nodded. 'Ten bucks.'

He grinned wildly. 'Ten bucks says she'll be broken hearted—'

'—and not interested in getting laid.' I finished for him, smiling back. See? I wasn't getting even near laid and I could smile. I had a great smile.

'Yeah, well, at least not by the guy who wanted to see the film,' he said. Then he frowned. 'What's wrong with you?'

'What?' I replied, smiling. This felt good.

He took a step back. 'What are you so mad about?'

My face fell. Maybe I just needed more practice. I turned

to the register to hide the flush that was creeping over my collar.

'Nothing.'

'O-kay,' he said cautiously. 'Well, there were three extra Mars Bars in the box today. You want one?'

'One? I'm having two or the bet's off.'

The evening went slowly. I knew I'd lose that bet but we put *Predator* on the dual screens and tucked into the Mars. By eleven p.m. I was feeling tired and more than a little queasy. That was when Sam called the shop and told me to meet him at the Hindley Street police station at nine a.m. the next morning. When I put down the phone I glanced at my reflection in the window.

Barry started closing the register. 'It's a dead giveaway that you're holding in your gut when you stick your tits out like that.'

'Shut up and count the money.'

'Slut!'

The woman who slurred at me on the street had bags under her eyes that could have carried my weekly shopping. I stepped cautiously around her as I approached the station. I was wearing Love Kylie undies with an Oroton bra and feeling sexy but classy. I hoped the bows on the pants didn't show through the thin material of my pinstripe trousers. I wore a red rollneck jumper with tiny silver star earrings and my hair was in a loose, tangled ponytail. A casual look that had taken me a half-hour to get right. This guy was messing with my mind.

That morning I'd had a call from Declan. He wanted to know why I hadn't called him, so I told him I was a shameless cradle-snatcher and that he deserved better. He was young enough to have more hope than bitterness so he just laughed, albeit slightly ruefully.

'Your call, Cass.' And that was it. Then we talked about the latest Nick Cave album and vowed to keep in touch. Boy, it was nice to be around people who'd never witnessed the indignities of bubble skirts in the eighties. Some things just seemed so untethered and simple.

A glass-fronted building under a video game arcade, the Hindley Street police station was currently marred by some obscene (and poorly punctuated) graffiti. I went inside and spoke to the officer on duty who directed me to a café four doors down. Sam was reading *The Australian* and drinking short blacks. I was more a cappuccino girl myself but I thought the day called for compromise so I ordered a long black and sat down.

'I know I said I'd leave you alone,' he said, 'but I've been thinking about what you told me last night.'

'Really?'

'I thought you might want some help finding out what's going on with the skinny chick.'

'You can do that?' I was surprised. I thought guys like Sam were busy hunting white-collar criminals and going under-cover.

'I've taken some time off work, essentially to deal with Neil, but I can help you out if you want me to.' He was being cautious. I took the cue and nodded.

'Okay. But first, tell me what's up with Neil.'

'I think you know.'

'I know he's doing drugs. He was always doing drugs. I'm guessing the drugs don't grow on plants anymore, and maybe he's not just spending his dole cheque either, but, other than that, I'm not ticking any boxes.'

'He's doing smack and I don't know how he's paying for

it. I'm just concerned he's in over his head. I'm trying to get him to a clinic.'

'Do they work?'

'Sometimes. If they want to clean up, it can work. The chances are better if they've got something to go to once they're clean. Something to do. Drugs are appealing when you're bored, directionless, insecure... Work and pleasure fill in the gaps in your life, make you feel better about yourself, more confident. Neil hasn't even finished uni.'

'He started uni?' I was shocked. Neil wasn't the motivated type. When we were together he'd spent his days watching television and his nights playing guitar. He was Bill and Ted and the whole Excellent Adventure rolled into one.

'Mum's worried, so I promised I'd help out.'

Mrs Tasker was always worried, but she had reason to be. The Taskers were a good, solid, middle-class family. Nice house in Toorak Gardens, big garden, pool. We all went to the same private high school. They holidayed overseas every few years. For a second as I sat there, trying not to stare at Sam's hands, which were broad and clean and apparently soft and I couldn't at all imagine them on my leg, a flash of jealousy flared up.

I really missed my parents despite our quarrels. They'd generally left me alone and I suspect were just bewildered by me—their cuckoo baby. I tried to picture my dad's face and it made me sad that I had to struggle. Eventually the feeling settled and I flicked my thoughts forward to the dry-out clinic.

'How are you going to get him there?'

'I was hoping you'd help me.'

'Ah.' Now I understood why he was being so nice. It wasn't because I was cute and my underwear sometimes matched. It was for Neil's sake. The disappointment must have shown on my face because he cracked a smile.

'Neil still likes you, Cass. Not in that way, but he respects you. He doesn't seem to have any friends and when you showed up that day I thought it was great. He knew you were up to something but he still appreciated it. Now he talks about you every time I call. About how well you've done and how he wants to meet Dougal and Oscar.' He caught the look on my face. 'I guess the dogs got scared away by the bird but I didn't tell him that,' he added, as I flushed in the glare of my big fat fib. 'I thought if I mentioned Jock he'd probably want to meet him too and it's always best to keep yourself distant from Neil. Last time he came around I lost seven CDs and a watch.'

His smile was crooked as he took a quick sip of his coffee. I added two sugars to mine when it came. When he'd said I was a good liar earlier I'd thought he meant pretending to my parents that I was studying for exams when really I was sitting in a tree watching the Sting 'Dream of the Blue Turtles' concert because I was too young to get in. I'd told my parents I was at a friend's sleepover. Irritation flared but I pushed it aside. So what if he knew I'd lied about my full life?

Then he looked me in the eye and I quickly crossed my legs. 'So! I decided we can help each other out. I'll back you up finding the anorexic and you can help me with Neil.'

I had no choice. I couldn't walk away now. I almost regretted getting involved but I had a feeling Sam's anecdote about Neil was just the tip of the iceberg and I wanted to help. The Taskers were good people. Neil was a good person. He'd just been transformed by heroin. Like a vampire; they might look the same, but they're no longer the same person.

'Okay,' I said, and my fate was sealed. I slugged the coffee as a chaser to my fear and grabbed my bag. 'Let's go.'

'I was hoping you'd say that.' As he stood up, I wondered if he had a gun tucked under his jumper somewhere. I was more of a knee in the groin kind of girl myself. If I got close enough before I fainted.

We pulled up a few metres in front of the bus stop around the corner from Daniel's place. I was riding shotgun in the Saab with Sam sipping a takeaway coffee—his third since the station café. I had no idea how he stayed relaxed with so much caffeine throbbing through him, nor how he resisted the urge to go to the bathroom. I'd had glimpses of something else in him, something more human, but he kept it well hidden.

We'd looped the block and it looked like no one was home at 17 Riverside Avenue. There was no light on in the front room, nor any sign of the dog-walker. I told Sam about Daniel's sick day, but as there was no way of checking the garage we had to assume he was at work. Or did we?

I borrowed Sam's mobile and rang the number Helen had given me for Southern Mobile Phones. Daniel picked up on the third ring.

'Hello? Daniel Glass speaking.'

I rang off. Well, he was nasal but alive. And not in bed. I definitely should have tried this earlier. It was all clear for Tennis Shoes.

'There's no point staying here,' Sam said. 'We'll get called in again by the Neighbourhood Watch.'

'I never got spotted,' I said, keeping my voice light.

'You're a woman.'

'What difference does that make?'

'Women aren't usually seen as dangerous.' He glanced at me. 'Of course they can be, some more than others, but it's not typical. A man in a car on an empty street stands out a mile. He could be a stalker, a burglar, a killer. A woman in a car looks harmless, waiting for her husband.'

'Hey. I didn't just sit in my car thinking I'd be fine because I've got breasts. I dressed up. I went to the park. I talked to the neighbours. I thought it through.'

'You trespassed, spoke to a neighbour under false pretences and broke into a house.'

I swallowed my anger. 'How about we park down the road, opposite the bus stop? Tennis Shoes probably came by bus last time, and if so, I'm guessing it wasn't a once-off.'

'Good idea.' He did a U-turn and we parked in a side street, nose towards the main street intersecting Riverside. He tuned into Radio National and I sank into the leather upholstery. Three buses pulled up, no Tennis Shoes. My eyes started to water from staring at the bus shelter.

I kept re-crossing my legs to prevent pins and needles. Sam hadn't moved from his relaxed pose. He hadn't even pulled the seat back from the steering wheel. The silence hung in the air as I struggled to stay alert.

'So, what do you want to do about Neil?'

'I want to book him into rehab in the Adelaide hills next week but they won't take him. He's run away from there too often before and they can't risk wasting the bed. I'll find something.'

'You've spoken to him about it?' I was surprised. I thought my job would be softening the approach.

'No, that's your job.'

'But he's got no choice?' I confirmed.

'No choice.'

I stifled an exasperated laugh. 'I'm sorry, I thought I was going to help him, not bully him. I thought we were going to try to make him see what he needed, not just make him go.'

'We are.'

'We are what?'

'Going to help him.'

'Yes, but will he want to be helped if we bully him? He's never responded well to being told what to do.'

'No one does, but sometimes it's necessary.'

I laughed, but it sounded bitter. 'Think about why he is where he is. He's defensive. He doesn't fit in. He's never fitted in. He knows that. He might harbour some real desire to be a normal citizen again, but he probably feels he's gone too far.' I kept my eyes on the shelter as another bus pulled away. Nothing.

'If you want to give him a life buoy,' I went on, 'you can't throw it at him and order him to grab it, especially if there are other options that look like they might be a hell of a lot more fun. You have to throw it to him and urge him. Maybe for your mother. Maybe for the future. But never, ever bring up the past, or what he's done. How he's ruined his life, or his education. You'll just make him defensive. Just throw it to him as a friend. Help him grab it because it'll be good, not because you think it's the only way he can save himself. Otherwise he'll throw it right back at you.'

'This is exactly why you're the perfect person for this job.'

I sighed. 'Okay.' I couldn't understand how Neil had stayed screwed up for so long, but I had a window into what it was like. I remembered the desperation to be different, to live my own life, to fall away from everything average and conservative. And I did it. And I stayed a loner right up until I fell in love with the big man on campus in second-year university and suddenly I became Ms Perky.

I swapped my long black skirts for short denim, my thick black stockings for sheer, my Doc Martens for pink jelly sandals. Then, with every boyfriend, I swung around between looks and tastes and personalities again until finally I finished university, worked for a few years in dead-end jobs, moved to Melbourne for the six bastard months and realised I had no idea who I really was, what music I liked, what things I wanted to watch on telly. I was a girlfriend, not a person at all.

On my return, I stayed away from boys and went to the movies on my own until I realised I loved action movies and not the horror movies I'd been renting with my previous boyfriend. Depression fell off me as I started defining myself. I made a list of all the movies I had to see and my spirits lifted again. Then I watched telly until I hated most sports. And loved *Buffy the Vampire Slayer*. I hated live bands but loved ambient music. I hated whiskey but loved gin and tonics.

Then I rented my pretty apartment and bought all my favourite things. Hence, the Visa bill and me sitting and waiting for a stranger to get off the bus.

'A penny for your thoughts.'

'That's so clichéd!' But I laughed. 'They're worth more than that anyway.'

'Really?' He turned towards me and smiled. 'I'll give you five bucks.'

'Ten.'

'Eight-fifty.'

'You were meant to say seven-fifty.' I smiled. 'You'd be hopeless in a drug deal.'

'I am hopeless in a drug deal, but I'm great at extracting information. Now spill.'

'I was just thinking about how I came to be here.'

'How did you?' He turned to me.

'Something to do with realising I hate watching the cricket, but sometimes the World Cup soccer isn't so bad.'

'Really, you like the World Cup?'

'I like the guys in their shorts playing in the rain.' I sat up quickly. 'Not as much as seeing Ms Slimfast though.' I pointed to the street as Tennis Shoes emerged from behind the bus shelter. Sam turned around. 'She must have got off that last bus. She's been behind the shelter.' I opened the car door and then hesitated. 'What do we do now?'

'Would she recognise you?'

I thought of the deli. 'Yes, she might not remember, but I shouldn't risk it.' I shut the door again.

'A guy on an empty street behind a woman will attract attention.' He started the engine. 'I just want to see where she goes.'

'She's going to Daniel's house,' I said. Blood pounded in my ears as I thought of actually catching her doing something illegal. 'I just know it.'

'Never assume anything or next minute you'll be up in the witness box and it'll all fall apart with one good defence lawyer. It's a ruthless business.'

'So it's a business now?'

'Well, it's more than a job.' We raced down the suburban streets, hitting Daniel's street opposite the deli, then we slowed down as we approached the house. The street was empty. Disappointment made me slump as we rolled past the house, only to see a glimpse of jean-clad leg as the front door slammed shut behind her.

'She's inside!' I grabbed my seatbelt in excitement as we rolled to a stop. 'Just wait. We have to catch her leaving and then follow the bus.'

'Okay, but we'll have to be careful. This isn't the perfect surveillance vehicle.'

'It's the perfect chick magnet though.'

He looked at me in surprise. Heat flushed my cheeks but I said nothing.

'I don't really go for "chicks".'

'It didn't look that way the other night at the club.'

It was his turn to flush. 'I was there with a friend from overseas. He was really keen on going out. I don't go out often. After I, well, I didn't have the best night and I guess I got a little drunk.'

'A little frisky too.' But I was buddy-teasing. He looked so uncomfortable that I laughed. 'You couldn't have had a worse night than me. I was stuck with my high school night-mare—two chumps with an IQ lower than their alcohol content wearing a dress that made me feel like I could be giving out handjobs for a hundred bucks. I'd really stepped into high-class hooker zone.'

My voice hung in the car. I guess Josie was right, sometimes I do get a little cynical. I try too hard to be funny and then it just offends someone, or everyone. Like now. Although I suspected I'd just grossed him out. I held my breath.

'You could have got at least one-thirty. The shoes alone could get you an extra five, ten if the client's partial to spike heels.'

'I had a friend at uni who used to let guys lick her boots for a hundred bucks at Salon Sin.'

'I used to go undercover at a brothel suspected of laundering cash. I had to talk to girls about how much I liked it when they wore plastic. As a cop I had to find ways to keep them in the display lounge.' He glanced in the rear-vision mirror. 'Which is the room where the girls parade in a row so guys can pick them like a chocolate bar. One night one of them offered to, er, wrap me in Gladwrap.'

'Nude?'

'Nude. Like in *Bad Boy Bubby*.'

'Great movie.'

'Great Gladwrap. I declined, by the way.'

'I'm disappointed.'

'I bet she wasn't.'

I looked at him. He was watching the rear-vision mirror, so I let my glance slide over his thick blue cable-knit jumper, his blue jeans, his slightly scruffy hair. He'd shaved, but he looked relaxed. He'd look good in Gladwrap. Jesus I was desperate. I rubbed my eyes. 'I've got to go to the toilet. Don't you?'

'No.'

'Okay, I'll be back in a sec.' And I took off for the public loos in the park. It was only as I emerged that I noticed Penny playing on the jungle gym with a bunch of kids some twenty metres away. I walked sedately, looking at the ground, praying she wouldn't notice me. I reached the car, slipped into the seat and sighed.

'Problem?'

'No problem.'

'You've got to learn self-control or you can bet that the suspect will turn up just as you take off for the nearest service station for a slash.'

'You mean to say you've used the bottle?'

'The bottle?'

'The portable toilet bottle.'

'We're not talking about this,' he said firmly.

'Must have been awkward.'

He stared stonily ahead and we sat in silence. I was just thinking about Josie and her snob addiction when Sam sat up. 'She's headed our way.' I slunk down in the seat, but he reached over and grabbed me before I'd settled. 'Sit up, it'll look suss.'

His hand was still on my jumper as I sat back up and his fingertips grazed my right boob as I moved, but there wasn't time for an awkward exchange as Tennis Shoes streaked past.

'She moves pretty fast for a hungry person,' I said, trying to ignore the electricity in my right nipple that could have charged a small town.

'Maybe she's naturally thin.'

'Maybe she's naturally hungry,' I thought about lunch and my stomach growled.

'Looks like it's catching,' he said. When she reached the end of the street Sam started the car. We pulled out and caught her sitting in the bus shelter. I checked my watch. She'd been in Daniel's house for only thirty-eight minutes. She probably had her routine down pat now, whatever she was doing. Sam turned left at the first intersection, did a U-turn and parked.

'What do we do now?' My instincts told me to get a sandwich, but I didn't want Sam to think I wasn't up for professional surveillance work.

'If we go back to waiting in the street opposite the bus shelter, we won't be able to turn right and follow the bus in time, the traffic is too fierce on this street. I'll reverse back as close to the corner as possible and wait in the car. You take this.' He handed me an orange plastic vest from the back seat, a camera, notepad and pen.

'Take photos. The council gig worked well for you last time. It was a good effort. Be invisible. Pretend you're measuring the spaces between poles, fences, stuff on the road. If anyone asks, which they won't, you're preparing for an overhaul of the streetscape. They're planting new trees, just make it up.'

We reversed back towards the street as I slipped into the heavy orange vest. I walked back to the street. It was about two hundred metres to the bus stop and I made notes, mainly trying to remember song lyrics and then write them down. There was film inside the camera but I didn't think Sam would appreciate me wasting it so I used a soft press on the button.

When I got near the bus shelter I remembered the deli again and a spiral of fear clutched my stomach. In the rush we'd ignored the fact that she'd seen me before. I pretended to make notes while facing the other way and then slowly walked back the way I came, paying particular attention to the gutter. Eight minutes later the bus came by and as I turned around to measure a tree it picked her up. I speedwalked around the corner, then kept walking quickly as the bus passed me. As I turned the corner, I leapt in the car, then we slipped into traffic.

We followed the bus for twenty minutes, pausing in side streets and near shops when passengers alighted. None of them were Tennis Shoes until we reached Malvern, a suburb of good shops and cafés, five minutes away from Josie's bar.

We passed Josie's street and kept going when suddenly the bus stopped and Tennis Shoes jumped off, walking quickly up the street. We drove into a carpark outside a butcher's, keeping the engine running until we saw her take a left, then followed, idling again as she went through the leafy streets. We pulled out just in time to see her walk into a house not unlike Daniel's.

This one, however, had a musty look. The grass was speckled with dead patches and the paintwork looked aged, but it was an expensive suburb and the curtains in the window, while closed, looked clean.

'Looks like she's home,' commented Sam.

'Ninety-four Zachary Street. The home that food forgot.'

'I think we need to get you something to eat.' Sam reached behind him, under a wet weather jacket and the orange vest, and pulled out some sandwiches, cokes and muesli bars.

I fell on them in relief. As I pulled the plastic wrap off a salad sandwich, Sam held aloft the notepad I'd been using. 'Say I'm the only bee in your bonnet, make a little birdhouse in your soul?'

'It's a They Might Be Giants song,' I muttered, relieved I didn't get a chance to write down the lyrics to Madonna's 'Erotica' that had been swirling in my brain most of the day. 'I had to write *something* down.'

He leaned towards me and my heart thumped up a notch as I swallowed a chunk of tomato.

'You have lettuce in your hair.' He picked it off, then flung it out the window.

'He broke up with me.' Josie had been busy interviewing bartenders and now the winning candidates were cleaning cocktail glasses behind the new stainless-steel bar.

'Carl?'

'Yes.' Josie's expression was flat and I could see the tension around her eyes.

'Why?'

'Why? Ah!' She swept her hands around herself in a grand gesture. 'Who knows? Maybe it was because I work most nights. Or because I earn more than he does. Or because I don't want to cook for him when I get in because I've been cooking all day at work. Or because now I'm about to hire a second cook full-time and I'm not considering his lazy brother-in-law Boris the Wanker. Or because I like reading the papers on Saturday instead of going to the football with him.'

'Oh.' Or maybe because you're being flirty with other guys? I kept my mouth shut for my own safety. I'd seen her swing that bag and it was ugly.

'I know you're relieved. So's Zara. You could have told me he was a wanker.'

I laughed. 'I did!'

'I know,' Josie shook her head. 'I just didn't listen.'

'He was good-looking. And he had a nice car. I've made that mistake myself.'

'That was before you were reformed. Now you never make relationship mistakes.'

'No,' I said cautiously.

'You never go out with losers.'

She was heading somewhere. 'Not anymore, I guess. Hit my quota.'

'So what about Sam Tasker, the biggest dweeb in all Alaska?'

I stifled a laugh. 'Zara told you about that?'

'A little. Not as much as your face does though. You're pink as a berry. You've got a right to be, too. Your ex-boyfriend's brother! The guy who used to speak to you in Klingon.' She laughed as she saw my shocked face. 'Oh, that's right, he stopped after a while. Then he read *The Lord of the Rings* and switched to Elvish for a year and a half. He nearly failed his finals because he wrote half his essay in Elvish without realising! You told me all about it one day when we spotted him in town. You hid behind the Malls Balls to avoid him.'

I was speechless. I'd forgotten just how nerdy he'd been, and how cruel *we'd* been. Even in my teens I'd been a cocky little bully sometimes, picking on anyone further down the food chain. I suddenly remembered dialling the Taskers' number and pretending to be Gandalf when Sam picked up. I turned a shocked face to Josie. 'I said "Fool of a Took!" And then I called him Sam Gamgee.'

Josie shrieked with laughter, clutching her stomach. The two men behind the bar were pretending to ignore her but the taller of the two had a smile tugging at his lips. I took a big sip of my gin and tonic and tried to laugh, but couldn't. I was the bitch from a teen movie. And Sam was the hero, the underdog made good, whom everyone sympathised with. God, how awful!

I drained my drink and Josie calmed herself just as the taller bartender came over with a tray.

'I thought it might be a good time to try out a cocktail,' he said. He placed the tray down on the wooden cube in front of us and went back to the bar.

Josie was still recovering as I took a glass. 'Thanks, Nick,' she said. 'What's in it?'

I wondered if Josie had noticed his smile. Tall and dark, with a lazy posture and sparkling eyes, he was the opposite of her usual conquests. Someone had hard-wired her brain to accept only spoilt, slightly podgy, arrogant rich kids. It was a shame.

'It's called the Vodka Dialogue. Gordon's gin, Absolut vodka, Bacardi Limon, blue curaçao, butterscotch schnapps, lime juice and sugar.'

'We'll never make it out of here alive.' Josie wiped the mascara from her cheeks in the reflection of a nearby stainless steel vase and held up a square chunky glass swimming with wedged limes. 'To you and Sam Gamgee.'

I clinked glasses. It felt nice to sit there with her. And I was glad she'd broken up with Carl. I glanced back at Nick, who was watching Josie out of the corner of his eye but quickly went back to the glasses when he caught my gaze.

'So what have you been up to today? Busted any bad guys?'

I told her about Sam's deal and the tail to the house in Malvern. We'd waited there for an hour before Sam dropped me home and planned another trip the next day.

'Another date?'

'It's not a date,' I said huffily. 'It's work.'

'When are you going to speak to Neil?'

I frowned. 'I think tomorrow. He was out today, so Sam's keen on pinching him tomorrow.'

'Pinching him?' Josie tried not to smile but it broke out.

I laughed. 'Cop talk.'

We drank another cocktail and I told her about Zara's crush on George at work and she told me how she'd decided she wouldn't be dating for a while. I didn't laugh, because she looked so serious, but I knew, as I've known every other time, that it's hopeless. She's a guy magnet: it'd be like not buying clothes when you work at Kookai.

Josie's mobile rang and, when she answered, her expression told me it wasn't great news.

'We're not open until ten tonight. No, she's not here. How did you—?' She glanced up, peering out through the glass front. 'Oh, okay. Five minutes.' She clicked off and then turned to me. 'It's Malcolm. He wants to ask you something.'

'You should have told him to go home. Is he coming over?' Josie had never let Malcolm befriend her like I had and thus he never broke through her icy cool. It drove him crazy. She was the perfect friend for his fictional self-image but she'd have nothing to do with him.

'Tell him yourself. He's here.' She nodded towards the front door. She must have got a good deal on the bread.

I swore and got up as he burst in.

He looked happily around him and then sat down next to Josie without a word. She was usually generous with her time, but she had very little for Malcolm. How he got her mobile number was a mystery. She shifted slightly away from him and I prayed silently that he wouldn't order a drink. The empty glasses were sitting on the table and it would be very rude indeed to refuse him one. But maybe rudeness was what was necessary.

I glanced up as Nick descended on the table. 'Here you go,' he said, putting more drinks in front of us. 'I know you have to leave in a minute, Sir, otherwise I'd offer you a drink. Josie has to help me organise the menu for this evening.' And then he was gone. Josie glanced up appreciatively as he moved silently back to the bar but Malcolm looked annoyed.

'I didn't come to interrupt,' he said and for a second I felt sorry for him. Just for a second. I knew he was shifting tactics as he realised he didn't have long. 'I just wanted to ask Cass something.'

'What's that then?'

'Well, that woman you were with. Can you give me her number?'

'Why?' I was surprised.

'She was gorgeous. So mature, so sophisticated. Just the sort of woman that would suit me.' He sat back with a swagger and I stifled a laugh. But who was I to get in the way? Helen was dating a drip with relationship issues that stretched all the way back to adolescence. She deserved someone better, or if not better, different.

I wrote her number down and handed it to Malcolm.

'I didn't think you'd do it!' whispered Josie.

I smiled like a Medici handing out gold coins. *What the hell?* 'It's all right,' I said. 'Helen must have eaten a bad scallop because she seemed to find Malcolm attractive too.'

'She did?' Malcolm's swagger disappeared and he sat up. 'Really?'

'Uh-huh.'

'I'll call her tonight.' He got off the couch, much cheered, and nodded towards the kitchen. 'How's that bread coming along?'

'Very well. Thanks, Malcolm.'

Maybe he wasn't so bad. Maybe Malcolm was just lonely, an outsider, like Sam. Perhaps he too would grow into a slightly scruffy, delicious, well-dressed heart-throb. Or was that heart-breaker? I looked at Malcolm's white rubber trousers as he made his way out of the café. Then he turned as he reached the door, saying, 'I'm gonna get laid, ladies!'

Josie put her head in her hands and I threw a rubber coaster at the door. Then we both lunged for our glasses in relief.

We were outside Tennis Shoes's house. I was waiting in the passenger seat, playing the wife waiting for her husband, while Sam went on a mission. No one would suspect he was anything except a father looking for his son's dog. He even had a photo. He wore blue jeans, an orange Country Road windcheater and a worried expression. He went to three houses before knocking on Tennis Shoes's place. I pretended to read a book, but flicked my gaze towards Sam at every opportunity.

He looked nice in orange. No one looks nice in orange. This morning I noticed how cool he was around me, how reserved, and it made me feel strange. Was it sadness? Lust? Regret for bullying him? More likely a giddy cocktail of all three. With a humility chaser. No wonder I felt a little dizzy.

He was forced to work with me to help his brother. There was no chemistry, just resentment on his part and desperation on mine. I was superficial and undeserving. If this was a John Hughes film I would get my comeuppance. Perhaps I would, soon enough.

'Maybe he's forgiven me,' I muttered doubtfully to myself as the front door of her house opened to his knock and he spoke to whomever was framed in the sliver of space. Then the door opened wider and he leaned casually against the frame, talking. I craned forward but couldn't see who he was speaking to. What should I do now?

I flicked open his glovebox. No gloves. A map of Yorke Peninsula (probably a romantic weekend away), a water bottle (half empty), a packet of generic painkillers, three pens, a torch and, I peered closer, a packet of tampons. Tampons? I slammed it closed. Tampons indeed.

My memory leapt back to a guy years ago. I'd met him at a concert and this was date number three. He lived alone in a nice house and had broken up with his fiancée of five years. He'd told me that he hadn't seen her for months but at some time during the evening I went to the bathroom and there was a clear, crumpled tampon plastic wrapper on the floor by the toilet like the skin of a bug. The rest of the bathroom was spotless. In the scheme of things it was nothing, but it just felt wrong at the time. And then suddenly everything else had felt utterly wrong along with it.

I'd left before coffee, pleading a headache. He called a few days later and said it wasn't going to work out. It was a ghost memory, but it still hurt. Relationships are pain. You're always worried they might wake up the next morning and realise they don't love you anymore. The risk factor is too high. So I've decided I'm investing in Definite Undies rather than Possible True Love. There might be only a one-in-six chance of losing in Russian Roulette but who the hell really wants to play?

So was it guilt that made me feel drawn to Sam? Maybe it was the car.

I blinked from my reveries as I caught sight of him walking down the path. He strode back to the driver's door and slid in.

'So?'

'I didn't talk to Tennis Shoes.'

'Who *did* you speak to?' I was excited.

'I spoke to her reverse.'

'Her *what*?'

'Her reverse—a large, shy, frightened woman called Justine who had no idea where my dog was because she hasn't left the house in eight years although she smelt like a lavender bush.'

'Really? And by reverse you mean—?'

'Her opposite. Where Suzanne is bones Justine is flesh. And she treated me like I was Luke Skywalker returning from the Battle of Yavin. You remember.' He looked over at me, his eyes bright. 'The night we watched it on Neil's fifteen-inch telly, when Dad bought a video player and we thought it was so great.'

'*You* thought it was great. I was getting my hair braided by your crazy neighbour.'

'That was long before you and Neil were dating. You'd come over because Mum was lending your mum something. Wool or something to do with embroidery.'

I stared at him, surprised he remembered, and even more that I did. 'That's right,' I said, slowly. 'She wanted the pattern for a William Morris design. I thought it was a Dylan Thomas design and everyone laughed at me.'

'Not as much as they did when we watched *Star Wars*.'

I laughed. 'Only because you wore your Stormtrooper helmet,' I said. 'I haven't seen *Star Wars* for years.' The memory of Sam in his helmet was suddenly very clear. The new Sam was remarkable, but there was still a glimpse of who he'd been. A shadow of his other self suffused his features with youth.

'And you can't. It's now called *Episode Four: A New Hope*.'

'You haven't changed.'

'Some things never change.' And that was when it happened. He looked at me and I flushed from scalp to toe. Prickles came up on my neck. Then he sat back and the moment passed.

What the hell?

'The walking Liver Cleansing Diet, whose name is Suzanne, moved in a month ago under very odd circumstances.'

'Tell me!'

He adjusted his seat.

'She arrived on Justine's doorstep in a wedding dress. Deserted her own wedding, apparently. Sounds like a scam to me.' I nodded as he went on. 'Sure sounds like a scam. A woman who hasn't left the house for that long isn't likely to open her door to just anyone.'

'She told all this to a man who lost a dog?'

'I have ways.'

'Yes, I know. And some people call them fibs.'

'Others call it subtle interrogation to get answers. I was very good. You should have seen me.'

'I wish I had. Did you woo her with your manly charms?'

'Only if by manly charms you mean desperate loneliness. I've just moved from Brisbane and Kimbo, my son's golden retriever,' he held up the picture of a very soulful puppy, 'is my only friend.'

'My God, no wonder you had girls on your lap the other night.'

'Girls. Girls are easy. It's women you have to worry about. Hormones all wild, trying a *High Fidelity* to regroup, quizzing ex-boyfriends, and assessing their chances of mating in the next half decade.' He looked over at me and laughed.

I recalled the day in the car after catching up with Neil and cringed. 'Very funny.'

'Justine didn't think so,' he said, his voice light. 'She was worried too. "Mad people out there," she said. I had to agree. Even I know some crazy women. When all along it's obvious what the problem is.' He looked over at me. 'She just needs to relax a little. Stop making shit up. Be herself.'

'I don't *make shit up*, as you call it,' I said steadily, but the heat had crept through from my face into my voice. 'No more than you, anyway. You and your fake son and your fake emotions. It's no worse than me shifting the truth aside in order to make the situation fit. I need to expand reality so people can tell me what I need to know. Why's my job so different to yours, anyway?' I noticed his expression and waved in exasperation. 'Sure you have a gun and everything, you can call back-up whenever you want, but I just have my brain and it's not always reliable. Sometimes things come out that are not strictly true, but it works and I've never been busted for stalking.'

'Only because I chose not to report you.'

I sat up, furious. 'You only tailed me because your family's fucked up. The neighbours spotted you after I don't know how many years of training but they never rang me in because I did it well. You just can't admit it. This is bullshit. You're just pissed off because of the past.'

My words hung in the air like a fart.

'This has nothing to do with the past. My family's fine. It's just Neil who's in trouble.' His voice was tight.

'Yeah, okay,' I said, making clear nothing was okay, mainly because I'd flown off the handle, but I needed time to work it out. 'I have to get back home.'

'Gotta walk the dogs?'

I rolled my eyes and made a little huffing noise to indicate my sophisticated exasperation and he started the car. We drove in silence while I cursed him to a lifetime of celibacy and undiagnosable illnesses. But he'd clearly never had a real tiff before because he kept talking. Had the man no idea about argument etiquette at all? I needed that frosty silence to maintain my rage.

'Can we just stop by Neil's place on the way back?'

I didn't know what to say and I felt a little adolescent just ignoring him, so I nodded. 'Fine.'

It was only when we pulled up in front of his house I noticed the removals van. 'Is he getting a flatmate?'

'The other bedroom's full of hydroponics that I had to

pretend weren't there!' He caught my look. 'Sometimes it gets really boring reporting your own brother. Maybe he's moved out.' But we saw the men dragging a big sideboard inside and all the boxes in the hallway as we walked up to the house. Then I noticed the front door.

I fingered the deep grooves in the old wood panelling. Flakes of wood came off in my hand around the cuts that criss-crossed at head height. Someone had had a real go at it. With something sharp. 'Did Neil have a dog?' I asked. 'A very tall and angry dog?'

'No,' Sam said firmly.

'Did he say anything to you about this?' But it was clear he was in the dark as much as I was.

'No, he was fine the other day. I thought he liked living here.'

'When did you last—?'

'Four days ago.'

We poked our heads in the front door just as the men came out. They didn't know when the previous tenant had moved out, but they gave us the number of the new one.

Sam dialled the number. Over a crackling line the new tenant told him that she was renovating the place on a reduced rent and gave him the landlord's number. There was no for-warding address, we discovered Neil owed the landlord six weeks' rent, and the door issue wasn't improving his mood either. Sam promised to pay whatever was owed and then rang off. He slipped the phone in his pocket with a tiny sigh. There was no hint of the adolescent Sam. This one looked sixty years old as he returned to the car and then thumped the steering wheel with his fist. After a moment he gave me a tired smile.

'Good old Neil,' he said.

'Good old Neil.'

He drove me home and refused the offer of beer or tea. I felt useless and, in truth, annoyed with myself and the world. I'd lost my temper with Sam just as we were getting along. I was twenty-nine going on twelve. I was the one who had to prove something to him, not the other way around, and I was making no progress at all.

'Your nose is all pink,' said Josie.

'And your eyes are all googly,' added Zara. 'How many of those cocktails have you had?'

I'd been there an hour when Zara turned up. Having abandoned the kitchen for a night of meet-and-greet Josie pulled a newly filled cocktail glass towards her.

'Only three,' I said. 'And three is only one more than a couple. A couple is a regular drinking amount. You make me sound like Rumpole of the Bailey.'

Zara readjusted herself on the stool. 'Certainly you have his nose.'

Nick was making us cocktails to drown our various sorrows. Me for having a crush on an ex-Stormtrooper, Josie for being dumped by a loser and Zara for having made no progress at all with George. Other than that, our careers were soaring and our lives were as shiny as our noses. Sure, sometimes it's men who make our worlds go around, but only sometimes.

It was past eleven and the lounge bar was filling up. Josie watched as I fumbled in my bag for lipgloss. 'Cass, I think you're drunk.'

'I'm not.'

'You are. You just glossed your nose and it's shiny enough.'

I turned to scowl at her and something caught my eye. Sam was fighting his way through the crowd.

'Argh.' I dropped from the chair, grabbing my bag. 'Don't let him see me.'

'Who?' Josie whipped around.

'Sam! He's here. And I'm drunk.' I raced to the loos and, as I turned at the bathroom door, I caught Zara waving him over. She looked a little bewildered but she was holding up well, considering he'd baked himself into such a tasty treat over the past decade. I paused for a second to watch his reaction to Josie, the woman who could seduce the feathers off a duck, but he barely glanced at her.

Five minutes later, I'd re-tied my hair into a ponytail that swished my back and my red lipstick was firmly in place. Earlier I had changed into a short black dress with a high turtleneck and a soft leather coat bought before my Visa bill finally made me feel queasy. I didn't look so bad. I was having a good hair day at least.

'I knew it had something to do with ladders and something to do with sandwiches,' said Zara as I approached. 'I woke up with the sweats. Horrible.'

'What was horrible?' I asked, giving Sam a brief smile as I put my bag on the bar.

'My dream last night. I was eating a greasy sandwich that made my hands slippery, so when I had to cross this pit, my hands slipped on the fence surrounding it. I knew I was going to die and it freaked me out.'

I made sympathetic noises while trying to keep my hand from brushing a speck of lint from Sam's jacket.

'I thought I was going to die once,' said Sam.

'In the line of duty?' Zara looked pale.

'No, in the line at the seven-day supermarket. Some guy came in with a sawn-off shotgun, only he slipped in a puddle of juice and cracked his head on the Samboy chips stand. They caught it all on security video, including me protecting myself when he waved the gun around.'

'How did you do that?' asked Zara.

'I hid behind an old lady buying a carton of cigarettes. I figured she was on her way out anyway.'

Zara looked stunned until Sam laughed. 'I'm joking. I did flinch though. They kept the tape and they ribbed me about it for weeks at the station.'

'I thought police were used to guns,' I said, recovering.

'Police in Texas are used to guns. Police in Adelaide are used to occasional spitting.'

As the music softened we could hear someone shouting near the front door. Sam slid off his stool and moved towards the front of the bar just as a loud crash pierced the track like an ill-advised remix. I slid through the crowd behind him, and it wasn't until about thirty people had poured through the front doors that we saw everyone else had gathered around something on the concrete floor inside. No one was doing anything, but they were all shouting loudly.

'It crashed through the window!'

'I heard a bang. I thought it was a gun.'

Sam grabbed a cloth napkin from a nearby table and turned the brick over. There was a note held on by an elastic band but I couldn't get a look at what it said. He walked quickly outside—the street was empty.

Nick and Josie passed around free drinks as James, the silent bartender, started sweeping up glass. We moved the remaining crowd to tables and booths away from the window and then returned to the bar.

'Weird,' I muttered as Sam called in a report to the police.

'Do you think it had anything to do with Amanda and her thugs?' asked Zara, a frown creasing her features. I'd told her about Amanda's loose tongue but had assumed it was all over. I realised now that I was just being naive. Anyone who'd drive someone off the road had worked themselves into quite the vengeful frenzy.

I shook my head, but I was worried. Nothing like this had ever happened before and the thought of Tony threatening my friend, or her business, because of me made the cocktails churn in my stomach. No wonder PIs were always chugging antacid on the telly.

When Sam rang off I told him about Amanda's thug friends and about Gus sending the car around that night.

'Gus Stamp is a good cop. I'll let him know what happened. And I'll give him the brick.'

'You're not going to look into it?'

He shook his head. 'I'm on holiday, remember.' He unwrapped the brick. 'But I think this message is probably for you.' He turned the brick over, revealing the words 'Marriage is sacred'.

'You think this is from Amanda's fiancé?'

'Either that or a bizarre ad campaign for the local wedding reception centre.'

Sam's phone rang again and, as we helped Nick and Josie hand out complimentary nuts, Sam took me by the arm. I tried to pretend I wasn't getting the full body blush as he whispered in my ear.

'That was Officer Williams, from the northeast division. Neil's been picked up for possession and possible breaking and entering. I have to go down to the station.'

'Do you want me to come with you?'

Our eyes connected for a second. 'Thanks, but this is my problem.'

'Actually it's Neil's.' I was aware of Zara and Josie bustling around us but I could smell his aftershave over the smoke and sweat and sweet smell of vanilla candles in the windows.

'Whatever, as long as it's not my mother's.'

I nodded.

'So, what are you doing here, anyway?'

'I thought there might be a good chance of running into you after the day you've had.'

As I opened my mouth to ask him why, he turned and left. A vacuum must have opened up around me because within seconds Zara and Josie were by my side.

'Christ, no wonder you've been wiggy!' Zara's eyes were gleaming. 'I forgave him his chess indiscretions the moment he smiled at me.'

'He makes Vin Diesel look like a eunuch,' said Josie.

'Neil's been arrested,' I said.

'Again?' Zara frowned.

'True.' I was worried, probably because Sam was. Maybe Neil would go to prison again, something that probably wouldn't help his habit, or his attitude.

So I wasn't the happiest girl in the world, but I wasn't miserable because I still had hope. While it sounded like a message on a crappy fridge magnet, I also knew that sometimes it really was hope for love and a career (and perhaps a hacker breaking into the Visa company files and erasing my debt) that kept me going. Without some hope for salvation and change, there's just a black hole in your life and I couldn't see that there'd be much hope for Neil in prison. I wouldn't wish that on anyone, even Neil, who once told me I had 'significant hips'.

'Well, in either case, you'll be needing one of these,' said Josie and handed me another Vodka Dialogue. That was the moment when Helen and Malcolm came into the bar together, laughing and looking a little enamoured with each other. Oh, strange and ugly love, you have found suitable host bodies.

I swilled my glass and vowed to chase up Amanda's fiancé the very next day. I had mace, sixty-four pairs of underwear and was beginning to realise you couldn't prepare for anything in life. I was perfectly armed for a surprise attack. And I hardly ever got the shakes.

'So why do we have to wear sunglasses? It's not even sunny. They look stupid with Versace.'

'We're staking out a house, Malcolm. We have to keep a low profile.' I looked down at his puffy jacket. 'And that's *fake* Versace.'

'Top quality fake, though,' he said, holding out a well-stitched tag. We'd been waiting in my car outside Amanda's house for three hours. I don't know what I was hoping for. Maybe a delivery of illegal weapons. I'd seen Tony go in ten minutes ago and by the look of the shadows behind the curtains they'd gone upstairs for a quick shag.

Malcolm crossed his legs and sighed. 'We'll be spotted in a second in these wire frames. They're so eighties.'

I'd decided to bring Malcolm because I didn't have a Kevlar vest, but from the moment he'd jumped in the Laser he'd been pain in the bum. He'd agreed to come along on the proviso that I'd talk about Helen, and had called me just when I was leaving the house that morning to get gossip. They'd looked pretty cosy the night before at the Easy Lounge, but I could tell he was worried. He knew she was seeing someone but he had no idea I was investigating that someone. Professionally there wasn't much I could say, but it was good barter currency to look mysterious whenever he mentioned her name. I wasn't getting laid, so I had to get my fun where I could.

I'd called Sam first thing in the morning and he'd told me that Neil had been busted for possession in a grimy share house in Salisbury. The breaking and entering charge had been dropped due to lack of evidence. Unfortunately he was being held on priors for assault and Sam wasn't in a good mood, so I rang off, but not before telling him to call when he had any news.

'You get lucky last night?' I tried to imagine the physically intimidating Helen and the rather scrawny Malcolm together and failed.

'You know I didn't.' He stared out the window, then smiled tightly. 'She liked my car though.'

'Oh, that'll get you far.'

'I know,' he said, seriously. 'Chicks dig cars. She's a little uptight for my tastes, but sometimes they're the best kind. When you undo the strings it all comes loose, you know?'

'Sure, Malcolm.' I scrunched down in my seat. I'd just spotted Tony and Amanda leaving by the front door. Amanda was wearing yellow: shoes, A-line skirt and halter-neck top. She looked like a genetically enhanced ladyfinger banana. Tony looked huge, and he gripped her hand tightly before they jumped into the green Holden sedan in the driveway.

I put the car into gear and followed them down the street, all the while with Malcolm trying to smooth his hair into a central spike.

I swiped him on the head as we turned onto a main road. 'It's never going to happen, Malcolm. You have curly hair. Curly hair doesn't lend itself to a mohawk without serious gel.'

'I used gel. Hard Rock fucking gel.' He belched discreetly and sat back. 'Hard Rock, my arse.' He paused and, as I glanced around to change lanes, I saw him smile smugly to himself. 'Now, that's true.'

I suppressed a laugh. I'd seen his bum one night at a spa party. It was wide and hairy and wasn't his best feature. Even his chest was more appealing. 'Once again, it's *never* going to happen.'

'I'll have you know, my arse has been the source of some serious admiration from girls.'

'What? Admiration that it hasn't just slipped off like a huge marshmallow?'

He turned to face me. 'Look, I can tell you're still pissed off at me. Do you want me here or not? You're not doing me any favours. I could be home—' he paused, '*doing stuff.*'

I glanced at him in surprise and realised I wasn't really still mad at him. Maybe I was just harbouring resentment. I looked closer.

No. He was just really annoying.

'Sorry,' I conceded as I streaked through an orange light and then slowed behind a BMW as Tony weaved between lanes ahead of us.

He grunted. 'I'm sorry, too. About that rumour. Which had nothing to do with me, of course.'

'Helen's boyfriend isn't that good-looking,' I said.

He sat up. '*How* not good-looking?'

'He reminds me of a young Daryl Somers.'

'Really?'

'And he wears Dr Scholls around the house.'

'Those ones with the bobble soles that massage your feet?'

'Nope, just the slip-ons. With socks. Like a German tourist.'

He smiled. 'I wear Peter Alexander ugg boots.'

'I knew you would.' I popped a musk Lifesaver to keep my expression steady. We drove in silence, coming into the city, when suddenly the sedan indicated left and turned into a big ten-storey car park above a department store.

'Shit.' Now what? I pulled in behind them and grabbed a ticket. They swung wide and then we did the storey circuit until they found a park on the fourth floor. Tony was the

type to wait five minutes while a little old lady packed away
her shopping and warmed up her car. Malcolm put the time
to good use sorting through my cassette collection.

'You have four compilation tapes here,' he remarked, after
stacking them neatly beside the empty juice bottle and jar of
hand cream in the glove compartment.

'Uh-huh.'

I was concentrating on not drawing attention to us, which
was tricky as we were now hovering five metres behind them.
I tucked my hair behind my ears and pushed the sad *Risky
Business*-style Ray Bans up my nose. 'They're all good,
though. One of them has Hot Chocolate,' I said.

'I know. And one of them also has the Nolans. This one's
techno,' he said, holding it up. 'This is *industrial* techno, the
other one's Triple J rock and this is soppy love songs. They
all have song listings on the cases. In *different* handwriting.'

Tony pulled into the space and I had no choice but to
glide carelessly by. Malcolm seemed unaware of how close
we were to blowing our cover. My heart was thumping as I
turned up to the next level.

'And?' I was getting impatient. I was trying to figure out
if we'd fit in the 'small car only' space but I took a chance
and nosed carefully in, locking up and slamming the door as
Malcolm stuffed the tapes back in the glovebox and scrambled behind me. As we reached the fourth level walkway, I
peeked between floors.

'They're by the lift,' he whispered behind me, making
me jump.

'Thanks.' I slowed until I could see they weren't looking

my way, then grabbed Malcolm by the puffy shoulder. We ran, bent double, to a row of cars five metres from the lift.

They weren't paying any attention to us as we slipped between cars in their direction.

'You go,' I whispered, pushing him forward. 'They won't recognise you and we won't know where they're going if we don't follow the lift.'

'They could be going anywhere.'

'I know.'

'You said it wouldn't be dangerous,' he hissed.

I waited while he fidgeted with the toggles on his cargo pants.

'Well, um. What does Helen wear to bed?' he asked sullenly.

'I have no idea but I'll find out for you.' I waved impatiently at him. 'Go on. I'll try to find you. Keep behind them. Now go,' I pushed him out and he straightened. He really was gormless and I felt a rush of sympathy, but then I caught a glimpse of his wobbly bottom and ducked down behind a black Jeep Cherokee. He reached Amanda and Tony just as the light above the lift rang and followed them awkwardly inside.

As soon as the doors closed I ran to the door to the stairs and took them two at a time. Excitement crawled through me as a plan formed in my mind. I tripped as I hit the second landing but kept going. John McClane in *Die Hard* would have kept going. Only John McClane also wore sissy boy singlets under his clothes and managed to turn them into macho wear. If I had to bandage my feet with my shirt I would be left running around in a purple Bendon bra with yellow daisies and I figured that probably wouldn't frighten anyone. On second thoughts maybe the poochy bits of boob that now sat in my cleavage might scare someone a little.

At each door I ran the length of the narrow corridor that led to the floors of the department store and on the second floor I spotted Tony's big head above the toasters and breadmakers in the electrical section. I couldn't see Malcolm.

Gus had once worked as a security guard in Myers and I knew where the cameras were, what was and was not acceptable in a department store, and what happened when you broke the rules. I also knew from many hours of bored conversations at DVDWorld that Tony liked shagging in the change rooms. Especially after looking at lingerie (and not having to pay for it). Sure enough, after browsing through the kitchen section they headed straight for the undies.

After selecting a red corset and black G-string they made a move for the change rooms. After two minutes there was no sign of them, so I grabbed a red bra and slipped in with a backwards glance. One of the attendants was just returning to the base station. I could hear low grunting as I entered the rooms.

I walked hastily back to the woman just as she pulled out a bunch of bras for hanging. I had to move fast. Tony wasn't a man for foreplay, or endurance.

I pointed towards the change rooms 'Excuse me, I was just in the change rooms and there's a couple,' I leaned forward with my eyes wide and whispered, '*doing* it. In there. It's disgusting. I'm going to complain to management.'

To her credit, she looked genuinely shocked. 'What? Doing *what*?'

'Having sex,' I said. 'In the change rooms.'

She looked frantically around her. 'I'll call security.' She dialled and spoke hastily into the receiver, all the while keep-ing an eye on me.

'Call more than security,' I said when she rang off. 'I want you to call the police. It was offensive.'

She looked at me warily. 'You want to press charges?'

I figured I could always leave before the cops arrived. 'Maybe.'

'Because management will be on my back if the police turn up. Makes the store look bad.'

'And I guess fucking in the change rooms just adds a whole lot of class?'

She picked up the phone just as Malcolm arrived breath-lessly at my side. I shot him a warning glance and he spun around, feigning interest in some large tummy control undies.

A customer dumped a pile of singlets on the counter when security turned up in the guise of a grumpy balding Harvey Keitel type. Perfect. The attendant directed him towards the change rooms but he charged towards me.

'You saw what?'

'Heard,' I said, pasting on a shocked look. 'I was in the change rooms trying on this.' I held up the bra and he blushed to the ears. 'And I heard some people doing it next to me. It was awful. I thought this was a quality store.' He nodded, as if I'd just given him orders to call in the bomb squad, and marched off.

'You stay here,' he called back as the woman behind the counter started dealing with the singlets. My heart was thumping as her attention was diverted; I grabbed Malcolm and we walked quickly back through to the lifts.

I dragged him behind a mannequin just as Harvey Keitel brought Tony out, gripping his upper arm. Amanda trailed behind them, looking mortified. Her yellow halter-neck was untied and she clutched the strings to her throat. I noticed cheerfully that the yellow looked particularly bad against her red face.

'What happened?' Malcolm whispered.

'I heard them fucking in the change rooms.'

'Christ.' He stopped in front of the cardigan section. 'Really?'

'Yes. Really.' We took the stairs to the carpark. My ankle hurt but I was itching to get away. I just had to hope no one gave them a very detailed description of me. Next time I'd go to better lengths to disguise myself. Fingers crossed there wouldn't be a next time, but I was beginning to realise the daily horoscope in the paper didn't really have the power to predict everything that would happen to me. I'd just have to stay alert.

I silently cursed Malcolm as we headed towards the car. 'So where did you get to?' I asked. Then I noticed the bag.

Malcolm had the decency to sound sheepish. 'I followed them into haberdashery but then I saw this amazing shirt.' He pulled a slither of brown silk from the tissue paper inside. 'It's Dolce&Gabbana. I saw it on *Sex and the City*. It's very "street".'

I kept quiet until I found the car, and slipped inside. There was no sign of Tony and Amanda. If nothing else they'd have a hefty parking fee.

'So you went shopping,' I said quietly as I pulled out.

'Uh-huh. I know it wasn't part of the plan, but frankly I didn't think we had a plan.'

I shot him a dirty look. He was right.

'You didn't need me,' he went on, 'and you know I get distracted by clothes.'

By the time we pulled out into the street I had calmed down a little but my breathing was still unsteady. The adrenaline was starting to kick in and it was making me a little nerved, like drinking too much coffee on an empty stomach.

'So, anyway, as I was saying,' he pronounced, as though busting Amanda and Tony had been an unfortunate interruption in the daily serial which was Malcolm and his life. I don't think he understood *The Truman Show* because he always felt the world revolved around him anyway. 'I was wondering about the compilation tapes.'

'Hmm?' I unclenched my teeth. I'd been concentrating on not driving the car into a tree. I could kill us both. People would understand.

'Who made them for you?' He smiled at me, unaware of the near-death experience blossoming around us

Focus on the road. Avoid trees. 'Malcolm,' I said, gripping the wheel and consciously softening my jaw. 'Why would I tell you about my ex-boyfriends after "the incident"?'

'Hey!' he sounded hurt. 'I keep telling you it wasn't me who said that about you and the dud blow job. I just passed it on. *And* I apologised.'

'Yes, about five minutes ago. And only so you could get information on Helen.'

'But I came along as your right-hand man. You lied. You told me you had all this gossip so I'd protect you. But you've got nothing.'

'You went shopping, Malcolm.' I loosened my grip on the

wheel again. 'And I didn't want you to protect me,' I lied. 'I can protect myself.'

In truth I hadn't even taken the lid off the mace, let alone thrown a punch. Probably I could have poked Tony in the eye with a pen, or criticised Amanda's fashion sense. She was touchy; it might have worked. 'Shopping would not have helped if something had gone wrong.'

'I *always* shop.'

'And I always lie,' I said wearily and pointed the car towards home.

'You should have brought up Tucker Moore,' said Zara. 'Just so you could have seen his expression when you told him about the modelling. He would have been so jealous!'

'Jealous because Tucker was such a dumbarse,' I said, picking at a bowl of rice crackers. 'If Malcolm was only a few IQ points lower he wouldn't talk so much. It'd be so much better for him socially. That was Tucker's gift to the world. Silence.'

'That and those eyes.' Zara feigned a swoon. She was on a long lunch break and hadn't made any move to leave. The George situation at work was apparently getting her down and she'd taken to lapsing into silences that ended with a long frown and often a blush. Avoiding work wasn't going to do her any favours, though. Maybe Josie would be more helpful than I had been. None of us had any relationship qualifications. If we were applying for the job as Zara's love counsellor, we'd both fail the interview and our CVs would prove to be bogus.

'Eyes are overrated.' Josie was making us all hot chocolates as we were waiting for the window repairman to finish up.

I agreed. I couldn't even remember what colour Tucker's had been. He'd been my boyfriend for about six months five years previously and I'd taken some expensive party drugs since then. Impossibly good-looking, he'd made me the industrial techno tape.

'And remember Steve?' Josie laughed as she reached for the chocolate sprinkles, exposing a lip of black lace bra. She prepared things for us like we were paying customers and it always gave me warm prickles in my scalp. Little kindnesses like that could knit together to form a sort of comfort on days like today when I felt rather unloved.

Maybe not everyone needs love, I thought, then remembered Sam and winced. Sometimes I missed being looked after, but friends were a very decent substitute, and they generally didn't surprise you over dinner with: 'Look, you know how much I love you, but I've met this girl…'

'Steve, the internet genius?' laughed Zara. 'Oh, he was *so* cute. Wasn't he the one who tried to spell out the alphabet on your clitoris?'

I nodded. 'With his tongue. He only got to P. He was very good.' *He'd had loads of practice.* It really was no wonder I wasn't in a relationship. Everyone I'd dated had done something to make me cringe, despite the often excellent sex.

I took the cup from Josie but was clouded with memories. Sam had been crowding my mind all day. Sam and every boy I'd ever kissed. Had I done anything to equal some of their dishonesties? I struggled to remember.

Past sentimentalities and cruelties loomed up in equal parts. A glimpse of a depressing picnic, a wonderful roadtrip, a cold glare, a flash of hurt, a heart beating beneath my ear on a lazy Sunday. I remembered an impromptu trip to Sydney with Steve when I realised that if I ever returned I would most probably be alone, and the cold, prickly fear of it.

Suddenly it had been horribly clear that this man at my side over dinner, laughing at my lame jokes, owed me nothing. I was the one who knew about his nightmares but his family were the ones who got to keep him. I could barely remember the sex, but I could have sketched the scene when Steve dumped me. He'd broad-sided me at a concert, telling me at the bar after a couple of vodkas that he had decided to move back to Sydney. I'd struggled not to cry and pretended it was the smoke machine.

It was not just the fact that I still loved him, but that he'd seemed so confident, almost cheerful, and I'd been so surprised. When had he looked at me and realised he didn't love me? That he didn't want to go beyond P? Was it before or after Sydney? Had I been laughing at someone else's jokes while he'd been planning his future without me, without even the possibility of regret? Was I ever the ex-girlfriend that other girls dreaded to hear about? Was I a ghost in anyone's life?

I forced a smile as Josie plopped down on the couch and felt a sense of maudlinness creep through me like a chilled breeze. I'd opened my mouth before she'd slipped off her six-hundred-dollar mules.

'I used to equate love with Wonderland,' I said quietly.

'As in the dance hall?' Zara laughed, flicking a glance at me, but stopped at the tone in my voice. I could feel a deep sadness descending but was powerless to stop it. 'Wonderland, as in Alice in…' I casually sipped the chocolate but it burnt my tongue.

'It started with the rabbit. Whenever I was recovering from a relationship breakdown, I'd tell myself all the time that what I missed was the cocoon we'd built, the habit of seeing him, the plans, the hand-holding, the sleeping together, the tooth-brushes in a glass by the sink. I'd woven this huge rug of a love-life together with all my hopes and dreams and fantasies and romance. Some of it was based on what he'd do and some of it on my interpretation, or prediction. The habit. Then I started calling it "the rabbit" because I was reminding myself so often to ignore those emotional habits that made my life so good.

' "It's just a rabbit," I'd tell myself. A rabbit that embod-ied all the hopes and dreams of love that seemed like intoxicating magic. That's Wonderland, right?' I asked, keep-ing my voice steady despite the pinching in my throat. 'A rabbit and magic? So then to me it just seemed like stuff patched together. It wasn't real so much as a place I'd made in my mind. A boy I'd created as perfect, whom I seemed quite capable of doing without once the magic had lifted, once the rabbit went away.'

Zara and Josie were silent for so long that I laughed, but it came out as a croak.

'God, that's terrible,' Zara muttered after a beat.

'It's true.' Josie's voice was serious. 'You miss the lifestyle as much as the love. The warmth as much as the person who created it.'

'I'm depressed,' said Zara.

I cleared my throat. 'I need a cocktail.'

'So do I.' Josie got up. 'Fuck the hot chocolate. Nick left the recipe for those vodka things.'

'It's only three o'clock in the afternoon!' Zara protested.

'Good enough for me. You in, Zara?'

'Okay. I can't go back to work after that depressing story!'

I was quiet while they clanked the bottles and glasses, filling the bar with cold white noise while my heart calmed itself. But I was stuck in love zombie zone. I tried to articulate it but I still felt strangled by sadness.

'Did you say something?' Zara called across the room.

I glanced up absently. 'Only it wasn't true,' I repeated with a smile. 'Sometimes it was Wonderland and sometimes it really was just love. The ache and yearning of true love.'

'Oh for God's sake!' exclaimed Josie and brought the tray over. 'Forget about Sam.'

'I'm not talking about Sam.'

'I know, but you're thinking about him. And you're thinking you're not worthy. Maybe not. You were a bitch.' She talked over my protest. '*But* you are no longer, and he seems bright enough to notice. He certainly noticed your arse in that outfit the other night.'

'What?'

'I saw it too,' said Zara, nodding. 'He couldn't take his eyes off you, and that's a challenge with Ms Sexpo here,' she said, indicating Josie.

'Really?' I felt twelve again but instantly better.

'Sure,' Zara said dismissively. 'I thought you knew.'

'You're a catch, honey.' Josie lifted her glass and we all clinked, then drank. I spluttered. 'It's very strong.'

'And so are you.'

I groaned. 'That's so corny.'

'I know, but you just keep doing a good job on this sexual

sleuthing gig and you'll have a great career, a terrific apartment
and a guy who may or may not have the serious hots for you.'

'He'll never do anything about it,' I muttered.

Josie turned to Zara with a smile. 'Well, then, we'll just
have to help him along a little, won't we?'

'No,' I waved my hand and the drink spilled. 'Don't do
anything! It's all under control.'

'Sure it is,' laughed Zara. 'Ours.'

And they clinked glasses again, only this time they were
empty.

I'd seen Tennis Shoes, who I now knew as Suzanne, leave her
Zachary Street house thirty minutes earlier, but it had taken
me that long to figure out my story. I had no idea if she'd
be gone for the day or if she had a job, but I was determined to talk to Justine.

As I walked up to the door I rehearsed my hastily patched-
together story. When Justine answered my knock, the words
fell away and I stood staring dumbly at her.

She was gorgeous and larger than life. She filled the doorway. Her huge eyes stared nervously at me and I felt a wave
of compassion because she looked so frightened. Was this the
face Sam had managed to lie to? Clearly he'd had more practice than me. As her eyes grew rounder I realised I had to say
something.

'I've been following Suzanne,' I blurted and the rose-bud
mouth opened slightly in shock. Then she paused, gripping the
door until her soft, round hands went white and she tried to

close the door. I quickly jammed my foot between the door and the frame and pushed against it so it opened a fraction more.

'I wouldn't have come here if it wasn't important, if I didn't think you were in some danger.'

I was bluffing, but I could tell I hit a nerve. Her expression softened just slightly and she released her hold on the door and stepped back. I slipped quickly inside before she changed her mind.

Sam was right: she did smell like lavender. In fact, the whole house did. I waited in the hallway as she locked up, taking note of the three locks I hadn't heard being opened and the absence of furniture in the hallway. As we moved down the corridor, I realised why. It was a narrow space and she took up a lot of it. Guiltily I thought of my own annoyance this morning over my little beer paunch. I could still buy clothes at normal shops.

She brushed past me as I waited beside the doorway to the lounge, but she went into the kitchen. I walked through the door behind her. She put the kettle on and sat delicately in a chair. I, on the other hand, misjudged the chair and fell heavily. Always the cool one, I thought, as I glared at the chair. On the table was an electricity bill for Ms Justine Carver. Okay, now I knew her full name.

'I knew something was going on,' she said quietly. 'Can you tell me? Are we in trouble?'

It was an interesting pronoun. She had a low steady voice, but there was fear there. I could see it in her eyes and the way she picked at the skin around her nails. 'I've been hired to investigate a "situation",' I replied. 'And now Suzanne's mixed up in it and the police are very interested.'

Her hair was a tangled mess on her head and one curl fell down softly onto her shoulder as though in slow motion. I stared, fascinated as it bounced in place, then settled. She appeared not to notice. 'How mixed up?'

'Break and Enter. Possible burglary.' I left out my own indiscretions and, suitably relaxed by my own faux moral high ground, assumed a stern tone. 'She's been seen entering a house on Riverside Avenue. Does that address mean anything to you?'

She paled and glanced down. 'That's where an old boyfriend of mine lives.' She waved her hand impatiently, although I'd done nothing. 'Well, not boyfriend as such. More of a school yard crush. Anyway, he hurt me and I fear she is trying to take revenge.'

'Is she your partner?' I asked, but her expression told me no.

I tried to imagine the circumstances of Suzanne's arrival. If Sam had been right, the wedding dress had been a clever trick. Or a convenient and perfect key to another life. Although Justine had opened the door readily to me, she may well have been a good deal more cautious before meeting Suzanne.

She blushed. 'No, no. She lives here. We share this house,' she gestured around her. 'My mother left it to me.'

'How long has she lived here?'

'Probably a month.' But she seemed unsure.

'And you think she's taking revenge?'

She nodded.

'How far do you think she'll go?'

Justine stared at me, fear blossoming in her eyes.

'How well do you know her?' I asked. 'Why is she taking revenge on someone you knew at school? What happened?'

The questions seemed to steady her and she answered them in sequence. 'I had never met her before opening the door to her the other day. She had left her wedding. She was supposed to marry a young man called Adrian. He came from a different background. He'd hurt her very badly in the past but they had patched it up. He loved her deeply but she realised she'd end up hating him, hating his life and family, so she left the church before the ceremony. She knocked on my door because I was the only one with the curtains closed.'

'Why closed?'

'I don't know,' she said, looking thoughtful.

I tried to imagine the scene. Abandoning your wedding was such a soap opera thing to do. Did people do that in real life?

'Do you believe her?'

'I've read about scams in the paper,' she said steadily. 'Suzanne was pretty upset when she arrived. I looked after her. She's had no contact with anyone. That I know of—' she added '—since she arrived here.' Then she gazed out the window. 'I can't imagine how that must feel. To lose someone like that.' She turned to me 'What must her family be thinking? She just disappeared. It must have hurt him terribly.'

'He hurt her first, though, didn't he?' I reminded her.

'Yes, I guess so. He liked someone else for a while. I don't know if he did anything about it, but she seemed distressed. I guess trust is pretty important. Maybe he was untrustworthy.'

She said it like it was a disease you just caught.

'Maybe,' I said. She seemed to be mulling it over as though it had only just occurred to her. I remembered Sam's words.

'Do you work?'

She shook her head and silence fell. 'The kettle's boiled,' I said and indicated behind her. She got up and poured two cups. A sweet, empty smell filled the room and I realised I now had a cup of herbal tea. I hated it. I smiled politely.

'Biscuit?'

I shook my head and she came back to the table. I suddenly wondered if she was medicated or if this dreamy approach was just a symptom of her isolation, of the unhurried life in a house that smelled lovely and kept her safe.

A noise outside made me jump and I realised how awkward it would be if Suzanne caught me here. I stood up. 'I should go.'

'Are you going to arrest her?'

'I don't know. It's not really up to me now. It's a police matter,' I lied. 'I don't know what your relationship with her is, but it would be better for you to stay well clear of this. If she implicates you, as initiator of the break-ins, you could be in trouble. It would be better for you to be honest from the start. Can you trust her? Will she bring you into this if she gets charged?'

Justine came around the table towards me. Her eyes seemed moist, but it could have been the light. She shook her head. 'I mentioned Daniel to her once, when I was drunk. The next thing I knew, she'd brought some of his things over. I don't know how she found him. Then she described his girlfriend, his house, his underwear. She disappears all day. I never know when she's getting home. She gets angry with me, she's so moody.' She leant towards me as I hitched my bag on my shoulder and we both walked out into the hall. 'Sometimes she frightens me.'

I nodded for her to continue but she seemed lost in thought.

'Frightens you how?'

'She thinks Daniel, well, that Daniel and her ex-fiancé, Adrian, have something in common. But Daniel is grown up now. He's probably a lovely fellow, I don't know.' She seemed confused, dazed. I was tempted to say that her generous words about Daniel were not entirely accurate, but I kept quiet. One thing I'd learned from watching telly was to let people talk themselves through it. Don't interrupt in case you make them realise what they are saying and shut them up. I waited. Patience was a virtue and, God knows, I needed one of those.

'I told her how Daniel had hurt me and she kept, well, egging me on.' She suddenly looked right at me and she looked defiant, even though she spoke so softly, so slowly, that I had to resist the urge to step forward. 'You know how sometimes you can create something in the moment? Well, when we were talking, I—' She flushed. 'Well, I guess I've never really had *girlfriends* before.' She said the word as though it was reverent. 'And now I do.' She smiled but there was something there, something almost childlike. I felt a shiver run through me and clenched my hand to stop it shaking. She wasn't crazy, was she?

'It's very nice.' Her expression changed. 'But I guess it's not so nice anymore.'

'Why do you say that?' I thought *I* knew why, but I wanted to see if she did.

'Well, because of this, why you're here.' She indicated me with her soft, round hand.

'So you'll help me?'

She shook her head. 'No! She's my friend. My best friend.' And then she smiled so brightly the fat in her chins shifted. 'She's going to live here with me and we'll be friends for a long time.'

And I knew, then, that there was something very wrong. I didn't know if it was the smell of the house, of the wide, pink, dimpled flesh of her arms that made me look away, or the sense of depression that had sunk into my pores like dirt, but I could tell from her face that she saw things quite differently from me. She lived in another world.

'She's a very loyal friend,' she said, still smiling, and as I sat there, something must have moved through the light in the glass by the door because the hall seemed brighter and I realised her eyes were wet with tears. She blinked and looked away, but she was still smiling as though she were happy.

'Okay,' I said, as we walked down the corridor. 'I'm going to try to sort this out. Just make sure she doesn't hurt you. Don't say anything to her about this, about me coming around. It's very important. Do it for your own sake. You don't know what she's capable of.'

And then we heard a key in the lock and Justine pushed me so hard through the door to my right that I tripped on a corner of a rug and went sprawling.

The room was dark and I lay frozen, spread-eagled on my stomach as the front door opened some two metres from where I lay.

'Hi. What are you doing, waiting for visitors?' I'd never heard Suzanne's voice before. It was high, sharp, probably lent itself to whining. 'Yeah, *right!*' Then she laughed. A hard, cruel laugh.

'No, no. I heard a noise. It was you. I thought it was a mouse.'

'No mice here, you big lug. You keep this place so clean they'd starve.'

My heart was thumping so hard I thought they'd hear it banging against the floorboards. Then Justine took a step into the room and drew the door closed, enveloping me in darkness. The muffled sounds of their voices and Justine's heavy tread faded as they moved to the back of the house.

Praying this wasn't Suzanne's room, I lifted my head. There was a heavy dresser to my left. I lifted myself noiselessly so that my toes and hands were on the ground, then slowly slid into a crouch. The room was small and, as my eyes adjusted to the light, I realised it was indeed a bedroom.

A double bed mattress stood in the far corner, a wardrobe opposite the window to my right. If Suzanne had moved here suddenly she wouldn't have many clothes. As the door to the wardrobe was ajar, I stepped cautiously towards it and eased it open with my finger, revealing a dark array of clothes. I stood up and carefully pulled a hanger off the central pole, although even if the dress was Justine's size, this could still be a storage cupboard in a once spare room that was now Suzanne's. I swore under my breath. Why did I keep ending up where I didn't belong?

The dress was huge; a gaping floral affair with what looked like a drawstring waist. As I replaced it, I heard footsteps in the hallway and I froze as the door to the room swung open and Justine's face peered around it.

'Quick,' she gestured frantically. 'She's having a bath.'

I crept behind her, feeling exposed in the raw light as she fumbled with the locks and, within seconds, I was outside. She closed the door softly behind me and I hurried back to the car, taking off at lightning speed before I could even draw breath.

I hadn't seen many abusive relationships, but Suzanne had clearly seen the advantage of living with Justine. Too weak and insecure to defend herself, so grateful just for the company, that she'd put up with fear and cruelty. I felt filthy, not from sprawling on the carpet, but from seeing the hunted expression on Justine's face. Wishing once again that I had a mobile, I stopped at the first public phone I found, put my handbag on the counter and pulled out my wallet.

I called Sam at home. He cleared his throat before identifying himself and it gave me such a rush of affection that I gripped the earpiece more tightly. Lusting after him was one thing, but I knew I would regret it if I fell for him. I closed my eyes when I remembered yesterday's conversation and realised it was too late. I never remembered Steve without good reason.

'Sam, it's Cassidy. I was just talking to Justine. She says Suzanne is doing it on her behalf. Daniel, on Riverside Avenue, is an old school friend. I think Suzanne got it into her head that Daniel had done Justine wrong, and now she's acting as an avenging angel because she's bitter towards all men. She's also a complete bitch. She treats Justine like an idiot. She seems to think she can do anything she wants. She's mad.'

I took a breath and Sam jumped into the dead air. 'Hold on, Cass. Can you prove this?'

'You had pictures of me leaving Riverside. Do you have any of her?'

'Three.'

I smiled with satisfaction. 'Well, then. You can take her in on Breaking and Entering.'

'You watch too much TV. It's not that easy. A photo of her leaving a house doesn't exactly prove she entered illegally. And we'd need fingerprints or some other evidence. Did she wear gloves?'

I tried to remember. 'I don't know. But Justine might testify.' I remembered Justine's fear. 'Well, if I told her what was at stake.'

'Cass, I don't think that much is at stake right now. We can't really prove she stole anything, can we?'

'Justine said she brought home some of Daniel's things.'

'But did she return them?'

I hadn't asked. 'I'll call her,' I said, but I was starting to feel like a bit of an idiot. Not such a big change, but still irritating.

'Okay,' I said. 'I'll get proof. And I'll catch her at it. Oh, and I hardly ever watch TV.' I rang off to his protests down the phone. He was right, of course. But I was desperate. I'd have to ask Helen if Daniel had noticed anything missing over the last month or so. And I'd ring Justine.

Ten minutes later I had Justine's number from directory assistance. I'd call her the next day in the hope that Suzanne was out righting imagined wrongs. As I stuffed my wallet in my pants I called Helen and explained the situation so far.

'You're kidding,' she muttered when I'd finished.

'No, she's just doing it because of her own issues. It's got nothing to do with Daniel. But that doesn't change his problems with ex-s.'

'So she's just messing with his head? Or mine, I guess. I wonder if he's even noticed. He hasn't said anything to me. What else has she done?'

'So you can forgive Daniel for the other stuff?' I held my breath. I hoped not, for her sake. Maybe I was hoping a little for Malcolm's too. Just a smidge though.

She paused. 'I don't think so. I deserve better than that.'

'That's true, but don't do this because you've met someone new. New always looks appealing early on, but that feeling doesn't always last. It's much harder to have a good relationship.'

'We didn't have that great a relationship,' she said firmly. 'He was lousy in bed for one thing.'

'Oh?' Such was my surprise my mind went completely blank.

'And he grunted when he slept. Drove me crazy.'

'And you're using past tense.'

'It's definitely over. I'll tell him tonight.'

'You want to do me a favour and ask him if anything's gone missing at his place?'

'I can't do that. He'll know something's up. I told you early on I didn't want hiring you to come back and slap me.'

Damn. 'Okay, well.' I didn't know what to say. 'Good luck,' I added hopefully. Why did I feel so disappointed? Because I wanted to bust Suzanne. But I had very little to go on and no one to prove it. Sam's pictures meant little without hard evidence of theft.

'Send me the bill.'

'Okay,' I said and, in a daze, rang off.

I looked up to catch a flash of blue before pain exploded behind my eye. 'You stupid bitch,' a voice whispered in my ear before the phone booth slid away and a roar filled my ears. I saw nothing but light as I hit the ground. Feet pounding on the footpath made me remember Suzanne and I winced, waiting for another attack. But nothing came except blackness.

'Cass?'

'She's sleeping.' It was Malcolm's voice but I couldn't see him. It was dark.

'Someone turn the lights on,' I croaked.

'Can you open your eyes?'

I tried but they felt so heavy. I tried again but it was like peeling off velcro.

Then I felt a hand on my arm. 'Cass? I think she's awake.' The voice moved away, then swung closer. 'Cass, did you see who hit you?'

'Who hit me?' I repeated.

'Yes. Did you see them?'

'Blue car hit me,' I muttered. 'On the noggin.' Had I been drinking? What happened?

'You weren't hit by a car. You were hit by a fist. Did you see who was connected to that fist?'

I tried to shake my head but fireworks went off behind my brain and I winced. 'Go away.'

'She's okay.' The voices moved further away and then somebody lifted my head, put something behind it and laid me down again. Then they punched me again.

Or at least that's how it felt. Fear ricocheted me from the bed and voices and arms surrounded me. Someone was holding me down. 'Cass, it's okay. You're in hospital. They're just trying to treat your head.'

It was Sam's voice. I flickered an eye open and then squeezed it shut again. 'Turn out the lights.'

'She can't make up her mind. She never could. The blue shoes or the black? The Vodka Bar or the Soda Room? She's nev—'

'Just keep your eyes closed, Cass.' Sam cut Malcolm off which I was thankful for. If he started talking about how I couldn't decide between boys I would move like lightning. Lightning.

'Someone punched you in the face and you got knocked out,' said Sam. 'You've got a lump the size of a mandarin. Someone stole your bag too.'

I groaned. Well, there's ten tampons and a linty packet of Mentos I'd never see again.

'You want me to call in your cards?'

'I put my wallet in my pants,' I muttered. But no one moved to check. I adjusted on the bed to get it and realised my leg was rubbing against scratchy sheets. 'Hey! Who took off my pants?'

The room went quiet. Finally Sam spoke.

'The ambulance brought you in after an old lady reported you, er, lying there.'

'No one saw who hit me?'

'There was no one around when she got there. Just you, sprawled on the footpath.'

'So the *hospital* took off my pants?' I kept my eyes tightly shut and the silence in the room seemed to echo around me. 'What's wrong?'

'Well, it would appear whoever mugged you also took your shoes.'

'And your sunglasses,' said Malcolm.

'And your socks.'

A burst of laughter came from my left. 'You looked pretty funny in your jeans and T-shirt with your little white feet sticking out.'

I heard a noise, some protesting and then the door closed. 'Is he a friend of yours?' Sam asked.

'Ex-friend. Very ex now,' I muttered.

'Zara and Josie are on their way over. Malcolm's card was in your wallet. I found the girls through the Easy Lounge.'

'So who called you?' I winced at the thought of my unconscious self talking in my sleep. My long and rather detailed daydreams about Sam flooded back and I held my breath.

'The old lady called the station after the ambulance. I was in there getting some paperwork and I recognised the description of you.'

'The shoeless, mugged girl on the street sounded like me?'

'Yep.'

'You went through my wallet? It's lucky you didn't call Jock's vet,' I hissed. My jaw *really* hurt!

'I did, actually. But it turns out—not a close friend.'

The room was quiet and I peeked out of my less sore

eye. I squinted at Sam sitting in a plastic chair to my left, his head resting in his hand. He looked tired.

'Hey, Pirate Pete,' he muttered.

'You're pissed off at me.'

'Yup.'

I squinted at him. 'But I was just trying to do what I thought was right,' I croaked. My face *really* hurt.

'You were just going off half-cocked. If you'd given me a second I would have come with you and we could have spoken to Daniel, or Suzanne, together and sorted this out. It doesn't actually have to be a police matter.'

'Helen doesn't want Daniel to know she hired a private investigator.'

'Most people don't. We could have worked around it, though. Now we have to catch Suzanne doing something isolated from your involvement, in order to bring her in.'

I opened my eye further to see his expression. Hope flared. 'Really? You'll help?'

'I have no idea why you're so fixated on busting her but yes, I will help.'

'I'm suspicious.'

'Of her or me?"

'Pick one.'

'You should be suspicious. They're releasing Neil today and I'm hiring you to keep an eye on him.'

'No way!' I nearly sat up but the world swung wildly to the left and I fell back heavily on the bed. 'I'm injured. I can't be trusted to watch someone when I can't even see out of one eye!' I tried to be as indignant as possible, even though it felt like my jaw had a hundred three corner jacks stuck in it. I blustered my way through the pain. 'It's stupid!'

'That's why he's going to move in with you for a while. Just until I find him somewhere to stay.'

I exploded. 'Why can't he stay with your parents? Or you? I'm not having him. He'll hock my stereo within hours.'

'He's already hocked most of my stuff. And Mum's. The tough love counsellor says we can't take him back. But living with you will be the toughest love of all. It should put him back on the straight and narrow. I'll get someone to watch the flat, for your own sake as well as his. Kills two birds with one stone, as they say.' There was something in his voice that made me think twice before going on. The second thought was an ugly one, though, and I regretted it instantly.

'You think someone's after me?' I said quietly. My face was throbbing.

'You think someone punched you out and mugged you for that imitation Gucci bag?'

'Maybe.'

'I doubt it. Your wallet *is* still in your trousers by the way.'

'Where are they then?'

'In a tray under the bed. They said you have to stay in for another six hours while they monitor you, but then you're free to go. Organise someone to pick you up then. I've sent your car home.'

A nurse came in and warned me she was going to give me some painkillers, but the most pain I'd felt was in my arm as she slid the needle in. And I was in a lot of pain. I hate needles.

'You'll be fine in no time, love,' she said. 'Oh, no, don't smile. You have a graze the length of the Nullarbor Plain on your jaw. You move and a thousand drops of blood push up through the padding and we'll have to change it again.' I could hear her fussing around the bed, tut-tutting to herself. I hated her a lot.

'I'll call you tonight about Neil,' said Sam, scraping back his chair.

'Hang on,' I said with minimum jaw movement. 'I don't want him living with me!' Talking between clenched teeth made me sound childish and stubborn, which of course I was. 'I don't want it. Jock will gouge his eyes out.'

'Now you shush and do what your boyfriend says,' said the nurse. 'You don't want to have plastic surgery.' And then she laughed—rather evilly I thought.

'He's not my boyfriend,' I hissed loudly as the nurse left. 'He's my bloody nightmare.' I waited a few seconds. I could only keep my eyes open for short periods and I dreaded looking in the mirror.

'That's no way to speak about your boyfriend,' he said, and it sounded like he was smiling.

'Has she gone?' I whispered.

'Yes. Maybe they could sew your lips together,' said Sam cheerfully.

'*I can't live with a guy!*' I said, teeth still clenched. 'And not *Neil*. No way.'

'You want me to report you for Breaking and Entering?'

I realised I'd been scratching my thigh in annoyance and now it hurt as well, but not as much as my face. Damn him all to hell. I felt cornered and vulnerable. 'Fine. Bring him around after nine-thirty. I'll be watching *Alias*. And you'd better bring food. I only have girl things. Boys eat twenty Weetbix a day. I only have yoghurt.'

'Last time I saw you in the morning you had biscuit crumbs stuck on your face.'

I frowned. 'When?'

'At the Hindley Street café.'

'It was a health muffin.'

'A very gooey one. Anyway, he can change your dressings. Are you going to report this?'

'What?' I asked. 'There's nothing to report.'

'You call this nothing?'

I lay in sullen silence. What was wrong with me? I swallowed and it hurt. I was scared. And I didn't want to drag this out. Whoever hit me could have done a lot more. I would just have to be more prepared.

I heard Sam sigh heavily. 'Well if you're going to pretend this is normal, I can't do anything to find out who did it.'

'What could you do, though? Honestly?' I was angry but it was more with myself than with Sam. I bet I looked like shit too. An ugly, lily-livered dope. He was silent.

'See!' I said triumphantly, and realised how twelve years old I sounded.

Then the room filled with voices as Zara and Josie burst in. 'Oh, poor you!' 'Hi Sam!' 'What happened?' But it all seemed to come from far away. My legs felt like puffed-up helium balloons and the pain ebbed away. That felt good. Warmth seeped in instead and my leg felt instantly better. I smiled. 'Oh, it's like being at the pub.'

I opened one eye and Josie's face said it all. I felt like an angel but I looked like the Elephant Man.

After plugging me with more drugs, the nurses let me leave at seven-thirty. Zara brought me gingerly home and we sat on the couch, but not before she removed the large Venetian mirror over the television. 'I've never liked looking at myself while I'm a couch potato,' she said. 'But now you won't have to see your big, lumpy purple head lolling about.' I felt like an overfilled water balloon.

Then she fussed about me in a very pleasant manner and called work, telling them I had to have at least a week off because I had been mugged and bashed, which made me sound like someone who wore a beanie and said 'Strewth' a lot, then she made me some very sweet tea, which I dribbled down my chin.

I sat through most of this aware that I was smiling benignly. I felt like the padding went all over me. It was clear, like bubble-wrap, and I was cocooned inside. The television show raced by like a blur, everything astounding me in an open-mouthed, dull sort of way and by the time I heard Neil's knock I was ready for a glass of wine to continue the anaesthetic self-service.

Zara got the door. 'Hi, Achilles Neil,' she said and through my one eye I could see she was smiling. Sam brought him in and said he'd be back in an hour. I had easily resisted the urge to clean up the apartment. I felt exhausted, my face was being held together with a giant nappy and my eye was purple so I figured a spotless benchtop wasn't going to do much to improve my overall appeal.

'G'day, Zars,' Neil said as he brought in his bags. I lolled at him, grinning inanely. He flinched when he glanced my way. I got the feeling he was as impressed with the new living arrangements as I was.

'Er, Cass. Thanks for letting me stay. I'm sure it'll only be a few nights.'

'No kidding,' I slurred.

He had the grace to look a little sheepish, which broke through my Zen-like state, and left me irritated. He was one of those guys who looked like he needed sympathy, which was how he'd gotten away with so much mischief in the past. He played up to everyone, but would probably never admit it to himself. I got more and more annoyed as Zara offered him all my best stuff.

'Would you like a cup of hot chocolate, Neil?' she asked demurely and then poured it into my special Haigh's mug. 'Fancy a Tim Tam?' I scowled as he was fussed over like a returning soldier and not the ex-boyfriend felon he really was. I felt like yelling out that I was the sick one, but I kept passing out.

After a while I sat up and tried to behave with proprietor-style confidence. 'You can sleep on the couch,' I said without moving my new bandage too much. A few hours on it was fine, but eventually your own body weight put you at risk of muscle damage. It would ensure a short stay. 'There are towels in the cupboard in the bathroom. I'll get you sheets and blankets.'

'Thanks.' He smiled brilliantly and I hauled myself off the couch in a mini huff. Then I joined Zara in the kitchen and poured a glass of wine. 'Zara, you want one? Neil?'

They both demurred. Zara, I suddenly realised, because

she was leaving. Neil, because he was on methadone. The fact that I was the drugged-up alcoholic wasn't doing much to improve my mood.

Zara gathered her things together and left with a sympathetic smile. 'Be nice,' she ordered quietly at the door, then waved over my shoulder. 'And watch your wallet.'

I closed the door firmly, turned around and for a second my heart jumped. Neil was sitting in the same chair Sam had occupied, with his feet up on the magazines and a stiff arrogance to his posture. Was I getting the hots for the same guy over and over again, just slightly different versions?

'You have a really nice place, Cass. I'm sorry to hear about your dogs.'

'Hmm?' Then I remembered Oscar and Dougal, the fictional playful puppies. I probably blushed, but the wine and injury kept me permanently pink and flushed, so it had no impact.

'Sam said you had to give them away because of the neighbour complaining.'

'Ah, yes,' I fumbled and grasped at the lie gratefully. 'Mr Crabtree's a grouch. Watch out for him. I have a parrot now but he's asleep on my wardrobe. Okay,' I continued, warming to an idea. 'House rules. Mr Crabtree needs the windowsill and outside window cleaned each week. Maybe you could do that.'

'Sure,' he brightened. 'I like cleaning.'

I frowned. 'You do not. I saw your house.'

'I like cleaning now,' he said, faltering slightly but clearly determined to do the right thing. *Benefit of the doubt.*

'Great. I have to go out tomorrow, but while I'm gone

you can earn your keep cleaning up in here for a while.' I had an urge to leave, and I also wanted to know what would happen if I tried with the car outside the apartment to keep an eye on him. Was it police or someone Sam knew? It didn't bother me as long as they stopped Neil pissing off with my CDs.

'Sam said you had to stay home because of your, um, face.' He frowned, gesturing around his own chin as though I needed a visual map of the damage.

'Sam talks too much.'

'Yes, he does. Sam's cool, though. He's getting me some new clothes.'

'How old are you?' I huffed. 'Twelve?'

'Arrested development,' he said quietly.

'The band?'

'The condition. My counsellor said that emotionally I *am* still a child. That I haven't grown up. So actually you're right.'

I hadn't expected that. I sat down. 'What else does she say?'

He smiled. 'That I can't look after myself. That I can't be trusted. That I hate myself.'

'Do you?' I asked quietly, wondering if I had accidentally taken too many painkillers. Neil had never talked like this when we were dating.

'Sometimes. Most of the time. I've hurt everyone I've loved, including you.' He looked up. 'I didn't mean to. But now I have to take responsibility for it. That's step one. Accept your mistakes. Accept that I'm in crisis.'

'Sure,' I muttered. This promised to be a cheery stay.

'Your face must really hurt. Look at us. I'm broke, with

a one-hundred-dollar-a-day habit and I smoke pot for break-fast,' he held his hand up at my protest. 'I know, no smoking inside. And you... Well, you—'

Before he could say anymore I stood up. 'This is like a post-production party of *Les Miserables*. I'm going to get ready for bed. It's been a long day.'

'I can't get it up anymore either.'

'Oh for fuck's sake! This isn't Jerry fucking Springer.' I turned to Neil. 'We're roomies for a few days only. Not friends.

'Never friends,' I added firmly.

'Sam will be back any minute with the food and stuff.'

'I know,' I said, holding my head, relieved at the sudden change in topic. 'So you'd probably better give me back those painkillers.'

His expression shifted and he pulled the foil tray from his hip pocket. I took it silently and pulled the curtains closed on the city lights.

'And take a shower after he leaves. If you're cleaning any-thing tomorrow, maybe start with your clothes.'

'I'll tell Sam you're going out tomorrow,' he said slyly.

'And I'll just kick you out and they'll send you back to rehab,' I retorted. 'You've got two options, so take one. One day at a time. You sure as hell won't let people help you, but I'm not going to let you screw up my life as well. I can do that well enough on my own.'

I poured a glass of water with an unsteady hand, and went to bed. For the first time I wished my bedroom was sepa-rated from the lounge. I had a wardrobe and a cubic shelving system between me and the rest of the apartment, but the glow of lights from the lounge area still attracted my eye. I got up and hooked a coat on the second shelf and blocked the source of the light, then crawled back under the covers.

Ten minutes later I heard a knock on the front door. They talked quietly for an hour or so and then Sam left. I could hear Neil pottering about the flat as I drifted off to sleep sometime later. I'm embarrassed to say it felt oddly comforting, like leaving the television on while I napped on a Sunday afternoon. I cursed softly to myself as I disappeared into dreams filled with Tim Tams and some of the cast from *The A-Team*.

When I left by the front door the next morning, the surveillance car outside seemed to gleam on the street. The guy behind the wheel looked nonchalant as I walked towards the corner but, as I slipped into the deli, I saw him reach for something on the seat beside him. I went back out, ignoring the stares that my bandaged face attracted and went quickly back into the apartment by the back stairs emergency fire exit. When I got to my front door I could hear shouting inside my apartment. I'd only been gone five minutes.

I fumbled with my key and wrenched the door open only to see Neil in a pair of bright red pyjamas fighting off a wild-eyed Jock, who was going at him like a professional dive bomber. I stood admiring his form until I heard Mr Crabtree's door open to my right.

'It's okay, Mr Crabtree,' I said, trying to ignore the fury on his face, which quickly turned to horror as he saw the bandage. 'It's just my cleaner. He's having problems with the vacuum.'

Then I ran into the apartment as the front door slammed behind me.

The noise inside was horrendous. 'Jock!' I yelled as I rounded the kitchen island. Neil was stumbling through the lounge room, hands tearing at his hair while Jock was doing his best to audition for *The Birds*. As he heard my voice, Jock immediately abandoned Neil and flew to his post, feathers all awry. Neil continued flailing at his head. I walked quickly towards him and grabbed his wrists.

'Neil!' I shouted sternly into his wide eyes. He obviously hadn't even heard me come in.

'Neil,' I repeated more softly. He looked terrified. 'That was Jock, my parrot. Remember? You just gave him a fright.'

'Jesus!' He fell down on the couch. 'Jesus fuck! He just went for me! Fuck. I thought it was some fucking weird cold turkey thing!'

I looked around the room for the first time. The sliding doors to the desk were ajar and the cupboards in the kitchen were hanging open. 'What were you looking for, Neil? Jock was just being protective.' I thought about what Sam had said about hocking his watch and CDs. 'You steal my stuff to sell and of course Jock is going to attack you. I left you alone for five minutes. There might be someone outside but they're not going to protect you from me.'

He looked up between his hands, his eyes genuinely frightened.

'You were gone five minutes, Cass. I was looking for your cleaning stuff. I found it under the sink.' He pointed to the bucket by the swing door rubbish bin. 'I waited until you left because I knew you didn't think I'd do it. I was going to surprise you.' He shook his head. 'Honestly.'

We stood glaring at each other, each furious and martyred to the hilt. I weakened first, of course, because I went to a private school for longer than he did and get flustered pretty easily when it comes to guilt.

I glared at Jock on the post who was cleaning his feathers primly. 'Sorry.'

Neil leant back on the couch, gulping air, his thin legs spread, looking utterly exhausted. 'That's fine, Cass. I'm used to being untrustworthy. I'm just not used to being attacked.' He looked up with a tiny smile. 'Did I look like Tippi Hedren in *The Birds?*'

'Sort of, only you leapt about a little more, like in a rain dance.'

'Did you forget something?'

'Trying to head off Philip Marlowe outside,' I inclined my head to the door. But I could tell he didn't believe me.

'You didn't trust me.'

'You just said *you're* used to it. Well, I'm not used to living with an addict.'

'I haven't had a fix for two weeks,' he said. He looked stubborn. I was surprised.

'But, how did you get...?'

'Scoring for a friend.' He looked up. 'I know, it's lame, but it's true. I hate the stuff. I was coming off it when I just got so depressed. It feels better now. I'm smoking dope and the methadone helps. I was going to clean up around here in both senses of the word, I guess, and then go down to the clinic at lunchtime.'

I walked to the window and peeked through. The car was still there. I'd removed my bandage and replaced it with gauze and a few careful bandaids. The eye still looked a deep plum colour but it was already turning a little yellow at the edges, which was a good sign, although I wasn't going to get spotted by a talent agency today. Unless of course they were looking for colourful circus freaks. 'I'm going out the back way. If Sam comes by, tell him I went to get barbecue chicken.' I was getting nice and devious. Maybe this whole *Trainspotting* thing was rubbing off on me.

'At nine-thirty in the morning?'

'I like chicken.'

'Can you get me a banana fritter, then?'

'I'm not really getting chicken, Neil!' I hitched my bag up and left, frustration burning in my gut. Was this my life? Never knowing what I'd come home to? Feeling guilty for suspecting him, but being worried about my stuff all the time too? I walked down the stairs thoughtfully and slipped out the back door. Blinking in the sunshine, I walked straight into Sam.

'Bit early for hot chips, isn't it?'

I glared at him. 'You spoke to Neil.'

'Just called him. He said you were leaving and I thought probably not by the front door.'

'He's a fink.'

He waved his hand. 'Don't sweat it. I was on my way here anyway.'

'You don't trust me!'

'Would you trust you?'

'Yes,' I said indignantly but I could see his point.

'Well, if it makes you feel any better I threatened to cut off his allowance if he didn't tell me where you were going.'

'Well, then. He's a twelve-year-old fink,' I said, but then I remembered what he'd said the night before and blanched. 'He needs professional help,' I said, trying to be reasonable. 'I can't be responsible for him. I'm naturally untrustworthy.'

'Then you'll be perfect together.'

'It's different.'

'How? You could both go to jail, you're both lying, you're both ignoring your problems, and you both get away with it because you're cute and fun to be with.'

'He is not fun to be with!' I said, but I was staring at his face, which looked a little ruddier than usual. Was he blushing? He was wearing a V-neck jumper and white T-shirt. Suddenly I could picture his legs up on my coffee table, relaxing before a good old movie, like *The Big Sleep*. I blinked out of my daydream and glared at him.

'Don't glare at me. You can take a compliment.' He grinned and rocked back on his heels.

I thrust my fists in my pockets to stop myself pushing him over into the row of rubbish bins behind him. 'It's not a compliment to be compared to a twenty-eight-year-old drug addict.'

'You know what I mean.'

We stood staring at each other for a second and then I turned on my heel and went back inside the building. I stomped heavily up to the first flight and waited. The frosted glass that looked over the back alley didn't give me a view of Sam, but when I crept back down the stairs all was silent. I gingerly pushed opened the door.

'I've called in an order for hot chicken, chips and banana fritters at one o'clock,' he said, his arms folded across his chest as he slouched against the wall beside the door. 'I'm bringing it myself.'

I stomped back upstairs, clutching my heart and swearing softly to myself.

Zara called while I was watching Neil wash the windows from my vantage point on the couch. I had decided to redo my nails in honour of my boredom. I'd already done three loads of washing and remade my bed. I told myself it was good housekeeping, but I had suddenly gained the perspective of someone else looking at my life and I wanted it looking spunky. I looked like I'd fallen out of an aeroplane but at least my environment was pretty.

'So how's the share-housing?' she asked, her voice light.

'Grim. No wonder grunge fiction was such a bleak genre. It's like *Withnail and I*, only without the good looks of Paul McGann.'

She laughed. 'Oh, come on. You know Neil's a spunk. You used to find him irresistible.'

'Yeah, but I also lost sleep over whether I could afford a Choose Life T-shirt. Times change.' I walked the portable phone into my bedroom alcove and kept my voice down.

'It's just like *The Bold and the Beautiful*,' she said. 'You've just moved on to a different Tasker boy but they're both messing with your head.'

'I've decided to stay away from them both, but I can't avoid the one in my lounge room. He must have a spine of steel to sleep on that couch. But I'm not welching on my responsibilities. I made a promise to keep an eye on him and I will. I stick to my promises.'

'Sam caught you sneaking out?'

'Something like that.'

'How're the sleeping arrangements?'

'I was going to spend some money on a rather largish and more effective room divider. Any ideas?'

'Plenty. I saw a great cherry woodscreen in Freedom. You want me to pick one up on the way over?'

'You're coming around?'

'There's no way Josie and I are going to miss the dynamics tonight. Anyway, we have a plan.'

'What's going on?'

I was instantly worried. She sounded excited and Zara doesn't get excited often. It meant she was planning something for my own good, and her idea of good was always different from mine. The road to hell was pathed with good intentions. Or ex-boyfriends. Either way my toes were getting burned.

'See you at seven. How's your face?'

I touched the skin around my eye gingerly. 'I'm drugged up so I can't feel it much. I bit my tongue earlier.'

'You want us to bring takeaway?'

'Anything but chicken and chips.'

Sam turned up an hour later and soon the apartment was filled with the sweet smell of unhealthy living. I can't say I'm a big fan of the multi-national fast food conglomerate feast, but every now and then it just hits the spot. And I had a hell of a lot of spots that needed hitting.

We didn't talk until the bags were empty, then Neil quietly

went back to cleaning, this time wiping out the bathroom cupboards, and I discreetly adjusted my position so that my skirt had more room. It took advantage of the space and I wondered what Sam's ex-girlfriends had looked like. There must be plenty. Maybe he had a non-ex. Maybe she had eaten a salad for lunch today.

'Stop scowling,' Sam said. 'It's done now. You can walk it off when we chase Suzanne across the border.'

I looked up, but quickly avoided meeting his gaze. 'You think she's a crook?'

'I ran a check on her. Her name's Suzanne Reilly and she used to be an accountant at Grolsch & Deviner. Her story checks out too. Her ex-fiancé went on the honeymoon alone and came home with a divorcée. His family is completely freaked.'

'You found out all this on the police files?'

'I asked someone to poke around. Seems it caused quite the neighbourhood sensation. Gossip spreads. Adelaide's a big small town. She's got juvenile records a mile long. Shoplifting mainly. A couple of misdemeanours. She cleaned up her act.'

'Maybe emotional trauma made her revert back to old habits.'

'Or she just grew new ones. From what I can see, she's developing a taste for bad company too.'

I sat up. 'What do you mean?'

'She went to Daniel's again early yesterday.' I felt a little sick at the memory so I concentrated hard on his hair until the nausea subsided. 'Then she left again a few hours later. Went to a bar called the Blue Room. Opens at four o'clock and she was waiting in the café across the road. She stayed there for five hours. A little unsteady on her feet when she left, and she'd made some friends.'

I nodded encouragement but he just sat watching the sky through the window. I found a chip down the side of the chair and threw it at him. '*And?*' I demanded 'Who was she with?'

'Some seriously dodgeois guys.' He pronounced it doge-wah and I suppressed a smile. He was definitely more relaxed around me; the frosty cop was melting into a normal guy. A normal, cute guy who smelled too damn good.

'You knew them?'

'I wasn't watching her. A guy I know owed me a favour, so while I was making sure you didn't cash in your chips early on a suburban freeway I had him keep a lookout. I know the type. Facial hair, dirty jeans, hotted-up car. She took the bus home alone.'

I was excited. 'So now what?'

'We wait for her to do something stupid. Looks like we won't have to wait long. My friend called me while I was getting the chicken. Told me that when she left Daniel's she had a suitcase. Looks like maybe she got cocky.'

'Why d'you say that? What was in the suitcase?' I was so annoyed it hadn't been me following her that I had to sit on my hands. I really should brush up on my anger management skills. The urge to throw my paper bag full of soggy pickles at Sam was overwhelming. Mixed up with the urge to throw myself in his lap of course.

'Seems she went to a pawnbroker with the suitcase. She sold some nice pieces of men's jewellery and two leather jackets. And the case itself. You remember any jackets?'

I nodded. 'A long black one and a shorter brown one?'
'That's right.'

'He had at least one suitcase up on top of the wardrobe.
So what are we waiting for?'

'Nothing. We can bring her in whenever we want. I just
thought I'd let you know.'

Suddenly I realised what was going on. 'And I have to
stay here on my fat—and getting fatter—arse while your cronies
pick her up.'

'My, er, "cronies", as you call them, Al Pacino, can pick
her up according to Australian law and make sure nothing
happens to Justine in the process. I'll send a counsellor
around to her house too. The woman needs help. No one
should stay cooped up alone, especially when her first social
interaction for however many years is with a felon.'

'Maybe you should send Neil around there, keep her company,' I said dryly.

'I can still hear you, you know,' Neil shouted from the
bathroom.

'I don't care,' I retorted. 'I can hear you snore.'

Neil laughed. 'Well at least I don't burp in my sleep. You
sounded like you'd just finished a tray full of McHappy meals.'

'Oh, shut up.'

Sam glanced at me. 'You kids are adorable.'

'You shut up too,' I said and stood up. 'I think your visiting hours are over.'

'I brought some things for dinner. You want me to cook?'

'No,' I said hastily, imagining the cosy scene when Zara
and Josie turned up and cringing. I knew they would love it,
but worse, so would I. Despite the occasional moment, I

doubted Sam's interest in me. I was useful and probably added some kind of comedic element to his days, but what I feared most was my own lack of control. A cosy night in, with him cooking up some delicious treats like a brooding Jamie Oliver, was too much for my little heart to handle. I needed distance to resist embarrassing myself. A tall glass of Distance and a Sarcasm chaser. Cosy nights didn't lend themselves to self-protection.

'Thanks, but I can manage.'

'Okay,' he shrugged and got up. 'I'll call you both later.'

In a non-romantic way, I reminded myself. He's calling his brother and his brother's minder, not a girl he likes. There was just no way. 'Sure,' I said casually. 'Zara and Josie are coming over. I'm sure they'll hold Neil down if he goes for my throat.'

'I can still hear you, you know,' Neil shouted again.

'We know,' we replied simultaneously.

Embarrassed, I led Sam to the door but when he left I realised he was taking Neil with him, a police escort to the methadone clinic, so I took the opportunity to have a bath and soothe my swollen face with a flannel. Then when Neil returned alone, and I'd applied various creams and ice-packs, we cleaned out the kitchen cupboards. Life wasn't so bad. *Choose to be happy*. I tried to smile at the tin of bamboo shoots in my hand but it hurt too much.

'You sure eat a lot of pot noodles,' said Neil, stacking them in a pyramid on the floor. I pointed to the circle of cans.

'And *fruit*,' I said. 'I eat a lot of mango. Loads of vitamins in those.'

'Not so much in the Rice Bubbles, though, I guess,' he said, as he piled three unopened boxes on the edge of the sink.

'Yeah, because smack is such a healthy alternative.'

I stumbled up, my legs stiff and painful, and went through my mail. Too many bills again. Helen's money hadn't made a significant enough dent in my debt and not working at the store meant I was getting further behind. I suppressed the panic in my chest and took a deep breath. I would have to pay Zara for the bedroom screen but that would be my last purchase until I could legitimately find an eyelid to put shadow on again.

He's calling his brother and his brother's minder.

Three hours later I was woken by the doorbell and sat up with a start. I'd been lying on the bed wondering what to do next, 'My new life starts *now*' etc, when I must have dozed off. I patted my hair and pretended I'd been rearranging my shoes as Zara dragged the screen in.

We organised my bedroom corner so the screen blocked everything from the lounge room, and the shelving and the wardrobe faced each other at right angles. It was cosy but a little weird, like one of those faux bedrooms you create in the kitchen during share-housing days when you need to add another rent payer to the lease.

I was starting to worry that Neil would be here for a while. I liked having my own space, wandering to the loo in the nude, singing along to the Cranberries, wearing my old scuffed sneakers. With Neil here, I was always going to have to make a little more of an effort, just in case Sam turned up.

He's calling his brother and his brother's minder.

That night Josie made pasta with loads of pepper and Neil behaved himself very well. He cleared up and even did the dishes while we sat around talking about Amanda.

'There's nothing we can do. No one saw who hit you. Frankly, it could have been anyone.'

'Thanks a lot.'

'Well, it's true.'

'I know,' I said gloomily. My new career wasn't looking so great. My first job had come back to bite me on the bum and my second was now in police hands. It was a semi-success, but Helen was probably dating my dud friend at this very moment and I had slim hopes she would remember me fondly in ten years' time.

'So, that's why we've decided to get you a new life!' exclaimed Josie, suddenly clapping her hands.

I remembered Zara's perkiness on the phone. My heart sank. 'I'd forgotten. You guys are up to something.' My voice held undisguised dread.

'Yes. And it's going to be great,' Zara said.

I held up my hand. 'Hang on. 'Why are you guys so keen on getting me a new life? I just got attacked. I have to rest. My life is shit. I live with an extra from *The Bill* and my face looks like a colour chart. Next week I can have a new life, but right now I'm just trying not to get infected.'

'The only chance of you getting infected when we're finished is from a sexual disease,' crowed Zara with such untypical zeal that I flinched. My vision was so restricted now that my eyes hadn't far to go in order to narrow dangerously. 'What's up with you?' Then I remembered. 'Did something happen with George since I spoke to you last?' I leant forward eagerly.

'Yes, yes, we talked in the café yesterday and we're going out on Sunday, but that's got nothing to do with it,' she said hastily. 'We're going to help—'

'Hang on. You're going on a date?'

'Yes.' She smiled proudly. I didn't say anything and Josie gave me a look to confirm that she'd tell me everything later. It was hard to suppress my surprise, though. Zara had never gone on a date before. Not that I'd known about, anyway. And here she was dating a guy she really liked. But if that wasn't why they were here then I knew I was in for a nasty surprise.

'Tell me then,' I said wearily.

'We're going to organise some dates for you. We have a whole bunch of guys lined up. You need to see what's on offer. You're not getting out enough and it's restricting your options. So we've organised a roster.' She handed over a pad of paper with a grid on it. 'We've lined up all the cute, successful and smart guys we know and we've organised dates with them all until you find the man of your dreams, or,' and she glanced meaningfully over at Neil busying himself in the kitchen, 'until he finds you.'

Neil popped his head over the counter. 'It's a good idea. They're right. You have no life. You need to get out. I can't sit here all day with you. You'll drive me back to drugs.'

'Shut up.' I was furious. And mortified. Not just for my own ego, which was dying of a terminal illness as I sat there, but also because Neil would be sure to tell Sam I had been rostered on a dating regime. I might as well spray Loser on my forehead. A vision of him on the couch in that club with girls on his lap appeared before me and I went cold.

'I don't want to date all these guys.' I glanced at the list. 'Who the hell is Reggie Green? He sounds like a prat.'

'You dated *Frederick Jello*,' said Josie, grinning. 'Prats are actually your speciality.'

'Present company excepted,' shouted Neil.

'Included,' Josie shouted back.

'Fred was a DJ!' I said, indignant. 'He mixed a song just for me.'

'Reg is a metalwork artist,' said Zara, sounding annoyed. 'If this is going to work you have to be adventurous.'

'I don't want to be adventurous.' But even I could hear the tremor in my voice. My friends had to fix me up. Like throwing animals together in a pen at the zoo and hoping they'd mate. I blinked rapidly. 'And anyway. No one will date me with my big purple pumpkin face.'

'By tomorrow night you'll be fine,' Zara assured me. 'Josie bought some green-based foundation to counterbalance the, er, purplish hues of your face.'

I glanced over at Josie, who held up a big Body Shop bag and grinned. I hated her.

'So tomorrow night we've organised a date with...' Zara glanced down at the notes. 'John Palmer. You're going to the Whatley. John is a lawyer. He looks a little like Johnny Depp, though.'

'How little? What's the rest look like?'

'Maybe Chris Judd?' admitted Josie.

I looked blank. 'A J-Lo ex,' she added.

'He had piggy eyes!'

'No lawyer worth their salt has piggy eyes,' said Josie. 'Good looks are part of the job requirement. You have to look trustworthy. He's very nice.'

I frowned. 'Is he one of your ex-s?'

'No, brother of an ex. Tom Palmer. Remember the trip to Noosa?'

Who could forget the trip when Tom wooed Josie with a week away and then asked her to give him a blow job on the beach? I cheered up. I'd always thought that sounded kind of fun.

'Well, okay.' I tried to keep the grumpy tone in my voice, but I couldn't deny I was interested. 'Who else?'

'Ben Henderson.'

'Who's he?'

'He's an architect. He's a little young.'

'How young?'

'Twenty-five.'

'She'll eat him alive,' Neil called out from the kitchen.

'Shut up! What about Declan? I can get a twenty-five-year-old.' I lied. Declan was an aberration. I tried to imagine twenty-five and couldn't. What had I been doing? It was only four years ago. I frowned. I'd been messed up. Maybe everyone's messed up until they hit thirty. I only had four months to go and then I was home free.

'Are you making tea, Neil?' piped up Zara as the kettle whistled like a train.

'Nah, just scrubbing off the caked-on food from a few saucepans,' he said and I blushed. Damn him for being such a born-again good guy. 'If you want some, I'll put it back on again.'

'Thanks,' said Zara and raised her eyebrows to me in a 'What a great guy he's turned into!' way, which was very annoying. She didn't have to live with him.

'What a crawler,' I muttered as I scratched at my belly.

'Hey Cass,' said Josie seriously. 'You're cute and smart and funny. You just don't give yourself a chance.'

'Yeah, if you've got it, flaunt it!' said Zara. Maybe George was a bad influence after all.

'Jesus Christ, it's the ya-ya sisterhood,' said Neil from the kitchen over the whistling kettle.

I shrugged. 'Okay.'

'Really? Okay?' said Josie.

I nodded.

'Great!' Zara jumped up and pulled chocolate from her shopping bags.

I hesitated, shaking my head as she offered me a row. 'If I'm going to flaunt it, it shouldn't wobble. I need to lose some weight.'

'Stand up.' Josie grabbed my arms and yanked me off the couch, then looked at me appraisingly as I sucked my tummy in and turned reluctantly. 'You need a new bra. That one's too old, I can tell by the shape of your boobs. But other than that, you've got a great figure.'

It was fine for her, all five foot eleven and Uma Thurman willowy. She sometimes just forgot to eat. I only ever forgot to *stop* eating.

'The only guys I know who like skinny women are the dopey ones who want to feel all macho and big. Any guy worth his salt would kill for you. You just need better posture.' She pushed and prodded until I was ramrod straight.

I plastered a big fake smile on my face as she rifled through my wardrobe, coolly selecting and discarding my life's collection. And then the phone rang. I picked up absently, brushing Josie away as she tried to see what I'd look like with a bob.

'Are you alone?' The voice was familiar but I couldn't place it.

'Who's this?'

'It's Sam, you dufus. I just saw someone enter your building. It looked like it could be one of Neil's cohorts.'

I glanced over at Neil as he packed away the dishes. 'He has *cohorts*? Who has cohorts?' I swallowed my frustration. 'What should I do?'

The room went quiet at the tone in my voice and as I turned towards the wall, hunching slightly over the phone, I caught Neil looking at me with a frown. Josie wandered back from my wardrobe and sat down on the couch, watching me.

'We're going in after him, but if he's a neighbour, we'll look stupid. So I'm just warning you in case something goes wrong. We can't do anything unless he makes a move.'

'What's going to go wrong? What move?'

The phone was silent. 'Sam? What *move*?'

Suddenly there was a knock at the door and I sucked in air.

'Someone's at the door,' I whispered, shaking my head. Neil came around the kitchen island.

Then the knocking became banging. And shouting.

'Neil, you fucker. Come out. I know you're there! You owe me money, you little shit!'

'How did he know Neil was here?' I squeaked into the phone.

'I don't know. But you just keep the door locked. I'm having trouble getting a park.' Then he rang off.

'You're *parking*?' I said incredulously into the dead air. There were no carparks in the city. Shit. Then I remembered Neil's front door. Yeah, right, Sam. I'm definitely going to open my door to the human Cujo. But he wasn't there to punch in the nose so I had to glare at Neil instead, who flinched and moved back into the kitchen alcove in a hurry.

I turned around to the frozen room. 'Don't answer it,' I whispered between the shouts.

'Fuck, no,' muttered Neil. 'That's Two Job Johnnie. He's so fucked on drugs he forgot I paid him back the money. He goes a little crazy.'

'Oh, really? Crazy, eh? Thanks for the tip!' I could feel my heart pounding in time to the noise on the door. 'You *promise* that you paid him back?' I said, knowing a promise from a junkie wasn't worth a whole lot.

'Definitely. I know because I sold my guitar to do it. He came around to my old place and tried to take the door down.'

He didn't have to tell me twice. It'd looked like he'd had an axe.

'What's the two job bit about?' I whispered between clenched teeth.

'He used to work for Frank Samson, the big property developer out in West Lakes. He did two jobs before someone dropped a roofing tile on his head. He's never been the same.'

'And the same was?'

'Crazy as a brothel on a Friday night. Now he's just plain angry.'

'Great.' We sat down on the couch while Neil stood in tense silence by the sink. We listened to the shouting and banging while flicking nervous glances at each other.

Then I heard Mr Crabtree's voice floating through the wall. 'What's going on? I'm trying to watch the news. How's a man to—' Something slammed against the wall and Two Job Johnnie stopped abusing our door and turned his attentions to Mr Crabtree. Mr Crabtree had never been so quiet before. Maybe he was dead already. I'd be in big trouble from the strata housing committee. I got up and walked over to my dining table. My heart was beating so quickly I felt faint, so I had to get my blood moving.

'You clean the windowsill today?' I asked Neil.

He nodded.

'Well, that's something,' I muttered. Then the cursing quietened down and shuffling and movement echoed through the walls. I sat nervously, imagining Johnnie positioning Mr Crabtree into a battering ram like in a cartoon, when suddenly a cold mean laugh replaced the abuse and then a door slammed. All was quiet. Then someone turned the news up loud enough to block out any noise. Someone who was not a battering ram.

Uh-oh.

Over the sound I heard a key in my lock. No one had a key except me and Zara and...

Shit.

I stood up and gripped the back of my dining room chair as I watched the handle on my front door turn. Before any of us could move, the door swung open and a short, wide little bull terrier guy stepped through and slammed the door behind him, pulling the chain across. Why the hell hadn't I thought of that?

Josie squealed from her position on the couch and Zara went white as a sheet. So much for the A-Team. We were more like the Z-Team. I was frozen in motion, unable to speak as he put the key I had dutifully given Mr Crabtree as part of our strata agreement on the little glass side table by the door. Why didn't I have friends who had weapons? Then I remembered the mace. It was in my bag, on my bed.

'So,' he said, triumphantly. 'Where's the little fucker?'

Before I had a chance to move, Two Job Johnnie had charged into the kitchen, slamming Neil into the freshly washed crockery. Neil recovered quickly and hurled a saucepan of hot water over Two Job Johnnie. The noise was deafening. Johnnie started to flail about, ripping at his hot, soaking clothes, making a lot of the same noises he had in the hall, only this time they were more like wailing than shouting.

Neil grabbed something from the counter and started spraying Johnnie with toilet cleaner. The wailing turned into a high-pitched noise only dogs could hear. My brain kicked into high gear at the sound. I took two steps towards my bed, with the bag and the mace, when Johnnie pulled a knife out of his pocket, then casually knocked Neil backwards with his arm. It made me skid to a stop as he ripped his own shirt off with one cut, took a step towards Josie, his chest and face a searing angry red, and grabbed her around the throat. I froze.

Neil lay sprawled against the cabinets. I could see him struggling to get up again.

'Don't you fucking move another muscle, Elvira.' He was looking at me. 'Neil?'

'Yes,' Neil croaked as he pulled himself up and came around the kitchen counter. He was fine.

'You Are All Fucking Dead Meat,' said Johnnie. And he said it like he'd seen a lot of dead meat.

Were there enough people in the room to suck out all the oxygen? I gasped for breath as the light glinted off the blade against Josie's throat.

Unfortunately, Jock took that moment to stir from his perch. I could see him out of the corner of my eye, but everyone else was watching Josie and Johnnie in their crude parody of a lover's embrace. Josie's eyes looked weird and I realised it was because her lids were peeled back from her face so you could see the whites right around her pupils.

I held my hands up in surrender, terrified that Jock would startle Johnnie into doing something stupid.

'Um, hello?' I cleared my throat and started again. 'This is my apartment.'

'Who the fuck are you, Elvira?'

'Cassidy Blair,' I said, sounding like I was in roll call. There was something horribly wrong here. I was trying to make conversation with a man about to slit my friend's throat. 'Could you please put the knife down?'

'Well, hi, Cassidy,' he drawled sarcastically. 'Pleased to meet you. I'm Johnnie and I'm fucking pissed off. And no, I won't put the knife down.' He peered closer. 'What the fuck's wrong with your face?'

'A lot.'

'Well, you sure uglified yourself.' He shook his head in disgust. 'Well, now, Mash Face. You figure I should slice your friend open or be fair and get stuck into the—' and he turned to look at Neil '–*fucking wanker* who burned me? I guess you're a fucking dyke, so you don't care what you look like, but I've got ladies to consider. I look like a fucking lobster. I feel like a fucking lobster. You are fucking dead, you little shit.' And he turned to glare at Neil.

To do that, Johnnie had to twist a little bit, and to twist, he relaxed the grip on the knife. As it moved a half centimetre from Josie's neck, Jock flew quietly to the coffee table, sat on the remote and the television leapt into life.

Everyone in the room, including Johnnie, whipped around towards the noise, Johnnie's hand slipped further away from Josie and in an instant she punched his elbow into the air and leapt off the couch.

Johnnie lost his balance with the upward swing and staggered backwards. I may or may not have yelped like a puppy, but it was enough to disorient him. He was still holding the knife, though. Still angry and still standing.

Josie sprawled on the ground next to the coffee table and scrambled away from him as quickly as she could. I knocked over the chair and took three giant steps toward Johnnie, who was now waving the knife around, perhaps trying to find something to plunge it into. He hadn't connected the bird on the table with the noise. In fact, he was staring at Jock as though he was hallucinating. Which maybe he was. He was a friend of Neil's and while he was built like a stove, he was short and a little freaked out. There could definitely be drugs involved.

So I hurled myself at him, flattening him with my size 12, occasionally 14, body.

And it *really* hurt. For a second I thought I'd fallen on the knife, telemovie style, but then I realised it was just my jeans cutting into my waist. There was a second when our eyes met, and I stared into his red eyes for too long. He grabbed my hair and then we were rolling on the ground, thrashing and punching and kicking until we hit the leg of the table. My hip caught the edge but by then my anger overcame the pain that seemed to be everywhere.

The noise was terrific. He'd boxed my ears and my puffy eye wasn't helping me get my sense of direction back so I just kept hitting him as he grabbed and kicked. My tunnel vision from one eye was filled with red. I was like one of the Fantastic Four, although my mutant skills were rather more obvious to the naked eye than expressed through superhuman feats.

So it wasn't until I'd punched him sharply in the balls that he let go of my upper arm. I rolled off him as he lay panting, rolled up in a foetal position. I clutched my head with one hand and half-shuffled, half-crawled away. He made a feeble grab for my ankle but I kicked out and he rolled over again, groaning.

As I sat back against the end of the couch I saw there were long black hairs on the floor around us. Lots of them. I touched my head but it felt like there was still enough hair left to distract people from my purple face.

And then I realised the room was full of people.

'Nice work.'

I looked up to see Sam grimly watching Johnnie on the ground. As Johnnie groaned and rolled onto his stomach, panting, Sam took the opportunity to cuff him.

'Jesus, fuck.' But Johnnie seemed resigned to his fate. He lay panting openly while I tried to gather my wits (and pat down my hair).

'I haven't fought that hard since I went up against Shotgun Simmo in '89,' Johnnie wheezed. 'Only Simmo didn't fight so fucking dirty.' He glared at me like it had all been my fault. 'I can't believe plum-faced Elvira punched me in the fucking balls.'

Sam stepped to his left and with one arm held me back from kicking Johnnie in the leg.

I looked up to see my old police friend Gus standing in the doorway. Gus was probably fifteen kilos overweight and in bad need of a haircut, but the expression on his face told me I looked worse than he did. I took some comfort that at least I didn't have to wear tiny pink hot pants and angel wings along with thousands of buff babes in the next Mardi Gras.

He gave me a quick hug, his expression saying 'We need to talk', but I feigned blindness in my one eye and smiled inanely.

He flinched and then helped Sam haul Johnnie to his feet.

'I let them in!' squeaked Zara. She was still pale and the pink in her cheeks stood out like little smarties.

When Gus and Sam had dragged Johnnie out of the apartment and Zara and Josie had gathered their things and left in a slightly more subdued fashion than when they arrived, Neil, Jock and I sat staring at each other across the coffee table. The cops had done a good job of clearing up, but I still felt a little shaky looking around my apartment and imagining what might have been. What the alternatives were to Johnnie releasing his grip on Josie, or me rolling around on the ground with a guy who'd once fought someone with a nickname involving firearms.

Sam had taken the knife but when I turned on more lamps it still seemed to glint off every chrome surface in the room in a rather unnecessarily sinister way, which made my heart beat a little too quickly. Sam had looked very grim as he led Johnnie away. There was an unmarked car outside, but it didn't make me feel safe. What was to stop the next guy coming in like last time? Fuck strata rules. I was keeping my spare key.

'You want a cup of tea?' Neil asked, turning on the kettle.

'No, thanks,' I said and stomped off to bed. I could hear him muttering on the phone for a while as I drifted off to sleep and just prayed it wasn't an overseas call. Helen's money wouldn't last much longer.

'I've left Daniel. We just weren't suited.'

Helen was thrilled with herself but I couldn't help thinking Malcolm had been rather a powerful catalyst in the destruction of their relationship. What relationship was strong enough to fight the appeal of a third party?

I missed someone warm to cuddle up with at night, I admit, but at least hot-water bottles didn't break your heart. I hoped Helen knew what she was doing. Certainly Daniel was the mayor of Dud Central, but was Malcolm going to make her feel better or worse in the long run? Someone should really write up a few more rules. Ten commandments clearly weren't enough in these trying times.

'Terrific,' I enthused. She'd called to organise payment for the extra work and I told her what was going on with Suzanne. I needed to look for more work. Maybe I should get business cards made up.

'And Malcolm has been lovely,' she added. 'So we were wondering if you wanted to come over to his place for dinner.

He said you hadn't had much luck in the, er, love department, so we thought we could—'

I jumped in before she tried to set me up with one of
Malcolm's dodgy friends, or worse, brothers. I had dated
Malcolm's younger brother, James Ferrier, before, and I wasn't
keen to repeat the experience. I figured I'd filled my quota
of dodgy gropes in the back seat of a Mazda RX7 when I
still thought coloured stockings were the go.

'A blind double date? Well, thanks, but no. It sounds
really great,' I tried to keep my voice light, 'but I'm pretty
busy right now. Maybe later. I'll call you, okay?' I rang off
before she could protest. I really had hit Über-spinsterhood
when people like Malcolm tried to set me up.

'Who was that?' asked Neil and I told him a little more
about my second job. We'd settled into an odd George and
Mildred-style living habit. He made breakfast; I chose the
music. He cleaned the apartment while I took a bath to soak
the muscles that had suffered from my fight with Johnnie;
then Sam came around and dropped off food, had a quick
chat and left. Josie had postponed my blind dates, so I had
one more day to recover and then I was officially desperate.

When you're alone, you can at least tell people you like
being single. Once you're set up on a date (and there'd clearly
been a rush on this idea) then it was obvious to all and
sundry that you're gagging for it. I might as well just buy a
billboard.

'What shall we do tonight?'

'I dunno.' I'd sorted out my drawers and wiped all the
surfaces in my bed 'room'. I was very bored. And listless too,
it seemed. I knew I should be tying up my loose ends with

work. Certainly there was stuff to do to make sure Justine
was okay, Suzanne got her comeuppance and Tony, well, Tony
got some kind of venereal disease, but frankly, at that point,
I just couldn't be bothered. I was pooped.

'Sam suggested we all go out.'

I looked over at Neil and then peered closer. He was
feigning something. Now, if I'd been a good detective I
could have suggested innocence, or enthusiasm, or even
sobriety, but really I had no idea. Who knew what was
going on in his teeny tiny brain? Maybe I wasn't so tired
after all.

'Go where?' I asked suspiciously. 'I thought Sam wanted
us to stay in.' I admitted to myself that Johnnie had rather
set the wind up me. The thought of leaving the apartment
made me nervous, but I was also twitchy to keep my mind
off recent events. And something told me I could find trauma
tenfold beyond the doors if I put a little effort in. And a
little make-up on.

'You always do what Sam tells you to do?'

'No!' I paused. 'But hang on. You just want to go *out*
because Sam said so!'

'Well, anyway,' he said quickly. 'What about the movies?
Maybe we could get some food. I'm sick of pot noodles.'

I sighed. 'Me too. Okay. As long as it's an action movie.
No bloody romantic comedies. They bug me.'

'I know,' he grinned. Sometimes I forgot he was the same
Neil who'd taken me to see *Total Recall*, introduced me to
English Ska music and taught me fellatio. Well, I'd try hard
to forget that last one.

By seven-thirty we were both sitting on the couch. Neil

was reading *Vogue*, fascinated by the new season's must-haves—'a slouchy shoulder bag' and 'one knockout piece on which to build your wardrobe', but I was sitting primly on the couch, my feet together and handbag on my lap, ready to leap up when the doorbell rang. I had cabin fever and the ocean swell was starting to drown me. I picked up a magazine and feigned interest in Penelope Cruz.

When Sam finally knocked twice, I slouched casually to let him in, leaving the magazine open to prove he had misunderstood me.

'Fashion tips?' Sam asked Neil as he walked in.

'"A tuxedo jacket is both classic and cheeky",' Neil said as he threw the magazine back on the pile. '"Especially when thrown over ripped jeans." Let's go. When's it start?'

We were seeing a rerun of *Barbarella*. 'Quarter to ten. We can pick up a bite on the way.'

I frowned. 'But that's hours away. We can sit down and have lots of bites all together in a row. With cutlery.'

Sam looked distracted as he walked over to Jock to say hello. Jock promptly leapt onto his shoulder and nibbled his ear. Traitor.

'Where are we going?' I asked, willing Jock to clean with more vigour, but he had started delicately rearranging the hairs that curled slightly around Sam's ears. I looked away before they were burned into my memory.

'I thought we could drop by Justine's place,' he said casually. 'Just to make sure she's okay. They picked up Suzanne this morning making another trip from Daniel's house. She'll be in court tomorrow for theft.'

I tried to feel happy but there was nothing except mild

relief that Suzanne was off the streets. She made everyone around her look like they needed step classes. And tummy control undies. 'Why us?' I grumbled unkindly. 'Why now? I want a glass of wine and some crusty bread that breaks my teeth.'

'Twenty minutes. We'll pop through, make sure she's okay, then skedaddle.'

'Skedaddle?' I laughed. I couldn't wait to get out of the apartment and sure, I was mildly excited about seeing Sam for the next few hours. Maybe tepidly thrilled. And getting warmer. Even with a chaperone it would be nice.

'Justine's the fat hermit?' asked Neil.

'Shut up, Neil,' I said. 'Don't be so judgmental. We're not ticking boxes. You want us to call you the fucked-up junkie?'

'Why not? Everyone else does,' he said cheerfully, picked up his battered leather coat and we left.

'Since when did you like Green Day,' asked Neil, leaning forward between us like a kid.

'Put your seatbelt on. And since I heard them last week,' Sam replied gruffly as Neil went through the CD folder at his feet.

'UFO? Air? What happened to Wagner? And boring old Cole Potter?'

'Porter,' corrected Sam. 'I went shopping.' I looked at the CD folder filled with shiny new plastic cases and felt a bit funny. Was he trying to impress someone? I really hoped Neil would feel obliged to me in some way and let me know if he thought something was going on with Sam and a supermodel.

If Sam had a girlfriend, I wanted to know about it. But then if he had a girlfriend, what was he doing out with us on a Thursday night? I smiled, then frowned. Because he wanted to save the weekend for his new love.

Fuck.

'I've got a date tomorrow night,' I blurted, then wished the words were back inside my mouth. 'I mean, sort of a date.'

'It's definitely a date,' said Neil. 'He's a lawyer.'

Sam's expression was unreadable but something tugged at his lips. 'You're dating a lawyer?'

'Yes!' And then I didn't know what to say so I hummed along to the song, getting it hopelessly wrong.

'What sort of lawyer is he?'

I didn't know, so I kept humming.

'A criminal lawyer,' said Neil and I whipped around to glare at him. How did he know? 'He's just been made a partner. He drives a cool car.'

'I drive a cool car,' said Sam.

'I'm dating Tom Palmer,' I blurted.

'John Palmer,' corrected Neil. 'Tom's the brother. The Noosa guy.'

'Right, right,' I said quickly. 'Anyway! I guess Justine knows about Suzanne getting arrested?'

'Don't change the topic. What's the Noosa guy got to do with it?' Sam flicked a glance at Neil over his shoulder. 'What happened in Noosa?'

'I dunno,' said Neil, 'but it made Josie really uncomfortable.'

'Josie dated this guy's brother? Are you guys in-breeding?'

'It's a legitimate date,' said Neil. 'He thinks Cass is hot.'

I stared at Neil in admiration. I guess he could stop

cleaning the flat now. The car was silent as we glided to a stop outside Justine's house. It was dark.

'Looks like she's not home,' said Neil.

'She's a fat hermit, Neil,' I said. 'Of course she's home.'

We all marched up the front steps and I banged on the door. It certainly sounded quiet. After a few minutes we walked around the house, but the side gate was locked. I thought about jumping over but it was too high and I had my best wool pencil-skirt on.

'Come on,' said Sam. 'I'll give you a boost.' He cupped his hands together as though I was a Charlie's Angel and could just backflip off his palms into the yard.

'Why me?'

'You want to be a PI? You gotta do the dirty work.'

'This isn't a job!'

'It's the residue of a job, which is the same thing.'

I sighed. 'Well, I'm not getting a boost!'

'Go on, Cass. What if she's in trouble?' Neil actually looked worried. The curtains were all closed and there was no light on anywhere. Maybe he was right, but I felt weird about this.

'Okay.' I scrunched my skirt up around my hips. Luckily I was wearing black opaque tights, otherwise my purple G-string would have got more of a showing than it ever had on the catwalks in David Jones. I held onto the top of the fence and got a leg-up, then hoisted myself over, only my skirt got caught on the top plank of the fence and a loud rip accompanied me on the way down.

'Oops,' said Sam. 'Are you okay?' He looked over the fence at me. He seemed to be smiling but it must have been the light.

'*Oops?*' I muttered, eyeing the ripped fabric. 'You say

"oops" when you spill sugar. You say "gift voucher" when you throw someone over the fence like a catapult and ruin their clothes.'

'It's okay,' said Neil, joining him. '*Vogue* says film noir French looks are back in. "Milan is crawling with thigh-high splits and the timeless sex appeal of that intimate glimpse",' he quoted.

I stared at him over the fence. How did he retain information in a brain annihilated by toxins over a long and relentless period of irresponsibility? Some days it was all I could do to remember my own phone number.

I followed the wall around the corner, found the back door and banged loudly. 'Justine? Are you in there? Hello?'

'Cass!'

I jumped, looking wildly around. It was Sam. I walked back around to the gate.

'Let us in!'

'Sorry.'

We all trooped back to the door and Sam peered through the back windows. 'Something's wrong.'

'What?' I looked around. Everything seemed fine. Quiet and dark, but fine. Not suspicious at all. 'Why?'

'I've got a funny feeling about this.'

I gave him a droll look. 'Okay, Han Solo. Tell us your theory.'

Then I realised Neil was missing.

'Neil?' I hissed.

'Up here.' Neil was on the roof. 'There's a skylight,' he whispered loudly. 'I can see something. I think it's your fat hermit.'

'Stop calling her that!' I raked my hair back from my face. 'What's she doing?'

'Either sleeping in the hallway or she's stoned and watching the carpet.'

'What?' Sam stepped back to look at Neil. 'She's on the floor in the hallway?'

'Yep, pudgy legs spread, face down. Maybe she fell over.'

'Maybe,' said Sam, but he was already moving. He picked up a brick that was probably used to hold the screen door open and plunged it through the kitchen window. He cleared the glass from the frame and hauled himself quite gracefully inside. I thought about my freefall into Daniel's bathroom and cursed my clumsy limbs.

I peered through the space but he was gone. Just as I was preparing to boost myself in after him, the back door swung open.

'I'm calling an ambulance. She's unconscious.'

I followed Sam back into the house and, while he was on the phone, turned on lights and cautiously stepped around the sprawled shape on the floor. Neil stepped in after me.

'Is she dead?'

'No,' I whispered, 'unconscious.'

The ambulance arrived about ten minutes later, long enough for me to realise that Sam was irritatingly good in a crisis, whereas I just developed what felt like a urinary tract infection. By the time I'd used Justine's loo three times the ambulance people had hoisted her up on a big trolley and taken her away.

No neighbours came out on the lawn like they do in the movies, and I felt even worse for Justine. Did no one care? Everyone needs someone to miss them when they're gone, even if it's just to hospital.

As we waited for the emergency glass guy to arrive, we looked around the kitchen. I didn't know what Neil and Sam were thinking, but I was absorbed. I hadn't paid enough attention the other day. Now I realised we were seeing her world and it had been the sky and mountains and stars for her for what... six, seven years?

The ambulance people said she'd suffered a mild heart attack, but, as I pilfered a raspberry tartlet from the jar on the table, I realised her heart had probably suffered for a long time. It was just the shock that sent her sprawling. The phone was off the hook and it looked like she'd just heard bad news when she fell. I guessed it was bad news about Suzanne, a woman she'd only known for a month, who'd clearly had her own agenda and seemed to treat Justine like an annoying servant.

Even though Justine was frightened of her, and she was virtually a stranger, I could see the fascination. With her strong personality, turbulent past and foreign body, she must have been intriguing. Justine's life had been empty and Suzanne had filled it. What made me feel sick was that Justine preferred a life filled with fear and emotional abuse than one alone; that she'd almost certainly been devastated by the call, not relieved by the freedom it implied. It was all too easy to imagine and, even if I had it quite wrong, I was caught in the net of her loneliness and dashed hopes.

After the window was fixed and we'd accepted that we wouldn't be seeing Jane Fonda having a hair-curling orgasm again in *Barbarella* we picked up some fast food. I realised the reason I had lost my appetite was not just that I felt sorry for Justine, but because I felt sorry for me, too. Selfishly, stupidly sorry for myself. No one spoke on the drive back.

I'd always held out hope that my current trend of cynicism (and occasional rudeness) towards the opposite sex was just a phase. A funny, quirky phase I could talk about later to get a laugh ('Remember when I couldn't get laid and I called it my celibate stage?' I'd shriek and everyone would convulse with laughter as I sat hugging my spunky, smart and kind lover). I'd always thought that I could get a guy if I just put in the effort, but maybe I didn't put in the effort just in case I failed. How brave was that?

Ultimately the possibility of rejection was an open door to the potential crazy, fat hermit lifestyle. At the bottom of my scorn and distrust, was there really a fear that I too would be discovered by strangers, sprawled on the floor of my apartment, in loose tracksuit pants, a smudge of chocolate sauce on my chin? And maybe an aged parrot pooing in my ear. Well, that just wouldn't do at all.

John Palmer was very polite.

'Hello Cassidy, nice to meet you,' he said and shook my hand. Which was sweet, I guess, only his hand was dry and cold—like sandpaper. I liked a bit of nervous sweat on occasions like these. Even a dash of twitching fingers or a shaky clearing of the throat helped me see that they too perhaps lay in bed wondering what awaited them the next day. I told myself he'd been sweating up a river on the drive over here but had carefully wiped his hands on his neatly pressed trousers before knocking on my door.

Neil and Sam had politely offered to pop out to grab a video, which I'd gratefully accepted. It had also been nice to picture them both watching *Hot Shots! 2* in my living room. No *Hot Date 1* for Sam, apparently.

It was like a job interview. I felt like saying my worst fault was being a perfectionist, or too much of a team player, but I figured that might result in some sort of sexual misinterpretation, so I clamped my lips shut and then turned them into a coy smile.

As I walked through to the kitchen I noticed him giving me the once-over. Guys should know that girls can feel this. It's just like in the movies, when the villain senses the red dot from a rifle sight tracking over his body, we can feel the glance sweep slowly over us.

Josie had come around before John arrived, smoothed my hair into a long black plait, made me wear a soft pink silk dress with a low neckline and peachy make-up on a foundation of greenish base to hide the discolourations from my misadventures. My eye looked fine after she'd played around with colours and curlers and liners and shimmer.

'Distraction,' she whispered as she sprinkled glitter in my cleavage. While it made me feel adolescent, it was delicious to have someone fuss over me with such care and skill and I realised how much I missed touch. The sensation of Josie brushing my hair, and delicately painting my face gave me goose-bumps all over and I tried hard not to let it show. I was a desperate spinster with a terminal case of skin hunger.

She lent me a long, slim-line black wool coat, but let me wear my own shoes. Then I'd walked around the apartment, stomach in, breasts out, as though I had a book on my head, until she was satisfied that I was ready. I had to admit I looked pretty good. I smiled into the mirror. In the afterglow of attention, the attractive, if outrageously curvy, girl looking back at me in the mirror made me smile. Maybe this could work. I offered him a drink.

'Just water, thanks.'

Okay, so if I have a glass of wine, does it make me nervous, or an alcoholic? Well, I figured that if it made me an alcoholic, then we were just not suited and it would all be over quickly and painlessly and I could take off my dominatrix shoes with the ankle straps and crawl back into bed, ready for the spinster fairy to come and take me. I hear she's very beautiful.

I brought the drinks over and we sat rather awkwardly on the couch. We were due to leave in a few minutes, really, but I wanted to show off my apartment. I confess I had it in my head that if I impressed him early with the good things then he had a chance to ignore my significant hips and less than cool CV.

A rush of warmth towards Neil for cleaning the apartment so beautifully made me smile until I caught John's look. He was staring at Jock.

'Does he fly?'

I nodded.

'Does he talk?'

'Not often,' I said. John still looked like he was watching a murder take place.

'Why's he here?'

'He's my pet,' I said slowly.

John seemed to gather himself up, like a human shopping bag of emotions adjusting itself after a milk carton had become unbalanced. 'Oh, right.' Then I realised there was a little *American Psycho* in him. A little? A lot? It was all spooky.

'Okay.' He paused, scratching his neatly combed, slightly foppish hair so a bit stuck out at right angles. 'I have a dog.'

I relaxed. 'Really? I love dogs. What kind?'

'A labrador. Jessie, she's three.'

'Oh, they're gorgeous,' I enthused, grinning like an idiot as I finished my drink. 'They're very playful.'

'Oh, I don't let Jessie play. She's a house dog. I train her every day and we take walks after work. I bought her to meet women but the only women in the park are heifers in sloppy jumpsuits. Jessie and I stay well clear.'

I stared at him. 'Heifers?'

'Fat. You know the type,' he smiled at me conspiratorially. I looked around. Was he grinning at *me*? 'They let themselves go. But, other than that, the park's a great place.'

I couldn't take my eyes off his face. I couldn't believe I was going to have to have dinner with this guy. I gripped my bag tightly, swore delicately under my breath and then fake-smiled my way into a quick exit from the apartment. I was going to kill Josie.

We locked up, me glancing wistfully at my quiet, offence-free apartment before allowing John to whisk me off in his red convertible. A voice in my head was screaming, 'Throw yourself bodily from the car! Save yourself!' but there was also another little voice telling me that if I could do this, I could do anything. Literally *anything*. I just hoped no one saw us together.

He took me to a restaurant that had been written up in the previous weekend's paper. During dinner I changed the topic from relentless and snooze-worthy law to the three different Gucci bags Sarah Jessica Parker sported on the latest episode *of Sex and the City*. John seemed to know more about the show than I did and I momentarily conceded perhaps I'd judged him unfairly. He'd allowed me to choose the wine and he'd even pulled my chair out when we were seated. But I had been too hasty. Damn my gullible heart.

'I love that show. It just proves that women can be as bad as men. My last girlfriend was always griping that men are always either cheating on someone or thinking about it, and it's just nice to know someone has the guts to expose how hypocritical chicks can be.'

'But the power of the show is to reveal idiosyncrasies and truths,' I said desperately. 'There's no right and wrong, no one's perfect. Everyone makes mistakes.'

'Exactly.' He grinned, and then his gaze dropped into my cleavage as though his eyes were on springs. 'You know, Cassidy, it's nice to have a decent conversation with a girl. You really *challenge* me.'

I figured challenge was the latest hot relationship sensation in *Ralph* magazine, or his therapist told him about it.

'Great!' I enthused. It would certainly be a challenge living this down. I glanced nervously around the busy restaurant for the third time and my eyes settled on a familiar head, facing away from me. I couldn't place it. With brown, sensible hair and a blue blazer, it was sitting with a dumpy girl who seemed quite happy to keep talking through her sheer enjoyment of the main course. It was only when the head turned to answer a question from the waiter that I realised with a jolt who it was.

Daniel.

Daniel? On a date? Well, I guess if he and Helen had broken up... And Helen was dating Malcolm... But something seemed wrong. If Helen broke it off, how did Daniel line up a date so fast? Maybe it was a work dinner, or she was his cousin? And why did she look familiar?

I nodded while John told me about how difficult it was being a lawyer and 'having a really creative side'.

He told me all about how he liked to read. How he'd collected all of Dick Francis's work, and John Grisham, while I watched Daniel and his date and nodded pleasantly.

The girl paused in her monologue to put her hand over his and then she shrieked with laughter loud enough to interrupt John's story of the old school reunion.

John looked over his shoulder in irritation. 'Christ. Some people behave like they're at the bloody football!' And he laughed as though we were both in on the joke. I mugged a smile and finished my pasta. The waiter kept filling my glass and I was getting that tingling, utterly slozzled feeling in my toes. And everywhere else.

We finished another bottle and even shared dessert—hazelnut ice-cream with meringue—but my attention jumped between John and Daniel, although the former didn't appear to notice. He popped off to the loo to answer his mobile phone at one point and I realised I was relieved to be alone—not the best sign. I also suspected he'd grown used to women ignoring his self-involved, arrogant manner, probably attributing it to their 'issues'.

Daniel and the blabbermouth left soon afterwards, and my boredom factor crept upwards until I was itching to get home and relax my face from my polite smile and light-hearted chuckles at nothing. After John dropped me off with a cold and clammy kiss I could almost hear him calling his mates on his mobile from the car, bitching about the heifer he'd just fed.

But when I got inside, there were two messages on the machine, one from him.

'Hi Cassidy. I've probably just dropped you off and politely kissed you on the cheek and promised to call, but I just wanted to say how much I enjoyed your company. I hope we see each other again soon.'

'Wanker,' I muttered. I'd read the same article in *FHM* last month listing just such a call under 'Guaranteed to get you laid'. The other message was from Helen.

'Hi Cassidy,' she said, sounding rushed and ending every sentence on a high note, as though it was a question. 'I just ran into an ex-girlfriend of Daniel's today and we got talking. I'd always thought she was a bitch from hell, but it turns out she's quite sane. She had some interesting things to tell me about Daniel. I just thought you'd want to know. Call me.'

I was itching to call right then but it was twelve-thirty and some people go to bed at a sensible hour. Unfortunately, Neil and Sam were not familiar with this. They crashed through my front door twenty minutes later.

'Cass, Cass,' Neil fumbled at me and pasted a serious expression on his slackened features. 'How'd your date go?'

He was drunk. And I realised in a rush that drunk people tell secrets. Had he spilled to Sam that I'd been set up? I might as well get a voice mailbox number and book myself into a match-making agency.

'It was fine. Thanks.' I sighed, watching Sam fill two glasses of water. His posture was loose and his natural soap and cologne smell had been replaced by smoke and sweat. One tipsy Sam was worth a thousand sober Johns. 'You guys tied one on?'

'We just had a few at the Grace. Shot some pool.' Sam's

voice was steady as he handed the glass to Neil, who flopped about like a puppy.

'Should he, er, be drinking while in treatment?'

'Probably not,' said Sam. 'In fact, definitely not. But he was being annoying. I thought it would settle him down.' Neil went to sit on the couch, slipped and fell on the floor, laughing.

'I guess it didn't work,' Sam added.

'I flirted with girls,' Neil announced proudly.

'Teenage girls,' Sam corrected. 'And I'd say your success rate was fairly low, although you covered enough ground that you couldn't help but get a nod from someone.'

I laughed. 'You got a nod? Ha!' I checked myself. I was definitely drunk too.

Neil smiled. 'Frida, like in ABBA. She has my number.'

'You mean my number.'

'Yes, she has *your* number,' he mugged. 'We all have your number in fact.' I watched Neil carefully. Suddenly the mood had changed. 'We know what you're up to,' he muttered bitterly into his glass.

'Neil,' Sam warned, but it was too late.

'Everyone knows you're just looking after me to ass, assua—' He corrected himself. 'To get rid of your guilt.'

'What guilt?' What was he talking about?

'Breaking up with me. Breaking my heart. I never recovered.' And then he burst into tears. I stood there in shock while Sam sighed and went off to get tissues. I still hadn't moved by the time he returned.

'I never broke your heart,' I said slowly when Neil had mopped up most of the moisture on his face. 'You cheated on me so many times that I had no choice,' I added. 'I left

you at the Schutzenfest in a puddle of mud and beer after
you told me you'd fucked Desiree Simpson. You did it in her
father's Holden.'

'I know,' he snuffled. 'But she was a slag. I *loved* you.'

'Oh Christ,' Sam sighed and dragged him to the couch.
'Go to bed.' He was angry.

'He can bloody stay with you,' I said, realising my hands
were on my hips. The night really wasn't getting any better.

'He can't.'

'Why not?'

'He just can't.'

I got a sick feeling in my gut, imagining some spiffy
blonde in aerobics gear getting narky with Neil for using her
fake tan. 'Well, he's moving out tomorrow. I've had a shitty
night. Oh, a great date,' I added hastily. 'But a terrible, um,
headache. He's your brother, you handle him.'

'I was paying you to look after him,' Sam replied slowly.

'Well, I haven't seen any casino chips yet, so let's just call
it even. He cleaned the place and now he's pissed me off.
It's time to go.' I threw a cushion at Neil's drooping head as
he slumped on the chair, went to the bathroom and slammed
the door.

I loudly brushed my teeth, washed my face and stalked
back to my enclave. As I curled up in bed I realised Sam had
left and Neil was lightly snoring on the couch. I hoped they'd
both have worse hangovers than me in the morning.

But, as I figured out when I was nineteen and still had not
developed a washboard stomach after adhering to my *Dolly*

diet for six weeks, not everything goes quite to plan. Neil's body was better equipped for a toxic overload than mine and he woke me at nine-thirty with a tray of perfectly buttered toast and chocolate milk.

'Headache,' I muttered, pulling the doona over my head as he put the tray beside me.

'I know,' he whispered. 'There's Panadeine Forte on the tray. Eat the toast, drink the milk. I'll get you a Berocca.'

He left and I sat up enough to choke down the pills and the milk, swallowing down the gag reflex and then cramming my mouth with toast as I fell back on the pillow. Crumbs covered my face as I continued to swallow and cram. He brought back the Berocca and I blinked back the image of all the colour mingling in my stomach.

'You're a guts,' he said, eyeing the tray.

'No guts, no glory,' I replied between bites. Ten minutes later the gloom had lifted slightly and in half an hour he'd put the Sundays on the stereo and I felt well enough to sit up and brush the crumbs from my ears and clavicle.

I hadn't pashed John, so that was good. Then I remembered the argument with Neil. Was Neil being nice to me so he wouldn't have to live with Sam? Why was Sam so reluctant to have Neil stay? Stolen items were becoming less of a threat and Neil was his brother after all. It must be an aerobics girl. I rolled over in the bed and pulled the covers over my ears.

I dozed through the sound of visitors and phone calls, but I just couldn't be bothered rousing myself to find out what was going on. Hopefully Neil wasn't organising a shooting gallery in my apartment.

Half an hour later Neil came and knocked on my wardrobe. 'Cass? You awake?'

'No,' I mumbled into the pillow.

'Josie's here.'

'I can tell her myself, you dope,' she said, breezing in and plonking down on the bed. She pulled back the covers. 'Was John a dud?'

'No. *I'm* the dud,' I said. 'John's just a wanker.' Probably he was a fine man and I was dead inside. I pictured a dried old bit of seaweed sitting inside a bottle rattling around in my gut and then I realised I didn't feel sick anymore. I sat up.

'He was really a complete wanker.'

'Neil played me the message he left.'

I nodded. Urgh, it made me ill just to think about it.

'I'm sorry he's a dick.'

I sat up. 'You *knew* he was a dick and you made me go out with him?'

'I hoped he had improved.'

'He hadn't.'

'Sure. Okay, well then. Tonight, you have a much better prospect. Lance Freeson is a graphic designer—'

I cut her off. 'I don't want to do it anymore. It's too hard. I'm tired.'

She shook her head. 'No, it's good for you. He's coming over at seven-thirty to take you to the B bar, the new revolving restaurant by the sea that's been refurbished, and then you're going to play Atari and shoot some pool at the Blue Room.'

'Oh, too groovy for me,' I wailed.

'You were probably looking for someone "more switched on" than John was, right?'

I nodded gravely. If switched on meant having a brain, then the answer was definitely yes.

'Lance is switched on. Like a floodlight perhaps, but it'll be good practice.'

'I'm not switched on. I'm shorted out. And I'm using these guys as target practice,' I moaned, rubbing sleep-glue from my eyes.

'Well, fuck it,' said Neil as he came in with a cup of coffee. 'They're using you too. Just make sure you come away with the biggest body count.'

'What are you still doing here?' I said as he put the cup down on my bedside table.

Josie looked between the two of us, frowning.

Neil nodded. 'I know. I meant to say I'm sorry for what I said last night. I can't remember, but Sam—' he indicated behind him, '—told me everything. I think I may have exaggerated slightly for effect. I like living here with you and I'll clean the house every day if that's what it takes. Sam's brought you over some presents.'

So Sam was here. I hoped he hadn't heard about my dud date. But the sense of embarrassment was overcome by curiosity. 'What sort of presents?' I hadn't even showered and I was a smelly old drunk. I shooed everyone away. 'Leave,' I gestured with my hands. 'Get croissants or something. I want to have a shower. And no bloody whispering about me behind my back.'

Probably I really was a smelly old drunk, because Josie went out and said something to Sam and then the three of them left. I threw back the covers and went to have a shower. There was a box on the floor in the living room but I didn't open it. It was just an ordinary cardboard box anyway, nothing special, nothing that said Haigh's or Crabtree & Evelyn. Jock followed me in and sat on the shower rail while I scrubbed off my depression with Body Shop mango gel.

Then I peeked in the box.

Groceries. And loads of pot noodles. Fuck them and the Saab they drove in.

By the time they got back, laden with croissants and freshly squeezed juices in paper cups, I was in jeans and a blue skivvy, filling up Jock's bowl.

I was nervous that I'd been rumbled and, what with Neil and Josie knowing my sad dating situation, it seemed inevitable that Sam would have the upper hand, having heard my regime for the next week or so. But when they'd put everything on the coffee table, moving the copies of *Vogue* out the way, he broke the silence first.

'I think I should tell you why I really would love it if Neil could stay.'

I looked up at the tone of his voice. 'Groceries are not presents.'

'I know, but there's chocolate in there somewhere.'

I nodded. 'Okay. Go on.'

'I know last night Neil was rude and seemed to have more baggage than Elizabeth Taylor, but he didn't mean what he said.' He nudged Neil, who shook his head earnestly.

'I really didn't.'

'And it would be good if he could stay here while he gets over this crucial stage in his, er, recovery.'

I let Jock hop up onto my shoulder for moral support

and sat on the couch next to Josie, who I suspected was restraining herself from nodding encouragingly at Sam, and saying, 'Go on, honey. You're doing well.'

'I can't look after Neil because I'm living back at home just at the moment,' he said. 'Neil isn't welcome there because of the tough love therapy, so there's really nowhere for him to go except rehab, which just didn't work last time and his counsellor doesn't think he needs it right now.'

'Hang on. Go back a second. You're living at *home?*'

Sam nodded, his face a mask.

'With your folks.'

He nodded again.

'Why? I mean, not that it's any of my business, but you never said anything.'

'I broke up with a girl and decided to move out. It was a bit sudden so home was the best place. I'm looking for somewhere now, but it's just taking me a little longer than I expected.'

'How long?'

'A year.'

'You've been living at home for a *year?*' I went to shake my head again but my headache was returning at a rapid rate. I was trying to reconcile the cool guy in the Saab with the sheepish guy in front of me who was hoping I'd help him out.

'Okay,' I said. 'I don't care. It's no big deal.' I remembered the tray this morning, and then the increasingly cheerful Neil around the house. And the fact that he was happy to watch *Just Shoot Me* when there was a rock documentary on SBS.

Jock combed my hair with his beak but he lost a strand when I nodded slowly. 'Okay, sure.'

Neil hugged me awkwardly and I felt embarrassed and slightly queasy. It would have been very poor form to spew right at that moment.

I went back to bed for another half hour and then remembered Helen's phone call. Gingerly I got up to call her back and found I didn't feel so bad after all. I sat on my bed with the portable phone cradled under my chin, pushing my cuticles back as she explained what Daniel's ex had told her. Apparently Susie had similar concerns about Daniel, but had no basis for it. She'd felt guilty of suspecting he was cheating on her, but she broke up with him anyway. Then she accidentally saw him at the post office.

'She followed Daniel and watched him through the window. She said it was dreadful at first—made her sick to her stomach. He bought about a dozen Valentine's Day cards and stood at the counter, five metres from her, going through his diary.' Helen paused. 'About a week later, she dropped around to his place to pick up a pot plant she'd left behind. She'd been nosy and peeked at the mail sticking out of his box and noticed that four cards with the same pink envelopes had been returned, and she memorised the names. She remembered one address, so she followed it up and called the girl.

'Apparently Daniel sends her a card every year on Valentine's Day. Sometimes he emails or calls her at work as well. She's in a committed relationship with someone else and doesn't give a fig about him. She sends the cards back, hoping he'll get the message, but he keeps sending them. She's asked him to stop, but he just doesn't get how messed up that is.

I bet that girl's partner was pissed off too. He's playing around with other people's lives.'

'Why do you think he does it?' I asked, rubbing cream into my nails.

'She thinks he's just locked into his teenage years, when he couldn't get laid.'

I thought about Justine pining for him at school. Fat, lonely Justine with no friends. Probably, to her, he was perfect.

'As he got older, he got better looking, but he couldn't shake the insecurity. He clings to them all like barnacles, apparently. Maybe he's trying to prevent himself from being alone, so he keeps the crowd of girls around. It's a bit freaky, but it's not illegal, or doing any harm. Except to his present relationships, I guess,' she added. 'Although if that weird girl hadn't started all this by making me suspicious, I might not have thought anything was wrong at all. He was very secretive.'

'True.' I couldn't help wondering if it was just better not to know. If Suzanne hadn't made Helen suspicious, Helen might have moved in with Daniel and they might have had a wonderful life together, never knowing all this garbage. Was it all just lies? Are hearts so easily broken?

We were silent.

'I guess you can't really trust guys,' she said finally, and I suddenly realised I hadn't asked Zara about her date with George and instantly felt guilty. When was it? Tomorrow?

'Maybe not,' I agreed. Certainly I hadn't had much luck. The ones I'd dumped because they were boring or stupid or annoying may well have been up to mischief too. I just didn't care enough to find out.

Then I remembered my date with John. 'I forgot to tell you. I saw him out last night with another girl.'

'Daniel?' Helen sounded surprised.

'Yes. She talked a lot.'

'I don't know who that might be,' she said, sounding thoughtful. 'Anyway, not my business now, although I am curious. I wonder if we've overlooked something all this time. Maybe he really was having an affair.'

I mumbled something noncommittal but I was curious too. I'd never slept with him so it was a little different to imagine how it must feel. Then I shook myself. I *knew* what it felt like. It felt *crap*. 'You want me to look into it?'

She paused. 'No. I don't care, really. Just an ego thing. But if you hear of anything, let me know?'

'Sure.' I put the cream away in the drawer and peeked out at my little gang. They were cleaning up the plates and paper bags and unpacking my dud grocery presents. I realised that I hoped Sam wouldn't leave before I had spoken to him but I couldn't resist prodding Helen. The temptation to get gossip was overwhelming.

'How's it going with Malcolm?'

'Great!' She cheered up. 'We're planning a weekend away. Daniel never wanted to go away.'

'Terrific. I'm glad,' I said, but silently prayed that the bed and breakfast, morning breath and every little thing that comes with a romantic night would not put too much pressure on wee young love. 'Good luck.' I rang off.

When I entered the kitchen, Neil was doing dishes and Josie was sitting on the bench, her long legs swinging as she idly dried the dishes. 'This has turned into the set from *Friends*,' I said. 'Don't you all have homes to go to?'

'Nope,' said Neil and Sam cheerfully.

'How's Justine?' I asked.

'The hospital says she's in a stable condition, but it's awkward. She's very unwell and her heart is under a lot of strain.'

'The poor woman.' I tried to imagine waking up in a hospital bed, not knowing if anyone would visit you. I reminded myself to go in the next day. I looked over at Josie, 'So what's your excuse for hanging out here, slacker?'

'Nick is handling the orders today. I'm shopping for new hostess clothes this afternoon. You want to get something for your hot date?'

'Another date with the lawyer?' asked Sam casually, and I feigned a laugh.

'No, he's a graphic designer. We're going to the revolving restaurant.'

It was his turn to laugh. 'Isn't that a bit tacky?'

Josie flicked him with the tea towel. 'You are *so* behind the times, Tasker. It's hot. If they served cocktails I'd be seriously worried. Cassidy deserves someone with good taste, something better than takeaway, anyway.' She smiled. 'You want to shop? Oh, and no underwear. You spend more on lingerie than Sam probably does on car wax.'

'Sure,' I said hurriedly. 'I need to get out of the house.'

'I guess I can't ask you to be careful,' he said and then suddenly he looked up. 'Hey! Neil, what did you say about Tony last night?'

'I dunno,' Neil said slowly.

'Last night,' said Sam, then he pointed at his brother. 'You thought you knew Tony.'

'No, no,' he replied as we all turned to look. 'It was Jessica.' He paused. 'My friend Jess works in the sex industry. She was talking last week about this big guy with this huge, er, penis, with a big vein down it, who comes in every week. He roughs her up a bit. She's spoken about him before and I hadn't thought twice.' I waved him on impatiently. 'Anyway, Sam told me about Tony last night and it actually sounds like the same guy.'

'No way!' I turned to Sam. 'How did you know about—'

Josie put her hand up. 'Um. I might have told him the other night when you were in the loos at the Easy Lounge.'

I looked at her quizzically. I didn't want Sam to know about all the dopey things I'd done.

'Okay,' I said slowly. 'So you think...'

'That we might be able to bring him in on something else.' Sam smiled. 'We can talk to this Jessica, see if we can get a match. We know all the brothels pretty well. We can just go in when we know he's there.'

'It's that easy?'

'It might be.'

'And then we can throw his filthy arse in jail?'

Sam laughed. 'No. South Australian laws are pretty unfair. If this Jessica co-operates, we'll have to negotiate with whoever runs it. Brothel owners and sex workers get punished much more heavily than the clients do.'

'But that's ridiculous. You mean the girls get fined more than the guys who pay to fuck them?'

'I guess. If you put it like that. And so delicately, too,' he said. 'But yes. Fines of five hundred dollars for being on the premises without a reasonable excuse are a little more favourable than the build-up fines for soliciting and loitering that the girls get done for on a repeated basis. We don't hassle them much anymore, unless they're doing something else illegal. Stolen goods or some sort of racket. It's amazing what goes on but most places are pretty clean. It's better to keep on good terms with them, and work together.'

'It's true,' nodded Neil. 'Jessica says they'll get a call beforehand, so some people who've been busted too often and risk going to prison can go home.'

'Really?' Josie's eyes were wide.

'Sure,' said Sam. 'There's no point wasting our time throwing them all in jail every week. We prefer to spend our time busting criminals who rape, thieve and disturb the peace.'

'Like me,' suggested Neil, and we all stared at him until he blinked and said hurriedly, 'except the raping business, of course.'

'Right then,' said Sam, clapping his hands and patting his pockets for his wallet. 'On that cheery note, I'll see what I can round up on the Tony front.'

'And we'll go shopping,' said Josie. I forced a smile. I wasn't much of a shopper, unless it involved underwear. I got depressed when things didn't fit, and when they did I got depressed because I couldn't afford them. And all that taking things on and off just got irritating after a while.

'Sure, great.'

Neil had decided he was going to make friends with Jock, so he went off into the corner and started whispering to him furtively. While Josie plopped down in a chair and flicked through my magazines, I let Sam out.

Except when we got into the hallway, he leaned towards me. The smell of his neck was intoxicating. 'How soon,' he said quietly, 'will you realise that there's nothing you need that you don't have?'

'Huh?' The sight of the hairs on his neck were making me giddy. 'Are you still drunk?'

He stood back, smiling in a slightly pained way, then walked off.

'Are you trying to say I shouldn't go shopping?' I called out, but he was gone.

I closed the door, stunned. Josie looked up and caught my expression.

'Did he try to kiss you?' When I didn't respond, she jumped up. 'He wasn't rude to you was he? What happened?'

I stared at her as she came around the couch and stood before me, daring me to send her out to box his ears, I imagine. 'No, nothing bad. He said something to me.'

'Well, what was it?' She stepped forward and took my hand. 'What?' She smiled again. 'Was it something sexy?'

I shook my head. 'No. Let's go shopping. I need some kind of therapy, maybe the retail one will work.'

'Are you sure? You look kinda funny.'

'I'm sure. I'd like to get something new to wear tonight. If this date is going to be anything like the last one, I need to be someone completely unlike myself to get through it. If I'm boring myself, I hate to think what I'm doing to others.'

'Well, something tells me you're not boring Sam. We'll get you something different, to make you feel different, but meanwhile you just act like Cass. That's better than half these dickheads could hope for.'

I smiled gratefully at her as she gathered my bag and keys and we headed off, waving goodbye to Neil, who was whispering in the corner with a rather nonplussed Jock. I didn't think I could stand another dull date, so if Lance was anything like John, I was going to have to make my own fun. Again.

As it turned out, I needn't have worried. I said Neil could stay home when Lance arrived, but that he shouldn't stare if Lance was funny looking or had a ponytail, so he decided to have a bath and stay out of the way. I imagined all graphic designers had ponytails but Lance had spiky hair and a bouncy step, full of the vivacity of life. Or, in his case, recreational drugs. It was like going out with Tigger.

I'd slapped on loads of foundation so my face looked more normal, and borrowed one of Josie's vintage designer bags. I felt good when he knocked on the door. We chatted for a couple of minutes in the doorway as he bounced around, admiring everything and then swooping on my kitchen appliances, identifying everything from various home decorating spreads he'd seen. I admit I'd bought a few sucky designer things, but I'd always been brought up to buy the best, not because they were groovy, but because they were—well—the *best*. But Lance fingered my toaster like it was a sculpture.

'C'mon, Cassidy Blair,'—he kept calling me that—'Let's have a good time! I've brought the appetiser.' And then he bounced out of the kitchen and onto the couch, pulling out a bag of coke as he went. I knew coke. I'd done coke. I'd just never done it so blithely before.

'Um, actually, Lance, I think it would be more like an *un*appetiser,' I said, as he pulled out his wallet for a fifty.

He looked at me, disappointed. 'But Cassidy Blair, we'll get our appetites back soon enough,' he said, holding up a joint. 'This is just to get us to the restaurant,' (he said restaurant like he was French, rolling his Rs and adding a gutteral 'aunt' to the end), 'then we can have a joint and we'll soon be starving!'

What was going on? 'Did Josie tell you I was a party girl?' I asked, tapping my finger nervously against my thigh.

'Oh yeah!' He smiled at me as though he could see my peek-a-boo black lace lingerie beneath my hot-pink mini-dress. The dress was old but the black stiletto boots with the silver loops down the outside were new. Two hundred and twenty dollars new to my credit card too.

I shrugged. Fuck it.

'Excellent! Let's party, little lady!'

Suddenly I could hear laughter from the bathroom and Lance whipped around. 'It's all right. That's just a friend who's staying with me. An old, old friend. A social outcast, actually,' I added as I heard more laughter and splashing. Neil was having fun in my tub. 'Nowhere to stay. I had to take him in. A waif.'

'Sure, sure, okay,' said Lance, still unreasonably happy. 'So let's party.'

And I did. I partied all the way to the restaurant, on the terrace downstairs where we nearly set fire to the bamboo matting when lighting a joint and then again as we wafted into the lift and then the restaurant on a cloud of purple smoke. We sat grinning stupidly at each other as we ordered white wine on a pale blue leather lounge while they got our table ready. Lance seemed to know everyone there. While girls admired my new boots (able to identify the brand and catalogue page they'd featured in), I window-shopped the men, who had partied as hard as we had. By the time we sat down, the room was a stuffy haze of smoke and dopey conversations.

I can't remember the dinner very well, only that I did get extremely hungry and ate three courses and we drank a good deal of wine. We put it all on Lance's business credit card—'entertaining potential clients,' he laughed—then we swooped out of the restaurant in a big happy group and danced at some club. And I just got happier. I met a lot of people who all seemed thrilled to meet me too and we all laughed and joked and kissed.

At five in the morning I finally squeezed into a car with Lance and our new best friends whose names I'd forgotten and they dropped us off at my apartment. The street was grey and very shiny and I was starting to feel a little grey and shiny too, so when Lance kissed me wildly and then danced off to his car, I wasn't disappointed to make my way up to my door alone. In fact, I couldn't keep the dopey smile off my face.

Eight hours later, when Neil brought me the same breakfast tray and pills, I threw the pills down my throat and ignored the toast. Again, I wasn't hungry. I realised I couldn't remember getting into bed. I peeped under the covers cautiously. I had my pyjamas on, which was a good sign.

'Not hungry,' I whispered, and by the way Neil reeled

back I gathered I hadn't cleaned my teeth. I touched my face in confusion and he nodded. 'Yes, you still have glitter all over your nose and quite a healthy smattering of lipstick too.'

Then I needed to go to the loo. I'd been alternating between water and wine for much of the night and I couldn't really remember peeing at all. Suddenly I needed to go very badly and very often. After the fifth trip, I was so annoyed I left the door open.

'You're not barfing—' called Neil from the living room '— so I'm guessing all this bathroom activity is because you partied in a rather more Studio 54 way than usual last night?'

'Uh-huh,' I muttered and then flushed the loo. I wasn't embarrassed about Neil hearing me pee. He'd seen my undies and the refuse of my life, so when I marched stoically back to bed, I was surprised to see him looking worried.

'So I guess you really did "party little lady" as the good man urged?'

'Shut up!'

'Hey Cass?'

'Yes?' I yelled impatiently.

'Are we two weird people who live together and don't have sex? Like in *Will & Grace?*'

'Yes,' I said, stumbling through the room and falling back into bed. 'We definitely *don't have sex.*'

'No. And I guess I'm not gay.'

I lifted my head. 'Well, you're not are you?'

'No, no. Very non-gay. No gay guy would put up with me anyway. Can't—'

'Get it up, yes, I know,' I finished, slightly wearily. 'You revealed that earlier. It was just great to know. I'm sure it'll all come back to you soon enough,' I added and then fell asleep.

In my various jobs I've encountered a whole swathe of wankers. A plethora of socially inept, rude, often funny smelling and inevitably poorly dressed people. People who wear polyester slacks and comb their hair over the bald spot and then loudly criticise a passing group of girls for having legs shorter than Elle's. Women who screech at their husbands in public while wearing stilettos and ankle socks and then wonder why no one wants to take them to Paris for sex. Boys who wear large clown pants and call their friends their 'posse' and can't remember their girlfriends' names. And somewhere in there is a distant memory of beautiful people parading about as though they owned the world while treating less pop-ular beautiful people like Beta video players.

So, as I fumbled about that morning, washing the Chupa-chup goo out of my hair and using my two-hundred-dollar eye cream on my lips to repair them from all the kissing, I won-dered if in fact everyone was actually normal but that at some stage people, like me, had entertained the idea of being other than themselves for a brief time. Therefore, in such a mode, they made it appear as though the world was part-populated with wankers. Perhaps.

Even Neil kept a wary eye on me as I refused food for the fourth time and feverishly washed my pyjamas, sheets and clothes, cleaned out my bag and threw away the twenty-odd business cards I had acquired in my travels the night before.

'Spiritual cleansing?' he asked as I deleted Lance's message from that morning from my machine. He'd called from Chi-chi in Rundle Street, asking me to join him, Antoinette and Raji for protein smoothies.

'You'll be reading *Oyster* magazine and getting an electronic organiser any day now,' Neil called out and I threw the nearest cushion at him.

Things settled down, until Helen called at midday in tears.

'He's dating her!'

'Who?' But I knew.

'Daniel. He's been seeing her for months! They met at the Robsons' engagement party! That was four months ago!'

'So, what do you want to do?'

'Kill him!'

'But *you're* dating Malcolm,' I said, reasonably. I knew how she felt though. What a turd-burger.

'Yes, but he was fucking me and thinking of her!'

'Sure. Perhaps. But maybe he was fucking her and thinking of you,' I said hopefully. But I could see her point. 'Okay. Let's kill him.'

She sucked in a breath over the phone; phlegm and tears gurgled through the earpiece. 'Really?'

'No!'

She collected herself and whispered hurriedly, 'Well, what shall we do?'

I had no idea, but there was a burning sense of injustice in my gut. Probably it was the drugs eating a hole in my stomach lining, but someone had to get their comeuppance and it wasn't going to be me.

'I'll swing by and pick you up. I still have a copy of his key. I gather you're not at work.'

'I said I had diarrhoea.'

'Good idea. No one wants to talk about it when you get back.' I got her home address and hung up.

'Where are you going?' asked Neil as I hunched into a coat over jeans and sneakers. 'You're up to something. You never dress that badly.'

'I'm going over to Helen's place.'

'Helen with the boyfriend who can't let go?'

I turned to him. 'Do I talk in my sleep?'

'No, but you talk very fast when you're on drugs or drunk and collapsed on the sofa next to me hogging my blanket and smelling like a cigar room.'

I didn't want to know. 'Yes, that one.'

'The one you wanted to know all the tips about breaking into a house for?'

'Uh-huh,' I said, reluctantly.

He leapt up and pulled on the jumper Sam had bought for him when we realised all Neil's clothes reeked of cheap incense and reminded Neil of drugs. 'Well, I'm coming with you.'

'No, you're not!' I scowled and grabbed my bag. 'You're staying here.'

'Sam said you had to keep an eye on me, and you'll just get yourself in the shit on your own.'

'Sam said you have to stay here where it's safe. I know they can't keep an eye on the apartment all the time but it's something. Helen will be there with me, so I won't be alone.'

'Crazy Two Job Johnnie broke in here and nearly diced

us all into bite-sized pieces, so it's very unsafe even when Sam's around sometimes. And the only way Helen could help you out would be by sitting on someone or poking them in the eye with her great big nose.'

'You've never met Helen!'

'You mutter to yourself a lot too.'

'Oh, shut up.'

I locked up and jumped in my car. I drove around the block while Neil picked up some coffees from Cibo's and then we went the long way to Helen's place in Parkside, finding ourselves in dead-end streets so often that I was dying to pee by the time we got there.

Helen lived in a classic peach-coloured cottage, topiaries out front, neatly mowed lawn, cream curtains in the window. It looked like she took a lot of pride in conformity, which surprised me, considering her slightly aggressive professional manner. Somehow I'd imagined a concrete block and minimalist furniture. I ran in and relieved myself while Neil introduced himself and helped Helen lock up.

'Shit, what happened to your face?' she asked as I met them in the kitchen. I touched my cheek. I'd almost forgotten and hadn't put any make-up on except eye-shadow. It didn't hurt anymore, probably the side effects of recreational drugs. No one had commented the night before, although the glitter had a very distracting effect. There actually was no puffiness and the grazing had almost disappeared. I looked almost normal, except for what looked like a permanent blush and a slight leer.

'Neil got annoyed when I stacked the dishwasher wrong,' I laughed and he shot me an angry look.

'Don't joke about that shit, Cass,' he said, smiling re-assuringly at Helen. 'My friend Fiona got punched in the neck for forgetting the loo paper,' he added and then turned back to the windows. Helen stared at him, fascinated.

'Your locks are stuffed,' he said.

'Yeah, I can't be bothered using the key and now they're rusty.'

'Smash the glass, lift the bolt, crawl inside, take the stereo,' he pointed quickly around the room, 'box of CDs, easy to move and sell; good speakers, TV, video, DVD player. I'd leave the lamp, but take the microwave. You could even sell that fancy espresso machine. It'd take half an hour and you'd be wiped out. You might have insurance but you think you'd want to sleep here alone once that's happened? I might even shit in your loo without flushing. Just to say boo.'

He walked around the apartment, lifting things up and still talking steadily. 'Where are the lock keys?'

'In the drawer,' she said, not taking her eyes off him and pointing into the kitchen.

He got them and then found some WD-40 in the cupboard, spent five minutes loosening the locks and locking up, then told her to get a gardener in to cut back some of the foliage around the side of the house, so that her neighbours could see her property without looking directly in her windows, and we left.

On the walk out Helen took me aside. 'Is he an under-cover cop?'

'Thief and drug addict,' I reassured her.

'Oh, good.' She fumbled in her bag for a tissue and wiped

her nose. Her eyes were still red but she looked more together than she'd sounded on the phone. 'He's very smart.'

'I know,' I nodded, surprised. If he hadn't boiled his brain and skipped school, the man would probably be a genius.

'Good-looking, too.'

I laughed and watched Neil as he scoped the street. 'I guess you're right. But you're dating Malcolm.'

'Of course. Yes.'

I handed her the key to Daniel's house and we all drove off to Riverside Avenue together, with me casting nervous glances at Helen as she chatted to Neil about good stereo systems. It turned out Neil had finished two years at a sound engineering school before giving himself up to the drug lifestyle, so he was quite the expert. Clearly it had helped him make his selection in various houses around town too.

Neil talked about music the way Sam talked about, well, anything boring when he was at school. But Sam had stopped and Neil still did it. The diagnosis of arrested development was very fitting. I tuned them out as Helen listened avidly to Neil's advice on stringing new speakers into her bedroom and dining room. I felt a little sorry for Malcolm, dragging his bread around town fantasising about her nostrils.

We pulled up in front of the quiet house and Helen jumped out. 'Where are you going?' I yelped, wrenching my door open and pulling on the handbrake. Helen's eyes were blazing.

Helen leant in the window. 'I don't want you guys to come in, in case you get in trouble.'

'Helen,' I huffed, turning off the motor and hooking a

finger at Neil, who jumped out of the car with me. 'I'm already in trouble for B&E,' I said over the car roof. 'And so's he. We're felons on the run. We'll do back-up.'

'Okay,' she shrugged. 'You sit on the porch and bang on the front door if anyone shows.'

'You have a plan?' I asked warily. She looked determined and her nostrils were flaring wildly. I could almost see her brain ticking over with evil thoughts.

She nodded.

We walked up the steps as she went around the side of the house. I was feeling fearless. I was familiar around here now. Maybe my outfit didn't back me up as it once had, but I had little to lose.

I heard a funny noise and looked around.

'What was that?'

'Nothing,' said Neil innocently. But then, as I watched the road, I could have sworn I heard the first few bars of 'I am Woman'.

'Shut up, Neil.'

'I'm not doing anything,' he laughed, but he stopped.

'Nice neighbourhood.' He plopped down on the porch, his back against the post. I remained standing, watching the street.

'Sometimes it is. Sometimes there are kids around.'

He glanced over. 'Not the maternal type?'

'Nope.'

'So, no kids, ever. Not in the future?'

'Maybe in the future. I've changed a lot in five years,' I added. 'Maybe in another five I'll want a brood of little bastards. Although your mother would kill me if they were bastards.'

I laughed and then abruptly cut it short when I realised what I'd said. I opened and closed my mouth a few times but nothing got sucked back in and time did not turn back.

Neil laughed. 'Cass. Just let your subconscious talk. Now that it's out, you can't suck it back in. It's gonna live the moment.'

'I—' But still nothing come out. I was mute with horror.

'I know you like Sam,' he said. 'It's written all over you every time he's around. Not just your face, you walk differently, you mutter and pull your hair. I know that look. He's completely fucked up about it too.'

I was about to jam my fists into my eye sockets and rub the day away but I caught his last words just in time not to ruin the autumn eye-shadow.

'He's fucked up? Is he embarrassed? Christ.' I was mortified. Had I been drooling at him all this time? Had I no shame! I started to twitch, and then it turned into a full-on shake down. 'Why did you say that?' I asked cautiously. Neil took drugs. Maybe his vision and judgment were impaired. His brain must look like a big old sea sponge.

'Not that kind of fucked up, Cass. He thinks you're great. It's obvious. Haven't you noticed?' He stopped and stared. 'You haven't noticed!'

'Stop it!' My heart had gaffer tape all around it. I couldn't bear the possibility that he was teasing me.

'What are you muttering to yourself?'

'Nothing.'

'He does really like you,' he said slowly.

We were quiet.

'How do you know he, er, likes me?' I tried to flip my

hair casually but it got tangled in a ring. 'He just likes me because I'm looking after you. I'm just taking the heat off him.'

'Yeah, well. I guess if that were true he wouldn't be so damn hot under the collar when you're around.'

I had an image of a sweaty guy in the tropics pulling his collar away from his neck and couldn't match it with my image of Sam.

I was about to say something to that effect but Neil must have read my mind. 'I'm his brother. I know what's going on under that sensible haircut. And I know what effect you have on guys.' He laughed at my expression. 'You're not anyone's idea of a dream date,' he went on as I started to look excited. The smile was wiped right off my face. 'You're hard work and completely frustrating most of the time, but you're damn worth it and every guy worth half a banana knows that.'

I blushed so fast it prickled and I was about to say something so it wouldn't look like I actually believed him when Helen burst out of the front door and hurried down the steps. Neil pulled himself up and we all piled in the car.

As we pulled away from the curb, I was still all tangled up in the thought of Sam and the hot-under-the-collar stuff so Neil was the unexpectedly cool one, giving directions and warning me as I nearly jumped the curb in my flustered haste. I guess he'd been in a getaway car before and had an advantage. And he didn't give a fig about the electricity in my pants, so he was a little more sane than I was. I could have powered a microwave oven.

'What did you do?' he asked Helen as we headed home. There was no one behind us.

Helen was breathing very fast, so it took her a while to respond, but when she did, she turned to me.

'You remember that photo album in the dresser?'

I nodded.

'Well I just buggered the lock open and looked through it.'

'He won't notice you broke in?'

'I don't care. Who's he going to tell?'

'But then what? Did you—?'

'Oh yes,' she said smiling widely. 'When I was in love with him, I thought he was great. The only problem was, when you're not in love, you realise what someone's really like, and I realised Daniel was a poor substitute for an honest, kind, *loving* man,' she smiled, emphasising the last one and gazing at Neil who looked startled. 'So I punished him.'

'You cut up his clothes?' whispered Neil in reverence, his eyes like saucers. It seemed that he thought he was in an episode of *Sex and the City*. Without the stylist.

'No,' she smiled. 'Better, but just as adolescent, I'm afraid. Last week, he bought a whole freezerload of seafood for his birthday party. I was going to have to cook it, but I guess that's not happening. I tucked them everywhere I could find.'

'Is he frightened of seafood?' Neil asked in excitement.

'No,' she laughed. 'But you must know the old trick. He won't look for the damn things until the day of the party, which isn't for quite a while, and by then they will have all gone off.'

'So where did you put them?' I asked doubtfully. I couldn't help but think it was a bit gross. And childish. Didn't we want to be cool and sassy and tell him to fuck off? It was the equivalent of egging his house.

'Oh, I hid them everywhere,' she said airily. 'There're scallops inside hollow lamp bases, prawns zipped inside cushions, crabsticks behind the wardrobe, mussels tucked into the feet of his weights machine, lobster claws through the washing machine and crabmeat squashed into the base of the vase of dried flowers. The fruits of the ocean are now crammed throughout Daniel's house.'

It did sound pretty good, now she described it. We'd pulled up in front of Helen's place by the time she told us the rest. 'Oh, and I put bleach in his laundry liquid and set his alarm clock for three o'clock tomorrow.' We whooped but she interrupted us. 'And then I put flea powder in his hair drier.'

'He uses a hair drier?' asked Neil incredulously.

'A lot of guys I know do, actually,' said Helen. I agreed.

'And I read somewhere about putting powdered milk in the bed sheets, so I did that too. It curdles with the body heat and sticks to your skin. It's almost impossible to get out, apparently.'

'Christ, you're Satan,' said Neil appreciatively.

'I know,' she said, a big smile on her face as she got out of the car. 'Thanks for helping me. I feel great.' And then she winked at Neil, who blanched, and she quickly strode inside, grinning to herself. We drove off, alternately laughing and falling into silent thought.

'The debris of love,' said Neil suddenly.

'I know,' I agreed. 'It's like all excitement and dreams, all full of hope, and then you're putting prawns in their table lamps.'

'I'm depressed,' he moaned.

'Me too.' We lapsed into silence again and, as we drove through town, I caught sight of an all-too-familiar figure.

'There's Sam,' cried Neil before I could change lanes to

put more space between us. I didn't want to think about Sam right at that moment.

'Pull over, Cass. I want you to talk to him.'

Sam was walking along North Terrace, eating an ice-cream.

'I'm not pulling over,' I insisted, 'He's eating ice-cream.'

'So?'

'So he's relaxed. I'm not going to ask him all these awkward questions when he's relaxed.'

'Right, right,' nodded Neil. 'Wait until he's really tense. That should work.'

'Shut up.'

But then I got thrown a fate curveball: the lights changed and I had to pull to a sudden stop behind a ute.

'Swap seats,' urged Neil suddenly. 'You get out. Go and talk to him.'

'I'm not going to talk to him! The lights will change.'

'We'll swap seats. They did it in one of those *Lethal Weapon* movies and they were moving at the time. Just get out and I'll crawl over. You won't have to slide under me.'

'Thank God,' I muttered, realising I did want to get out. I wanted to see Sam. What the hell was wrong with me? I'd just seen how foul guys can be, how far we'll go to get revenge and how mixed up it all is, and now I just wanted to try again.

'Okay,' I huffed, pretending to be pissed off. If it didn't work out, I could blame Neil for forcing my hand. I grabbed my bag and opened the door just as the lights changed. Neil clambered over into the driver's seat and buckled the seatbelt with a grin.

'You do have a driver's licence?' I yelled through the window, watching the traffic out the corner of my eye.

'Yeah,' he yelled back. 'It's just not current. And don't blame me if you get pregnant!'

I whipped back around to face him, but he pulled out to the honking of the cars behind him. I stood, suddenly terrified, clutching my bag as vehicles swiped me from both sides. When I saw a gap I ran towards the footpath where Sam was staring open-mouthed, his ice-cream dripping down his hand, uneaten.

'What the hell?'

'Hmm? What?' I acted unconcerned as I tried to catch my breath.

'You were nearly killed!' he exploded. 'You just got out of the *driver's side*. Hey! That wasn't my brother driving, was it? He's not—'

'No, no. No one you know.'

'Oh.' He licked his hand free of the ice-cream. 'Good.'

He tucked the drips into his mouth. 'How did you go with Tony?' I asked, thinking I could plug that microwave back into my pants soon. I could power the city.

'Turns out Jessica works at a place we know fairly well. They're good. We do drive-bys fairly often and they keep us up to date with anything weird they hear about. In return, we don't bother them more than necessary.'

'No raids?'

'Oh, sometimes we try, but they're quick. They make every client drop their dacks, and no cop will go near that. They also don't touch the cash, so it's tricky for us to bust them. We can't get them on a lot of stuff unless we get testimonials from clients, and who's going to step up in court and confess to paying for it?'

He shook his head. 'As I said, it's all geared towards busting the girls and the owners. Most of the girls I know are fine with the work. Together, tough, and they know what they're doing. Most of them.'

I looked at him doubtfully. It must mess with their heads on a fundamental level, but I figured Sam saw messed-up heads on a regular basis and just measured them all in relation to each other. I wondered where I sat on that scale.

We walked along, Sam licking the ice-cream and me subtly trying to shift my jeans while walking so the seam didn't catch me in the clitoris. No point making things worse than they already were.

'So what will you do about Tony? Any chance of nabbing him?'

'Yep, Mugsy. I reckon we've got a bloody good chance of nabbin' 'im.'

I pushed him away with a laugh and he nearly walked into a postbox. Then I felt it. The sun was shining and the bullshit of the day just slid away and I felt brilliant. It wasn't just my pants that felt warm. This felt warm. He made me feel good.

'It's a gorgeous day.'

I stared at the clouds—white paintbrush strokes across the blue sky—when I saw something out of the corner of my eye and flinched.

Then I realised it wasn't a bird poop heading my way at all but Sam. And then he kissed me.

He kissed me and it was really nice. No, not nice. Fantastic.

It was all sticky lips and the sun in my eyes and soft kissing. Then he pulled away and I sucked in some ice-cream that had landed on my lip and started coughing. I bent double on the footpath, spluttering, but all I could think about, through the tears and the pain and the overwhelming sensation that I might suffocate and die right there on the street, was that I'd grabbed his jumper as he leaned towards me. I'd felt the small of his back under my hand—the indentation at the base of his spine.

He whacked me on the back a few times and I stood up, wiping my nose and sort of grinning.

'Christ,' he laughed.

I stared at him, speechless. Well, speechless and snuffling a little bit.

'Thanks,' I said, then flushed.

'Thanks for the kiss or for the back-slapping?'

'Um, both.'

'Well, then you're welcome,' he grinned. We walked on a bit further, me pretending to still be enamoured with the clouds but actually surreptitiously licking my lips and clearing my throat of potentially life-threatening dairy products. I was walking like a zombie in step.

'Where are we headed?'

'The casino.'

I laughed, then stopped when I realised he was serious. 'You're *betting?*' I was stunned. I tried to imagine him at the roulette wheel and it didn't fit.

'I feel lucky.' And then he kissed me again, only this time I was more prepared and I even kissed him back. I let my hand feel that spot on his back again, and I was glad of the sunshine and the fact that I wasn't wearing sunglasses because I could see the flush behind his ears as he pulled away. I was also glad I wasn't drunk because I could enjoy the warmth in my stomach that spread right through to my fingers, followed by a million freaked-out thoughts (What does this mean? He lives with his parents and I live with his brother—where will we have sex? Can I drive his car sometime?). And then I shook with nerves all the way to the casino, my kneecaps jumping about as I tried desperately to walk normally.

When we walked into the big room he took my hand and held it while he put twenty dollars on the chocolate wheel and won one hundred dollars. I felt a little giddy and had to lean on a chair for support. My heart was all jammed up, and I was watching myself from afar as I laughed and smiled and pretended to be cool, while all the time just wanting to kiss his rough cheek and run my hand through his hair. He smelt great. Then he bought me a glass of champagne at the tacky bar from a waiter named Peter and we laughed again. Like complete idiots.

The next day I woke up feeling the warmth of the world cocooning me, although my cheeks were sore, probably from all the endless, annoying, ridiculous, uncool grinning. Sam had walked me home and kissed me again at the door and Neil had just laughed at my expression and we watched crap TV all night.

After being sufficiently hypnotised by the box to calm the shivers of excitement every time I remembered Sam's lips, Zara called. As soon as she mentioned her date with George I was shamed into silence.

'Christ,' she said, a nervous edge to her voice. 'It wasn't that bad. We just went to the beach and then we kissed.'

'I'm so sorry, I just forgot. I'm a terrible friend.' I rushed in before she could agree, 'But you kissed!' I sucked in air. 'You kissed! Who kissed who first? Was he any good?' I paused. 'What about the whole not so "Mentos fresh and full of life" issue?'

'He tasted great. I tested, actually,' she giggled, and I restrained myself from staring at the receiver in wonder. Zara sounded positively girlish. 'I pretended to be interested in his shirt but really I just wanted to lean in a bit. He was fine. It was a good shirt, too,' she added. 'And when I leaned in for the test, he went all quiet. It was so cute! And I kept talking about the wine bar we were going to, or something, but I was watching his face and his eyes were all sort of misty. I think he likes me. He is *really* cute!'

'Of course he likes you! Who wouldn't like you?' I said, but then I realised it was a dumb thing to say because she hadn't exactly been fighting them off. It had always been my opinion that she was just not interested, that no one good enough had come along, but I was starting to realise there was a very good chance she'd liked boys before, and just hadn't told me about it. I had to wonder why not, but probably it was my fault so I didn't wonder for long.

But I was *so* glad for her. I turned off the telly after Neil went off for a bath and curled up on the couch while she told me about how he'd ordered the wine, really nice wine, and she'd felt a bit drunk, and how he'd kissed her again when he'd dropped her off and how they had planned another date this week. I think I had a goofy smile on my face around this point because Neil walked past and just shook his head. I wanted to explain this had nothing to do with his brother, but maybe a little residual bit of it did.

But I didn't say anything about Sam. This was her moment. When she eventually stopped talking, we made vague plans to see a movie during the week and hung up. I wanted to share this with her, and tell both Zara and Josie about Sam, but I was just too tired. And I wanted to get my life back to normal. I knew I had to get off this weird merry-go-round of peculiar events. Like kissing boys, and people hitting me. Maybe the kissing bit could stay.

The next morning the phone rang and Neil picked it up while I took a shower. I cleaned slowly, stretching in the shower because I'd slept funny. The muscles in my upper back were tight and I let the hot water pound on them as I shaved my legs. It was Sam on the phone.

'You want to take it now or call him back?' Neil yelled through the door.

'I'll call him back,' I shouted, feeling all hot and cold like before an exam, and turned off the water. Had we really kissed? It seemed like a dream. I put on some undies and a singlet, planning to do some yoga to get my back out of kink. When I called back, Sam picked up on the first ring.

'Good things are happening in a rush, Silenus,' he laughed. For a second I didn't know what he was talking about, and then I remembered the poem that night he'd come around after the surveillance: 'Give me sweet nectar in a kiss that I may be replete with bliss.'

I gripped the receiver tightly. 'What's happened in a rush?' I knew he wasn't just talking about us.

'Rosetta called me last night, from Jemima's.' I was silent, just enjoying the sound of his voice. 'The brothel Neil's friend works at,' he added when I still hadn't said anything. I tried to catch up. 'A guy matching Tony's description came in last night, so I called your mate, Gus. We went in and grabbed Tony under the Summary Offences Act. We squeezed in a charge, and it turns out he's overdue on some parking offences, so we can patch something together here. They'll probably be delaying their wedding. He hasn't even called his lawyer, he's so freaked.'

'Oh, good.' I tried to feel justified, but I felt goofy happy and there was no room at the inn. But then I remembered my face and felt a bit better.

'We'll never be able to make anything stick for the other stuff, will we?'

'No. There were no witnesses, not even at the Easy Lounge. No one I spoke to could give me anything. This will mess things up for him a little though, and I'll make it clear we know what he's been up to. Hopefully he'll lay low for a while.'

'Great,' I said absently. 'That's great.'

We were silent, and I thought I could feel the sexual tension in the air when Sam suddenly spoke. 'Um, Cass.'

'Yeah?'

'The hospital just called.'

'Oh, yeah? How's Justine? I'm going in to see her today.' I'd meant to see her yesterday but events had sort of taken over.

'Justine died.'

I sucked in a breath. 'What?'

'She died of heart failure late last night.'

'You said she was stable.' Shit. She died alone. 'Did she have any visitors?'

'No, but she was in observation for two days. No one expected it. Her heart just gave out. She never came around.'

I said nothing.

'Cass? Are you okay?'

'No,' I said. 'I feel terrible. I was going to visit her, but I got distracted. All caught up in my own life.'

'Everyone does that.'

'I know. Look, I've got to go.' I felt sick.

'I'm coming around later to drop off some stuff for Neil.'

'Okay, sure. That would be great.' And we both rang off. What was wrong with me? I felt sick to my stomach. I rubbed it thoughtfully. I could feel it curdling under my hand. Guilt.

I must have been sitting there for a while because the phone rang again, making me jump.

'Hello?'

'Cassidy Blair?'

'Yes,' I replied cautiously.

'It's Barry. Barry from DVDWorld.'

'Oh. Are you working mornings now?' I asked absently. I was trying to get back into the present day but it was taking a while.

'No, no. I'm at home. Alice from the afternoon shift called me to say that your old colleague, Amanda, rang all freaked out and furious. Apparently she's blaming you for her boyfriend getting arrested or something. What'd he get arrested for?'

He sounded serious and I jumped immediately into the present. My face. Arresting Tony. The brick through Josie's window.

'Oh Christ!'

'I know. It's weird, but then I figured that it sounded just like something that would happen to you. She came storming into the store this morning, looking for you.'

And that was the moment when I looked up and realised the front door was open. I could hear Neil splashing, singing 'I am Woman' as he cleaned the windowsill. His back to the hallway and oblivious to everything.

'So I thought I'd better ring,' he said, but his voice came

from far away as my hand dropped the phone. My eyes zeroed in on the short pink streak that filled the door frame.

'How did you—?'

Amanda slammed the door. She took three giant steps toward me. The whites of her eyes were pink and she was baring her teeth like a rabid dog. Her breath smelt as though she'd gargled with metholated spirits.

And then she laughed, all tonsils and fake tan. I could still hear Barry, all tinny, yelling through the phone and I managed to yell something back just as she bent down and clicked the phone off.

'Neil!' I screamed but I realised he was already banging on my front door. She'd even pulled the chain across. Visions of Two Job Johnnie swam before my eyes—I'd really underestimated Amanda.

'Cass!' Neil yelled from the hallway. 'What's going on?'

I tried to shout back but she slapped me in the face, right in the centre of my receding bruise. It star-burst behind my eye as she pushed me backwards, toppling me off the stool I'd been leaning my bum on. I sprawled on the floor, but the stool bounced and then fell. My head hit the metal rung as it came down.

Only seconds must have passed because when I came around, Amanda was still raging around the kitchen. I silently thanked my bank balance for not stretching to the magnetic knife board. The thought of blood made bile bubble up in my throat. I could only see out of one eye again. Damn it. There goes my next date. And then I remembered Sam and something flared in my chest. I struggled to stand up. Amanda was storming around the apartment.

'You fucking bitch,' she yelled. 'I know you had something to do with this! Nothing like this ever happened before I hired you. I am getting married and you can't fucking stop me. You're a menace! You have no morals. You take a job and then shake it like a dog with a bone. You won't give up until you've got him in jail. I know it was you.' On and on she went as my vision cracked and sparked as though the glitter from the other night had seeped into my skin and pooled behind my eyes.

I rolled over onto my hands and knees and started to crawl towards the door. My head felt huge, like a big puffy watermelon full of juice bursting to get out. I kept losing sight of the door. Then I realised she was crouched beside me and then it felt like someone had cracked the watermelon in half and the juice all ran out through my fingers.

She'd grabbed my hair and was trying to pull me up from the floor with it. My ears were full of noise and I struggled to stand. Then I saw a flash of light. I pushed out but she hit me again. I shoved her with all my strength and I must have connected because the pain stopped suddenly. My head felt really strange.

I staggered back, refusing to fall over again, because I knew I should run. She was moving fast but I was at the door before I could utter another word. Something warm was trickling down my face but I wiped it away and had thrown back the locks before I felt her grab me from behind again. I fell through the door as I heard a shout.

Neil.

I rolled over and shuffled backwards on my bum, wiping the goo from my head until I hit the wall. I knew I'd just cracked my head, that it was just an incredible headache, and that it was just blood, but I couldn't fight the sensation of trying to hold my skull together. The glitter was everywhere, like a Blue Light Disco inside my head. Only it felt like I was horribly drunk.

When I looked up, Neil was holding my wrists and staring into my eyes. I could hear a slow mewing and hoped it wasn't coming from me.

'It's okay. I've called the cops. Sam's on his way. I think the whole station is coming, actually.'

'Where—' I groaned.

'The girl in the pink took a blow to the nose.'

I gasped through the taste of blood in my mouth. 'But...' I sat up. I could see through my one good eye again and the goo had slowed to a trickle. 'But that nose cost her eight grand!'

'Well we can see how she goes suing me, then,' he said.

And then I saw Sam drop to his knees behind Neil and uniforms filled my doorway and I realised it was Amanda who was making the little cat noises. She would be very pissed off about her nose.

And it was only when Sam helped me hobble back inside that I realised I was still wearing my pink frilly undies and a singlet top like the Girl Mostly Likely to Die Horribly in a B-grade slasher movie. I guess the yoga would have to be put off for a while. My back had competition when it came to pain.

After the paramedics left and I had swaddling muffling my ear, I was wrapped up in my doona on the couch with a significant dose of painkillers softening the pounding behind my eyes. They'd put six stitches in my head and told me that I'd have another black eye, but I was too dazed to get annoyed—yet. Josie came over to the apartment with Zara and they stood staring at me from the doorway. And then Josie laughed, which I thought was a little unfair.

'See! This is what you get when you try to serve your own brand of vigilante justice.'

I told them all about the ice-cream kissing while Sam was outside talking to another officer.

'Well, thank God you don't have to date number three,' whispered Zara. 'It was Charlie, the struggling actor. He has a weak stomach and I think your face might have brought back his bulimia.'

Now that Amanda and Tony and Suzanne were tucked away in separate cells somewhere, I just wanted to sleep forever. Sam came in and slipped his arm behind me as he sat down on the couch. Maybe it was just the drugs, but warmth bloomed in my chest and I swallowed down the tiny bit of reflux.

'Replete with bliss,' I croaked into Sam's ear sleepily.

'What did she say?' whispered Zara with a frown. Out of my good eye I could see Neil leaning towards me.

'I think she needs to go to the loo.'

'You might think you're spry,' Sam said quietly to me, 'but you took a bad blow to the head. You're going to have to stay in bed for a while.'

I flushed but Sam just laughed. Then he squeezed me. Hard.

'Ouch.' I felt like I'd rolled down a very rocky incline.

'And it's going to hurt a lot more.'

'I know.' I was thinking about the prawns, and maybe a little about the current sleeping arrangements.

'I have four words for you,' I muttered. 'Real Estate Section.'

'That's only three.'

'Tomorrow,' I added. And then I may or may not have fallen asleep.

Acknowledgements

This book is dedicated to Jo McNamara and Anna Jackson for impossible kindness, irritatingly good looks, and mostly for helping me with the rabbits. My thanks go to ArtSA for supporting this story. The deepest appreciation to Jenny Darling for all manner of good things, Deonie Fiford for her excellent and perceptive editing, Lisa Highton for her wonderful enthusiasm, Ineke Hogendijk for her big ideas and everyone at Hodder Headline for putting so much into this book. Thanks to Ellie Exarchos and Greg Roberts for the gorgeous cover and also to Marcus Gillezeau for the video clip and Chris King from The Look. Thank you to Matt Thornton for the beer (and Steve Asparagus), Marcus Brownlow for unprecedented tech support, the Swashbucklers for the inspiration, Bridget Benny for being gorgeous (and very, very blonde), Katherine Brooks and Tom Russell for their patience, Sara Henschke, Richard Wiseman, Sputnik, Roger Zubrinich, Darien O'Reilly, Nick Linke and Cathy Adamek for their wise words and kindness, Jemima for the snuffling, and Sophie Brooks Russell for a whole bunch of stuff I'll tell her about later. Sean ('We've always got LA') Williams pushed me to keep writing even when the Visa bills kept coming in at a freakish rate, so thank you. My family let me stay when I was officially a drifter, an impossibly generous thing considering my mood, and for their kindness and patience I am continually amazed and grateful. Gregory Peck should get a grand thanks for setting high 'guy' standards and, on this theme, my sincere appreciation to Stuart Symons for the champagne, the Plex and his most wonderful, and unequalled, company. Finally, thank you to Ben Mountford and his family for letting me watch the sun set over the salt lake at Marion Bay. In my mind, I'm still there.

The Happiness Punch

4 cups Havana Club Silver Dry Cuban white rum
3 cups Gordon's or Bombay Sapphire gin
1 cup pineapple juice
4 litres tropical fruit juice
Quartered strawberries and raspberries

Serve in a classic fifties punch bowl.

When Cassidy Blair takes on her third job as sexual sleuth, she never expects to end up in the back of a shaggin' wagon with a has-been pop star called Jason Wilde, but Cass was never the best judge of character, or career for that matter.

Still recovering from the black eye and five kilos she gained on her last job, she just wants to eat some low fat yoghurt, take it easy and forget the whole kissing incident with Officer Sam Tasker.

Well, maybe not necessarily *forget*, but he seems to have dropped off the face of the earth and Cassidy's getting twitchy. And now that she's a bit in love and a whole lot broke, she's ill-prepared for the mysterious Ned Maxwell.

Cass stumbles into another hotbed of trouble in *The Happiness Punch*, the sequel to *The Vodka Dialogue*.

Coming soon in 2004

Kirsty Brooks is the author of *Lady Luck, Hitching: Tales from the byways and superhighways* and *Mad Love*. She has a journalism degree and is the Director of Driftwood Manuscripts, an assessment and editing agency for writers. She lives in Adelaide and is easily startled due to a caffeine addiction.

The Vodka Dialogue

1 oz Gordon's or Bombay Sapphire Gin
½ oz Absolut vodka
½ oz Barcardi Limon
½ oz Blue Curacao
½ oz Butterscotch Schnapps
½ oz lime juice
1½ tablespoons powdered (icing) sugar

Mix with ice, strain from cocktail shaker and serve in a highball with a quarter wedge of lime.